the last dreamer

Barbara Solomon Josselsohn

the last dreamer

a novel

LAKE UNION
PUBLISHING

Text copyright © 2015 Barbara Solomon Josselsohn

Published by Lake Union Publishing, Seattle.

www.apub.com

Amazon, the Amazon logo, and Lake Union Publishing are trademarks of Amazon.com, Inc., or its affiliates.

ISBN-13: 9781503949645
ISBN-10: 1503949648

Cover design by Danielle Fiorella

Printed in the United States of America

For Bennett, my one and only rock star.

Chapter 1

Hey, Stuart!

I read on the *Business Times* website yesterday that you've been named editor in chief. Congratulations! Seems like yesterday when we were churning out news stories together, doesn't it? I was intrigued by the article about your promotion—especially your decision to add more features to the mix. As you may remember, I always wanted to do more feature stories at *BT*. Are you possibly hiring freelancers? I'd love to speak with you about taking on some assignments.

Iliana reread the paragraph she had just written, then crossed her arms over her chest and strategized how to continue the email. She could suggest that she go into the city and meet with him in his office, but it could be he was too busy for that now and would prefer a phone call. Maybe she should just come out and pitch a feature idea in the email.

She knew she could come up with a good one. Back when she was a retail reporter at *Business Times*, the chief editor constantly said she had a great instinct for zeroing in on what mattered. And after she got promoted to editor of the retail section, she quickly became one of the few section editors who didn't need to check with him about stories she planned to assign. He didn't need to waste his time looking over her shoulder, he said. He knew he could count on her section to be strong and relevant, each and every week.

She switched out of her email and over to the *Business Times* website to see what the magazine had recently covered. The current issue had a news story about a promising fashion designer who had ditched a great job at Kate Spade and sunk all her personal savings into her own boutique on the Upper West Side. Iliana rested her chin on her hand and started to imagine how she might turn this news bite into a feature, just as her cell phone rang. The caller ID showed the number for the middle school office.

"Mom? It's me."

"Matthew? Are you sick?"

"No, it's just that my violin's in the car, and I have orchestra today. By the time I remembered it, you were gone."

You drove away so fast that I didn't have a chance to get it."

Iliana glanced at the clock on the computer screen. "Can you borrow one?"

"Mr. Finn said the school violins won't be tuned until the week of the concert."

"Can you use one anyway?"

"He said if I don't have my violin here by class time, I won't be in the concert. And he's dropping a half grade for anyone who's unprepared."

Iliana rubbed her forehead with her fingers. Unlike many of his friends, her fourteen-year-old son actually enjoyed playing the violin. She didn't want him to be kicked out of the concert—or lose half a grade, for that matter. And she did sort of rush away quickly after she dropped him off at school, along with her twelve-year-old, Dara. She had known as soon as she left that her failure to ask "Got everything?" would mean trouble. She had just been so anxious to capitalize on Stuart's promotion with a query that could help relaunch her career.

"Yes, I'm still on with my mom," she heard Matthew say, his voice aimed away from the phone. Then he turned back. "Mom, Mrs. Green says I have to go. Can you come?"

She sighed. "Okay, I'll be right there," she said.

Not wanting to waste time fetching her coat, she pulled her black cardigan closer around her and shook out her dark ponytail. Pulled-back hair was fine at home, but she didn't like the glimmer of gray that showed up around her hairline the week before her colorist appointment. Slipping into her winter boots, she ran back to the car and pulled out of the driveway, thinking more about her article idea. What questions did she want answered, what internal conflicts did she want to uncover? She wondered what could spur a young designer to leave a comfortable berth at a successful retail chain and set out on her own. Why take such a risk, and how did this designer come to be so brave? Was she born that way, or was she emboldened by something in her past? And what if she failed—what would she do then?

Driving up to the school's front door, she parked just beneath the "Fire Zone—No Stopping" sign. She didn't want to drive all the way to the parking lot—it was too cold and she was impatient to get back to her computer. She switched on her flashers, grabbed the violin from the trunk, and rushed past the security desk and into the office.

"Mrs. Passing, you're supposed to get a visitor pass," the secretary scolded.

"It's just to drop Matthew's violin off."

"And you parked in the no-parking zone," the woman added, gesturing toward the window.

"You're right, I'm sorry." Iliana deferentially pressed her hand to her chest.

"Because it's a fire hazard, you know."

"I understand, it's true—"

"What would happen if we had a fire this very minute?"

"I'll do it the right way next time."

"He's in eighth grade, not a baby."

"Thank you very much."

"Kids need to take responsibility for their own problems," the woman called as Iliana put the violin on the floor and hurried out.

Climbing back into the car, she waited until she had turned on the engine before muttering "Fuck you!" under her breath. Who the hell did that woman think she was? She considered contacting the principal or PTA president to complain. She even began composing the email in her head: *Mrs. Crane's behavior was rude and inappropriate . . .* But then she changed her mind. It made no sense to make an enemy of the woman. And anyway, she *had* broken two school rules, parking in the fire zone and bypassing security.

Driving home, she tried to visualize the photo of the designer that accompanied the Kate Spade article. Had there been something in her eyes that revealed what she was thinking, a tiny squint that suggested fear, a strong gaze that said she was up for the challenge? Iliana yearned to delve into the woman's story. Why had she taken such a major detour from a more standard career path? Was she having second thoughts? What kept her up when she was alone late at night? Iliana knew this was a feature she'd love to write. She loved digging deep into people and finding out what made them tick.

Back at the dining room table, she squeezed her fingers together to thaw them, willing herself to believe that Stuart would give her the assignment. She had been trying to make a go of freelance writing ever since she left *Business Times* a few months after Matthew was born. When she had time while the kids were little, and more often as they got older and more involved with friends and sports, she would routinely pitch articles and finished essays to women's magazines like *Redbook*,

Self, Working Mother, and *Real Simple*; major general-interest publications like *Consumers Digest*, the *Atlantic*, and *Parade*; and a host of others focusing on parenting, fashion, and health. She envisioned herself
as the next Gail Sheehy, Joyce Maynard, or Anna Quindlen, a smart
and affecting commentator on contemporary life. But she rarely got
a nibble. She had queried *Redbook* for a story on a single mom she'd
met through friends who was bravely coping with the demands of an
infant daughter with significant development delays—but never heard
back. She pitched the same story to a senior editor at *Parents* and was
told that they had a core group of writers they used for stories on child
development—but they liked the sample *Business Times* article she had
forwarded about mattress stores, and would she be interested in doing
a short bulleted list of what to look for when buying a crib mattress?

Of course she had taken the assignment, just as she accepted occasional uninspiring assignments from the local newspaper, whose editor had heard she once wrote about retail. She'd squeeze in visits to a
banner-bedecked mattress store on Central Avenue or the expanded
dishwasher department in Rye Appliances and do the writing—a short
description of the place, a rundown of the products, a quote from the
owner—after the kids were in bed. It wasn't all bad, actually. She liked
writing, and she liked getting an occasional paycheck, however small.
Still, it was almost unbearable that most of the publishing world had
written her off. Did her decision to leave her job when her family was
young have to define her for the rest of her life?

With her fingers warmed up, she returned to the email and began
her pitch—*How about a feature article on Darlyn Reese? She's not even
thirty yet, and she's left Kate Spade to go out on her own. Is this bold, or is
it youthful optimism run amok*—but stopped midsentence when a beep
on her cell phone signaled that her husband, who was in Chicago for
meetings at his company's headquarters, had sent a text.

You there? he had written. *Got a problem.*

Suspecting she'd regret letting him interrupt her but also knowing she'd feel guilty if she didn't answer, she typed back, *What is it?*

I need you to go to my computer and email me Presentation.docx.

Can it wait a few minutes?

No, giving a talk and I need it.

Iliana dropped her hands on her lap and sat back in her chair. Marc did this kind of thing a lot: I need a file from my computer. Can you bring my car in for servicing? I'm running out of preshave. Would you get that new suit I had tailored at Brooks Brothers? Sure, she was happy to help him out, and because she was the nonworking spouse, she figured it was her job to take care of these chores. But it would be nice if he acknowledged that she might be busy or maybe even just used the word "please." Sometimes she felt more like a member of his staff than an equal partner in their marriage. The corporate secretary to his chairman of the board.

She ran upstairs to his computer to quickly send the document, but of course it wasn't a quick chore at all. First she had to text him back because he had changed the password on his computer and she didn't know the new one. Then she ended up emailing him not only Presentation.docx but also Presentation1, Presentation1-A, Presentation1-A1, and PresentationRevised before he remembered that he had named the right document Discussion, not Presentation.

By the time she got back downstairs, it was past noon. There was no way Stuart's email was going out today. She needed to be on the school pickup line by two fifteen to take Dara to her orthodontist appointment before getting Matt from after-school math help and taking him to the library, where his social studies group was meeting. And before she could do any of that, she had to pack up some snacks for the kids to eat on their way to their activities, put gas in the car, buy groceries for dinner, and then drive twenty minutes to Tarrytown to drop off Matt's orchestra tux, since the music teacher had negotiated a discount for tailoring that depended on everyone going there. She had long ago accepted that her own day ended by early afternoon, and then the kids' needs reigned. It usually didn't bother her; in fact, she often reminded herself she'd be sorry when they went to college and the house was empty.

Still, it was frustrating—especially when she remembered that tomorrow morning she was having coffee with Jodi. The two of them had been getting together for weekly coffee dates ever since their sons were in the same preschool class, and Iliana needed and valued the friendship too much to blow her off the next day.

But that meant the email would have to wait until the afternoon. And if something else came up, another missing document or musical instrument, it would have to wait even longer. Iliana went to the kitchen to gather the snacks, stopping at the doorway to give a last look at her now-dark computer screen. It seemed she was always in a race to get something done and be back at the computer before it went dark again. And it always went dark.

Later that night, after the kids were fed, showered, and in bed, Iliana called Marc's cell phone. She wasn't surprised when he didn't answer—she knew his Chicago meetings went very late—so she left a quick goodnight on his voicemail. She always felt a little unsettled in the evenings during Marc's twice-yearly trips there for strategy meetings. She wasn't used to sleeping without him, and she missed him. She would be glad when he got home on Thursday. She had even been toying with the idea of planning something special for the two of them, maybe making a reservation for a romantic lunchtime tryst at a hotel near his office. It would be fun to have something different to look forward to.

Finishing up the message, she went back downstairs. She knew she should use this quiet time to return to her pitch, but she was exhausted and headachy from all the day's driving and decided to go into the family room instead and veg out in front of the TV. The remote wasn't on the coffee table—Dara had probably dropped it, as usual—so she got down on her hands and knees and felt around under the sofa until she found it, along with a few wisps of dust and some clumps of hair. Grimacing, she aimed the remote at the TV and began aimlessly flipping through the channels.

Suddenly a passing image caught her attention. Reversing course, she flipped back a few stations until she found it again.

Pulling herself up, she studied the familiar high school corridor on the screen. The image was dull and filmy, with none of the bright colors that characterized recent shows about teens. Some guitar chords sounded as the camera slowly zoomed in on a boy and a girl standing next to a wall of lockers, the girl with an arm folded around a binder, the boy leaning toward her, a backpack slung over one shoulder. Somewhere in her head, Iliana knew who they were, just like she knew the words to the wistful pop tune starting up very softly in the background. *It's a world of dreaming . . . it's a life of Guitar Dreams.*

"I've been hoping for the lead in the senior play all my life," the girl said tearfully. "What if Mrs. Brown doesn't think I'm good enough? What will I do then?"

"Hey, we thought our band was a total dream," the boy said. "And now we play concerts every weekend. You just gotta put yourself out there, you know? You just gotta start dreamin' to the max!"

He held out one hand, and she took it. Then he pulled her in close and lifted her chin with the knuckle of his other hand, smiling shyly, as if he knew that an all-out smile would be too beautiful for her to bear. Then he kissed her, once softly, and then again, as he moved his hands to her waist and she slid her free arm around his neck.

Eyes on the screen, Iliana lowered herself onto the edge of the coffee table, sending the remote tumbling to the floor. *Jeff Downs,* she thought. *Where the hell are you now?*

Chapter 2

Jeff Downs's face was once everywhere Iliana looked—on the poster that hung on her bedroom wall, on magazine covers at the candy store in town, on the cardboard that was folded around cassette tapes she would buy at the mall with her babysitting money. Jeff Downs, star of the TV show *Guitar Dreams*, with his wavy brown hair that cradled the back of his neck, with his deep-brown eyes and square chin, with the dimple that materialized on his cheek when he smiled and was so adorable, you almost had to cry when you saw it. His smile was a tight-lipped smile, an embarrassed smile, a combination smile-sigh. A smile that said he would gladly walk away from all the attention, if only he could be alone with the girl of his dreams, sharing a slice of pizza perhaps, or walking on the beach.

She had seen him for the first time on TV when she was Dara's age. He was in a jeans commercial, playing the part of a teenage boy who brings his friend home to play basketball, only to discover that his friend and younger sister have huge crushes on one another. The friend and sister start to flirt in the kitchen, while Jeff tries to get his pal to take an interest in a can of soda, a bag of chips, or the basketball stats in the newspaper, the way he usually does. But today, the friend asks the sister to go for a walk, and the two of them leave the house. The camera then switches to Jeff shooting baskets alone on the driveway and missing every shot, while an announcer declares, "There's no going back. Reese Jeans."

Iliana rushed home every day after school that spring, doing her homework while keeping an eye on the TV, waiting for the Reese Jeans commercial. She was certain that Jeff was just like the character he played in the commercial—a loner, an outsider. She was sure he would understand her better than anyone else, since she was an outsider, too.

The transition to sixth grade that year had been hard for her. The middle school drew from two elementary schools, hers and another one on the wealthier side of town—and her best friend from elementary school had moved to the fancier area over the summer. Iliana was shy to begin with, she didn't make friends easily, and it was painful to watch Lizzie embrace a whole new group of girls that Iliana had nothing in common with. They talked about fancy designer clothes they intended to buy and argued about whether the skiing was better in Snowbasin or Copper Mountain, places Iliana had never heard of. When one of them showed off her new tennis bracelet at lunch, Iliana was baffled. It looked like a fancy bracelet to her—what did it have to do with tennis? Still, with nowhere else to sit, she went to the same lunch table as Lizzie and her new friends every day, pretending that she belonged. And as she sat there, she daydreamed about Jeff Downs. She imagined what he would do if he were to visit her school during lunch one day. She was sure he would find the girls at the table mean and shallow. He would turn away as they gushed over a new blouse or bracelet. He'd look at her as she sat quietly at the end of the table, and he'd tell them, "I want to know what *Iliana's* thinking."

That July, Iliana read in *Teen* magazine that the "Reese Jeans guy" had joined the cast of a new TV series about four high school buddies who form a band called the Dreamers. Knowing that the show would launch in September made it easier for her to accept the end of

summer and the prospect of a new school year, the likelihood of finding no welcoming faces anywhere in the lunchroom, and having to sit
again, ignored, with Lizzie and her rich friends. In August, she checked
the shelves at the candy store daily, and was the first to pull a copy of
the new issue of *Teen*—with a full-color photo section all about the
new show—from the rope-bound stack. The photos were mainly of the
show's biggest star, Terry Brice, whose California tan and white-blond
hair had made him a regular on sitcoms and commercials. But it was
the one close-up of Jeff Downs that held her attention. She loved that
he was looking down at his guitar, and not at the camera. Was there any
better confirmation that he was just what she had imagined—modest,
deep, and a little brooding? She was convinced that he allowed himself
to get close to only a few people.

People like her.

The next morning, after making sure that Matt and Dara were getting
dressed, Iliana slipped downstairs and turned on her computer. Sure, it
was just a stupid TV show, and an old one at that, but she kept hearing Jeff's advice to the girl over and over in her head—*You just gotta
put yourself out there, you know?*—the same way she used to hear him
as she went through the motions at middle school each day. Opening
her email, she read her draft to Stuart, made a few revisions, added
a concluding sentence expressing the hope that they'd talk soon, and
pressed "Send." There was no point in hesitating; it was time to put
herself out there.

But no sooner had she dropped the kids off at school—double-
checking in the mirror that Matt had his violin—and parked near the
Scarsdale Café for her date with Jodi than she received a sobering and
unwanted response:

Wish I could say your idea would fly, but
that Kate Spade girl is hardly worth a feature. I remember you like profiles about little
people with big dreams, but they're pretty
old school these days. We need stories with
big names that can increase our social-media
presence. Now if you get your hands on
something like that, write it up and send it
over, I'll give it a look. And btw, thanks for
the congrats!

Sitting in the turned-off car, Iliana stared at her phone until her cold, ungloved fingers started to ache. Stuart had barely taken enough time to read her idea before flatly rejecting it. And though his note had a friendly tone, his characterization of her idea as "old school" stung. As for the end of the note—how could she get her hands on a story about someone famous when she was out here in the suburbs, her days filled with chauffeuring kids, dropping off clothes, and fetching preshave? He hadn't even raised the possibility of an assignment—just gave a vague offer to give her work "a look." She had been on the staff of *Business Times* for eight years, she had helped train him when he joined the magazine five years after she did, and he couldn't even say that he'd love her to write for him? He wasn't interested. To him she was a has-been.

She sighed. She had been down this road before, when her ideas were dismissed or rejected by *Redbook*, *Parents*, and all the others. And this was even harder to take, since Stuart was someone she knew. She could foresee how the next few days would go. She would study Stuart's email for an hour or two, trying to glean something positive from his response or hoping he'd email again to say he'd reconsidered. And then, when neither happened, she'd crash. She'd be miserable and angry for days, short with the kids and Marc, cool to anyone who crossed her path. She'd remind herself constantly that Stuart found her useless. And then she'd slowly wipe herself up off the floor.

This was not how she had expected her career to go. She had joined *Business Times* a year after college, moving there from an entry-level public relations job because she wanted to be in publishing. She thought that after a couple of years, when she had some professional writing experience under her belt, she could move to one of the big women's magazines. And a few years after that, when she had made a name for herself in the publishing industry, she could start on her book. Her idea was to find four people who had come to New York City and prevailed despite obstacles—a lack of money or education, extreme youth, or disapproving parents or families. She wanted her book to showcase the vast possibilities of New York, and to analyze the kind of determination that could propel people to extraordinary and unlikely success.

But somehow she never made it out of *Business Times*. It was a comfortable place for her, and she was content. She received lots of praise for sniffing out news or scooping the competition, as well as regular pay raises. The time she stayed behind at a press conference about West Side development and got a direct quote from Donald Trump, she earned a bouquet of red roses from the publisher and a bonus. Five years into the job, she got her promotion, which brought with it more money and prestige. She figured she had plenty of time to move to the next career stage.

Then along came Marc, and everything changed. She met him on the way home from a weekend getaway in the Poconos, and he soon became her top priority. Being in love consumed much of the time and attention she once poured into her job—as did planning a wedding, starting a household, moving to the suburbs, and expecting a baby. She returned briefly to *Business Times* after her maternity leave, but found that she missed Matthew terribly. She hated turning him over to a nanny every morning and not seeing him all day. She talked about it with Marc, who pointed out that between the cost of the nanny and her train commute to the city, they were spending a lot of money for a job she was starting to resent. So she left *Business Times*, taking a gamble that when she was ready to resume her writing career, the publishing industry would welcome her back.

She opened the door and stepped out, not even bothering to close her coat. The frigid air stung her cheeks and tore through her turtle-neck sweater. She stumbled into the coffee shop and stood near the entrance. She barely remembered why she was there, until she noticed Jodi waving.

"Hi, honey! *Iliana!*" Jodi called, which made everyone in the place look up. "What's wrong with you? You didn't even see me!"

Iliana tried to smile normally as she slid onto the opposite green vinyl bench. "Sorry," she said. "Just tired, I guess."

A waitress came over with a coffeepot, and Iliana lifted an empty mug. "No, it's easier when it's on the table," the woman barked. Iliana obediently put the mug down.

They ordered breakfast, and Jodi tucked the menus into their holder. "Tired, hey, I hear ya," she said, pouring a stream of sugar from the glass dispenser into her coffee cup. "And when you're tired, everyone annoys you more, am I right? I caught Ben loading the dishwasher last night, and he wasn't even rinsing first. Shit, why are husbands so friggin' lazy all the time?" Her golden-brown, artfully wavy hair cascaded forward, and she tossed it back with a forefinger.

"Actually, you're not supposed to rinse them," Iliana said. "Dishwashers today have sensors, and they need the food particles to read how dirty the load is, and—" She sighed. She once dreamed of being the next great female essayist of her time, and here she was, spouting boring facts she had learned writing about a local appliance store.

They were quiet for a moment. "Why'd you stop?" Jodi finally said, her lips turned down in a playful pout. "I love when you tell me that stuff. You're so good at explaining, that's why you're a writer. Any new assignments coming up?"

Barbara Solomon Josselsohn

"Not right now," Iliana said, reaching for a napkin. She didn't want to tell Jodi about *Business Times*. The rejection was too fresh, and the fact that it came from someone she once worked with was too humiliating to admit, even to her closest friend.

The waitress returned with their food, and Jodi cut hungrily into her eggs. "You're so lucky that you have the kind of career you can do from home," she continued, biting off a piece of bacon. "Not me. A lawyer who hasn't practiced in ten years? Ha! Like I have a prayer of ever being hired again."

Iliana looked up from her toast. "You don't mean that, do you? It's not true that *no one* would hire you, is it?"

"Yeah, it's true. Why pretend? The only thing I'm good for these days is making sure Ben has clean shirts, clean boxers, and a full stomach, so he can keep going to work and bringing home the bacon. Or at least bringing home the money so I can eat the bacon." She took another bite.

"And that doesn't bother you?"

"I like bacon."

"No, seriously."

She shrugged. "What am I gonna do? It is what it is."

"But you were a lawyer."

"I still *am* a lawyer, thank you very much. And I still get to practice once in a while, although mainly because I'm too wimpy to say no."

Iliana smiled. "What?" she said. "What did you agree to this time?"

"I couldn't help it!" Jodi rolled her eyes. "I ran into Chelsea Gold at the track last week—that will teach me to exercise in winter, right? You know her, she owns that store Chelsea's Home Details a few doors down from here?"

Iliana nodded. She had covered the opening two years ago for the local paper. It was an attractive but overpriced decorating store, with small pieces of weathered, antique furniture and knickknacks.

"Well, we stopped to talk and she's adding a location in White Plains and said she was nervous about some of the details in the lease, and when I told her I used to review leases, she asked if I'd take a look at it. 'Just a once-over to spot any red flags,' she said. She told me she was sinking all her money into the business, so she couldn't pay me, but if I found something in the store, she'd give it to me as a thank-you."

"Pretty nervy of her," Iliana said. "She hardly knows you."

"Yeah, but I'm like that, I start talking to someone on the street and before I know it I'm all into their business." She shrugged. "Whatever. I like real estate. I like contracts. And she's got some pretty stuff. Hey, as long as we're right by the store, let's stop in there. You can help me find my thank-you gift!"

Iliana shrugged—what else did she have to do?—and they paid the check and then walked over to the shop. A cheerful bell sounded as they opened the wooden door.

"Pick me out something nice!" Jodi whispered as she headed toward the back. "I'm just going to find her and say a quick hello."

The place smelled good, like cinnamon and cloves, and Iliana wandered through the narrow alleyways formed by stacked chests and breakfronts. Everything looked old and weathered, as though the whole assortment had been brought in from some nineteenth-century New England estate. Eventually she came to a small writing desk in the corner and stopped to run a finger along its pewter drawer handles. It had a deep cherry finish and roll-down top, and it reminded her of the desk her parents gave her for her twelfth birthday. Her father, who had sold stationery products for a living, used to love the whisper that sharp pencils made on paper placed on a fine wood surface. He found it sad that pencils lost their points so quickly.

She opened a drawer and took out the price tag. Seven thousand dollars. No wonder she never shopped here.

Jodi came up behind her. "Hey, what'ja find me?" she said. "This? This desk? Isn't it a little . . . I don't know, sentimental?"

"What? No, it's beautiful," Iliana said.

"It's not very practical. The drawers are so small!"

"It isn't for storage, it's for *writing*. My parents gave me one just like it when I was in middle school. My dad went to six stores before he found the one he wanted. He said it was the perfect desk for writing down my dreams." She felt her eyes filling with tears. Her father had died over a year ago, and she still missed him.

Jodi leaned over and rubbed her shoulder. "Come on, let's go," she said softly. "I can choose something later."

Outside, she adjusted her fringed scarf. "Could you drive the boys to basketball today? The floor guy's coming, and I don't know how long it will take."

Iliana nodded. "Sure, I'll take them."

"Great. And let me know when I should fill in for you."

Iliana nodded. "Okay. I will."

"Because that thing in New Jersey for Marc's company is coming up, right?"

"Oh, yeah. That's right. The flower thing." The owner of Marc's company had a wife who grew up in New Jersey, and each year she hosted a flower-arranging workshop at her family's estate for the non-working wives of the firm's male senior executives. Marc was ecstatic that she had been invited this year, because he thought it showed that he was finally on the partners' radar screen and might be in line for a promotion.

"You don't want to go? I think it sounds fun," Jodi said. She reached out and nudged a strand of Iliana's hair from her face. "What's wrong with you today anyway? You're not usually this down."

Through the store window, Iliana could just make out the desk that looked like the one her father had chosen, the desk that Jodi had called sentimental. "I'll see you later, Jo," she said and started for her car.

Back home, Iliana stared at her laptop as she had known she would, looking for something positive in Stuart's email. True, she thought, he had turned her down, but he hadn't said he wouldn't hire her, and he hadn't said she wasn't a good writer. Yes, his characterization of her taste in profiles stung, but maybe he was right—maybe magazines had to be flashier these days. And maybe there *was* some cool, well-known business star she could track down, now that she knew the kind of article Stuart wanted. Still, Jodi's lament hung in the air. Were lawyers who'd left the workforce to have their families really as unmarketable as she claimed? Was the same true of former magazine writers?

She turned away from the laptop and rested her head in her palm. It would take some time for her to think of a personality who would impress Stuart and then figure out how to get the interview. She would have to be resourceful—maybe reach out to women she knew who could put her in touch with celebrity businesspeople. Who did she know with those kinds of contacts? Were there any doctors or lawyers in town who might have famous people in their practice? Any PR people who had famous clients? Brokers or financial planners with helpful connections? She tapped her forehead with the pads of her fingers. *Come on!* she told herself. *You know how to chase down a story! Think! THINK!* But the encouragement didn't help. Nothing came to her.

Gradually her eyes wandered to the family room, and she saw the TV on the wall, as well as the coffee table where she had sat and watched Jeff Downs through four straight episodes of *Guitar Dreams* last night. Jeff Downs, the guy who had made her feel better about herself every week throughout middle school, even though she didn't even know him. She couldn't help but wonder how his story played out. He had had a career that took off fast and ended quickly—the show was off the air after three or four years, and she never saw him on TV again after—and she was starting to worry that her career was over, too. She wanted to know how he had coped and whether he'd been able to move on to something else. She wanted to know what became of him—and how he felt about it all.

She turned back to the computer and typed "Jeff Downs" in the Google search box. Her eyebrows lifted with curiosity as she hit the "return" key. But then she sighed, as more than eleven million results popped up, along with ads from companies claiming they could find his address, phone number, and arrest record instantly. This was not going to be easy.

Methodically, she read through the first page of Jeff Downs listings. There was a cardiologist in Tampa named Jeff Downs, as well as a police officer in Las Vegas and a professor of biology at Stanford. There was a pastor in Philadelphia and a few insurance brokers and financial planners in scattered cities. Sure, she could eliminate the basketball star at Syracuse University and the old man who just died in Buffalo—*her* Jeff Downs was neither nineteen nor ninety-three. But what about the others? Was the guy whose smile once drove preteen girls crazy now a doctor, professor, or policeman? Could he have invented a whole new life for himself after his star crashed and burned years ago?

She went back to the search box and typed in "Guitar Dreams," staring intently at the screen for new results. Up came a Wikipedia entry—wasn't there always a Wikipedia entry?—followed by a host of YouTube videos and several TV-centered websites. She clicked on the Wikipedia link, which described the show's origins and gave some information she already knew. But within the wordy copy, an unfamiliar tidbit emerged:

> After *Guitar Dreams* was canceled, Jeff Downs, once known as the Reese Jeans guy, moved to Maine to start a skiwear business with his brother, Jack.

Skiwear? Now *that* was an interesting piece of news, assuming Wikipedia was right. Googling "Jack Downs skiwear," she held her breath while the results page loaded and then clicked on the first link, which brought her to the home page of a website called JackDownsHatsandAllThat.com. Locating the "About Us" tab beneath a picture of a lighthouse, she skimmed the paragraph that appeared. Sure enough, it said that Jack Downs had started the company with his brother—but added that Jack and Jeff eventually parted ways, and Jeff moved to New York to start something called Downs Textiles.

Leaning forward, eyes glued to the screen, Iliana returned to her browser and typed "Downstextiles.com." Then she waited, tapping a fingernail against her teeth.

A few moments later another home page popped up, with a photo of a New York City showroom sporting multi-tiered racks with colorful blankets. Once again, she found the "About Us" tab and clicked. Up came a list of four company executives, with "Jeff Downs, President" at the top. She wondered: Was "Jeff Downs, President" the guy who dominated her imagination for two full years of her life—or just one of the other eleven million Jeff Downses sprinkled around the planet?

Iliana pinched her bottom lip and studied the computer screen, trying to think where to look next. How would she have tackled this sort of situation back when she was at *Business Times*? And then it hit her: *Business Times!* The magazine maintained a huge online archive of material about New York City businesses—everything from sales figures and profit estimates generated by the research department to small news articles that for one reason or another didn't make it into the magazine.

So she went to the BusinessTimes.com archives—but quickly found that they were password protected. That was a surprise, as they had been available to anyone back when she worked there. How could she get in? She supposed she could email Stuart and ask for the password, explaining that she wanted to research past stories so she could develop a pitch he'd like. But that didn't make sense—why would she be looking at old, musty stories if she were trying to come up with something fresh? She was going to have to think of another way. Was there anything she remembered that could provide a clue about how the tech people might handle online security?

She thought about the kind of security that existed when she was on staff. Back then, there were physical archives located in the building, and the entrance to the room where they were housed was locked. She remembered that there was a keypad outside the door, and the code to unlock the room was . . . the street number of the building! What was it again? She quickly went to the publication's home page and found it: 2251. Might the company have used the same code when they secured the digital archives?

She entered 2251 into the box—and sure enough, she was in.

She typed "Downs Textiles" into the search box. Three short items popped up.

Bingo.

JEFF DOWNS, FORMER TV STAR, STARTS BLANKET BUSINESS

(New York: Sept. 2, 1999) Jeff Downs, a star of the one-time hit TV show Guitar Dreams, has launched a textile business and opened a midtown-Manhattan showroom at 295 Fifth Ave. to display his line of blankets.

DOWNS TEXTILES MOVES DESIGN AND ADMINISTRATION TO WESTCHESTER

(New York: Mar. 26, 2008) Downs Textiles, the blanket supplier started by one-time TV idol

Jeff Downs, has opened a second office near his home in Mount Kisco, in northern West-chester. Downs, who has declined to talk about his past since leaving Hollywood, was unavailable for comment.

JEFF DOWNS, FORMER TV STAR, ADDS FLEECE TO BLANKET ASSORTMENT

(New York: April 8, 2012) Downs Textiles, headed by former teen idol Jeff Downs, has added a fleece line to its blanket assortment. The company said in a statement that the line would debut in Bloomingdale's.

Iliana sat back in her chair and took in what she had just learned—that after all these years, Jeff Downs was living and working just about in her own backyard. How about that! It tickled her to know that at this very moment, he could be sitting in his showroom in Manhattan, a mere thirty minutes away, or working at his Mount Kisco office, just a few towns north. He could be seeing the same clouds out his window that she was, hearing the same whoosh of wind that she heard maybe thirty seconds ago. The guy girls everywhere had daydreamed about, the guy she loved to *actually* dream about each night, the guy she had once believed would value her in a way no one else did—that guy could be about to order a muffin from the same Au Bon Pain she stopped at when she took the kids to shop in Midtown over Christmas break. He could be right next to her any day now, if she knew where he got his morning coffee or what train he took to work.

But what did that mean? It was the very question she had asked herself at least once a day when she was working at the magazine, the question that led to the exhilarating process of creation. You found information and you processed it, and then you built a story. What was the story that was going to come from all she had uncovered?

The clock on the computer said one thirty. She had to throw in a load of laundry and go to the cleaners, and then it would be time to get the kids from school. She closed her computer. *Jeff Downs is in New York*, she thought.

She couldn't wait to discover where that surprising news would lead.

Chapter 3

She was asleep when Marc came home that night, but the pressure from his side of the bed when he sat to take off his shoes woke her. She pushed herself up on an elbow and watched him kick his shoes into his closet, then grab the single empty hanger and thrust his suit jacket onto it.

"Everything okay?" she yawned. "You look upset."

"Did I wake you? Sorry. As long as you're up, though . . ." He went to his desk and switched on the gooseneck halogen lamp.

"Ooooh," she said, squeezing her eyes shut and shading them with her hand.

"Sorry, sorry again," he mumbled, taking his wallet out of his pants pocket. He placed it in the empty space on the surface of his chest of drawers, just like he always did. Then he pulled off his watch and put it in its usual position, straight and flat alongside the wallet.

"We missed you," she said, hoping that would cheer him a bit.

He nodded halfheartedly and walked over to the bed to plant a kiss on her jawline. "Missed you guys, too," he said. "In fact, I wish I had never left in the first place. Man, what a godawful trip."

"Didn't go well?" she asked.

With the tips of his first two fingers, he combed his short, ash-brown hair away from his forehead. "Damn contract. I knew it was trouble."

"What contract?"

"The swimwear chain we picked up in Seattle—those bastards added this outrageous exit bonus for the management team. I red-flagged it a thousand times but Angers said forget it. Then we present the thing to Connors this morning, and Angers makes like it's the first time he saw it. So I'm the moron lawyer who can't read a contract."

"It can't be as bad as all that," she said.

"I don't know why we're buying a swimwear chain in Seattle anyway," he grumbled as he pulled his shirttails out of his pants. "They don't buy swimsuits there, they buy *raincoats*." He balled up the shirt and hurled it into the wicker basket. "Now Angers says he's getting a conference room in a Midtown hotel next week so our project team can meet off-site and 'regroup.' I swear, I spend my whole life covering my ass. And then some jerk who's covering his *own* ass up and throws me under the bus."

"Everyone's edgy at these meetings," she said. "You're all exhausted and stressed. At least it's over and you're home. Things will look better in the morning."

"I don't know about that," he said. "I'm just gonna have to lie low and hope this whole thing blows over. Connors can be a real jerk, you know. You get on his bad side and bam, you're out."

Iliana shivered and pulled the covers up closer to her shoulders. It was scary when he talked like this. Lately it seemed that he really thought his position in the company was precarious. She worried that they had overreached when Dara was born and they bought a large house, failing to foresee the tightening economy and naively assuming that Marc's raises and promotions would continue to come quickly and easily. She knew that his responsibility to support her and the kids weighed heavily on him. She hated that he spent so much time feeling tense and worried.

"Is there anything I can do?" she said.

He pulled off his belt. "I'll be okay," he said. Then he pointed toward her night table. "Did you get a chance to call?"

She looked over to where he was pointing. It was the invitation to the flower-arranging workshop she had talked about with Jodi. "No, not yet," she said. "I will tomorrow, I promise."

"You've had it for a week already."

"I didn't mean to let it go this long." Getting out of bed, she pulled some clean T-shirts out of his suitcase. She hadn't been able to bring herself to do it. A flower-arranging workshop for nonworking wives sounded way too similar to lunch period back in middle school, and she hated to think that after all this time, she'd be back where she started, sitting near a group of rich girls with whom she had nothing in common. Just because she was a stay-at-home mom, it didn't mean she yearned to make centerpieces for dinner parties.

"You know that I'm up for exec, and if you don't show a little enthusiasm, it will reflect badly on me," Marc said. "Especially after this Seattle mess. Dan's wife was invited for the first time, too, and she called back the very next day."

"I'll call first thing in the morning," Iliana said, putting the T-shirts in his drawer. "Believe me, I know how great this promotion would be, and I'll be enthusiastic on the phone, I promise."

He sat down on the bed and began peeling off his socks. "How are the kids?" he asked.

"They're good. Matt left his violin again, and I had to go drop it off."

"Anything else going on?"

"Not really. I read in *Business Times* that Stuart got promoted to editor in chief. I'm trying to get an assignment from him."

"Yeah? What do you think they pay for an article?"

"I don't know, a few hundred dollars. Why?"

"It just seems odd to me that you had time for that and couldn't find a minute to call Jena Connors," he said.

"Come on, Marc, I apologized—"

"If you don't want to go, then don't," he said, taking off his tie and snapping his wrist to straighten it out. "I'll just stay in this job for the rest of my life. If I'm lucky enough to keep it. But Iliana, if things go right, this could be good money. I mean, the refrigerator needs to be replaced, the patio steps are falling apart, and we have two college educations coming up. Let's face it, the only way we're gonna have any real security is if I get promoted to the executive team. Without that, I'm just a dispensable lawyer on staff."

"I understand what you're saying—"

"Look, I gotta get back on the right track after this Seattle thing, and you have to help me," he said, hanging the tie on a peg on the closet door and adjusting the ends to make them even. "It's not about you or me, it's about our family, about this job that supports this life."

She closed the door so they wouldn't wake the kids. "Okay, *enough*," she said. "What do you want me to do? Do you want me to call now? I'll call right now if that's what you want." She picked up the phone.

"Tomorrow's fine," he muttered and went into the bathroom.

She put the phone down and stood outside the bathroom door. "It's just that this is hard for me," she said. "All I do every day is what you need me to do, you and the kids, and it's starting to make me a little crazy. I mean, if my life is only about backing you up, if our family depends on you having a wife who arranges flowers and does everything you need . . . if you're saying that's the person I *have* to be—"

He opened the bathroom door so quickly, she jumped back in surprise. "For God's sake, why is everything always about who you are and who you want to be?" he said. "Why can't some things just be the things you have to do?"

"Because everything I do is about who *you* are!" she said.

He shook his head as if to say she still didn't get it and closed the bathroom door.

Shaking, she left the room and went downstairs. In the family room, she curled up on the sofa and pulled the wool throw over her shoulders. She was mad at Marc, but before long she found herself questioning her actions and motives, the way she always did when they fought. She knew she had behaved childishly by not calling Jena Connors yet to RSVP. Marc was right—he was totally devoted to making a secure home for their children, and he never forgot that they came first. He was right to expect that she would help out in whatever way she could. She had happily quit her job to stay home with Matthew. That was the path she had chosen, and she had gotten a wonderful life in return. Wasn't it selfish to ignore the invitation and waste almost a whole afternoon pouting about a rejected article and then looking for an old TV star?

Still, it stung that he had made her feel inferior by bringing up money—*What do you think they pay?*—as if the meager amount that freelance articles typically paid made her feelings unimportant. If everything she hoped to do with the rest of her life had to be measured by how much money it would bring in, then she was sunk before she even started. The days when she earned a respectable salary, with the potential for additional promotions and raises, were long gone. But had she really given up the right to all of her dreams when they jointly agreed that a stay-at-home mom would be best for their family? Couldn't he see that writing something meaningful and having it published was a way of proving to herself that she mattered? She truly wanted to elevate Marc—to help make sure that he always felt he was important, appreciated, and capable of making a significant impact on the world. That was because she loved him. Didn't he want the same for her? Didn't he love her that much?

Jena Connors's invitation was sitting beside her computer the next morning when Iliana returned from taking the kids to school. Marc must have moved it there from her night table before he left for work. Sighing, she read the printed card again:

Please Join Me
For a Three-Session Lunch-and-Learn on Flower Arranging
Featuring the Incomparable Manhattan Floral Designer Miyako
And Members of His Acclaimed Staff
Thursdays, March 13, 20, and 27
11:00 am to 2:00 pm

Obviously it was a thoughtful invitation. And to some people, it would be a very pleasant event. Even Jodi seemed to think it sounded like fun. But to Iliana, it sounded like torture. She knew the women who would be there. She had met them at the company's periodic cocktail parties. There was Delia Braun, the woman who spent an entire evening complaining to Iliana and a bunch of other stay-at-home wives about how frustrating it was that her nanny could never properly pack the kids up for a weekend away at their beach house: "Why am I still reminding her to take extra swimsuits? I didn't mind it the first few times, but I was hoping that by now she'd be more self-sufficient." And then there was that other woman, Krista something, who for some reason decided to describe in detail exactly how she decorated the bed in her master suite: "I have a simple white duvet for a clean look, but then I place a red silk throw along the foot of the bed for a splash of color. And I have decorative pillows, with embroidered shams descending from the headboard in decreasing-size order . . ."

Iliana didn't begrudge these women their concerns or their passions. It was nice that they had built lives for themselves that suited them. And they had lots of friends who shared their interests. But she simply didn't. She thought she probably had a lot more in common with the working wives of the executive team, or the women who were on the executive team themselves. She'd love to lunch with *them*. But most of all, she didn't like people looking at her from the outside—*oh, Iliana, stay-at-home mom*—and thinking they knew her. It made her feel invisible, like the speechless blob she had been when she sat at the end of the lunch table bench in sixth grade, hoping that Lizzie or someone would notice her.

Why is everything always about who you are? Why can't some things just be the things you have to do? Many years ago, when Iliana was single, she had agreed to go with a friend to a singles weekend in the Poconos. The brochure listed mixer activities such as cooking classes, motivational talks, and risqué party games, and the hotel's entrance sported a banner claiming "Soulmates Are Our Specialty!" But despite her friend's insistence that it was all in fun, it took Iliana less than a half-hour at the opening cocktail party to realize she didn't belong there. The women were all giggly and flirty, the men smirked and nodded appreciatively at the women's antics, and while a few guys asked her where she came from or what she did for a living, she knew they weren't really listening to her answers. She hated that nobody was really seeing *her*.

Funny enough, it was at the bus station where her friend had dropped her off before heading to her home in Philadelphia that she met Marc, who had had a similarly disappointing experience at the resort. They recognized each other from the opening mixer and sat next to one another on the bus, talking for the entire trip. At the time, Marc was an associate with a small law firm specializing in corporate downsizing, and he said that while he didn't like helping companies fire people, he got satisfaction from preparing literature to make sure they knew about the benefits they were entitled to. Iliana found him thoughtful and smart. When he asked her questions about her life, she loved that he truly seemed to enjoy learning about her. They got back to Manhattan, and he asked her to dinner the following weekend. She loved that he didn't make her feel anxious or insecure about whether he'd want to see her again.

Iliana looked at the invitation. She knew that she should just pick up the phone and call Jena Connors to say she'd be happy to attend. It wasn't that big a deal to give up three afternoons to support her husband and their family, and to help put Marc in the best possible position to earn a promotion. It would be great if he could become a member of the executive team—and not just because of the money. He would feel good about himself, validated in the work he had done over all these years and the way his life had played out. That was what she was struggling with now. It was heartbreaking to think that all the work *she* had done had brought her to this place, a place where she served mostly as a support system for her family. A place where all her attempts to write and create and be published again amounted to very little.

She pushed the invitation away and halfheartedly turned on her computer. When the screen came back to life, she found the Google results page for Jeff Downs still open. A YouTube entry with a thumbnail photo of Jeff and his costars caught her eye. She clicked.

It was a video of the recording session for "The Best of Times," the Dreamers' most famous song and their only one to go platinum. The boys were all in button-down shirts, skinny ties, and tight black jeans, their long hair windswept from their faces. Terry Brice was standing at a microphone, mugging at the others and grinning with delight, but it was Jeff Downs, the lead vocalist, who stole the scene. He half-stood, half-sat on a stool, one heel on a rung, his eyes focused on his guitar as he sang:

> *When I pick her up on Saturday,*
> *And she tells me, "Oh, we're on our way,"*
> *And it's all so real, I have to say,*
> *It's the best time, the best time in the world.*

At the beach we'll walk along the sand,
And I'll kiss her soft and hold her hand,
And she'll tell me, yeah, that I'm her man,
It's the best time, the best time in the world.

The best time,
And I know it will last forever.
The best time,
And I know now our future is set . . .

Jeff's buttery voice lengthened every note, filling every word with intention. She could remember playing the song in her head as she sat at the edge of the lunchroom bench, next to Lizzie and across from Lizzie's new friends. She'd pretend to laugh at jokes she didn't get, jokes told at parties she hadn't been invited to, all the while thinking that the girl Jeff described in the song would one day be her.

Watching him on her computer screen, she wondered: Was he still so beautiful, with his dark eyes and square jaw? Did he still have that amazing smile? Was he happy—*could* he be happy? After all, he had been washed up as a TV star while he was still so young. How did he feel about being a blanket peddler? Was it a letdown after so much time as a star? Or was there something about being a regular person that was better, more fulfilling, than being a star? Was he happy with himself? Or did he spend his life second-guessing the choices he had made when he was younger? Did he have dreams that he could pursue only when he was out of the limelight, or had his only dream been to stay in the limelight forever? And maybe most important of all, what lessons about her life could she glean from his? If he had found a way to be happy as a blanket peddler instead of a star, could his story teach her how to be happy, too?

And that's when she realized she had to meet him. She had to find a way to sit down with him and get her questions answered.

But how? The articles she'd read online suggested that he was pretty reclusive. He wasn't quoted in any of them, and one piece had specifically noted that he never talked at all about his past. She couldn't just call his showroom and ask to speak to him. No doubt he had a receptionist who screened his calls. And she couldn't just show up there and expect him to welcome her. Without an appointment she'd be asked to leave the building before she even saw him. She supposed she could go to his showroom in Manhattan and wait until she saw him go in or out—but would she even recognize him? And if she did, what would she say? Please talk to me, I was once a big fan, I loved your music, I loved your voice, and when I read that you had a business right here in New York selling blankets . . .

His blankets! She sat up straight, clenching her fists—*that* was the ticket! She could gain entry to his life by requesting to interview him for an article for *Business Times*. She would go ahead and write the article and then sell it to Stuart. After all, Jeff Downs was a celebrity, or at least he used to be. Thousands of businesspeople used to watch *Guitar Dreams* every week, thousands of businesswomen used to love the dreamy Jeff Downs the way she once did. Certainly he was the kind of big personality that Stuart wanted to profile.

Fingers flying over the keyboard, she went back to the Downs Textiles website. She didn't want to waste time waiting for a return email that might or might not come, so she found the company's phone number. Barely breathing, fingers shaking, she picked up her cell phone, trying three times until she finally entered the number correctly. The line rang. She listened to the menu. Not surprisingly, there was no option to reach Jeff Downs directly, so she pressed the key for a receptionist instead.

A moment later, a pleasant voice sounded. "Downs Textiles, may I help you?" She froze. Was she really going to ask for him?

"Downs Textiles," she heard again. "Hello?"

"Yes, hello!" she blurted out. Her voice was shaking, and so was her body. She pictured all the adrenaline that was surely pouring into her bloodstream. "I'm a writer working on an article for *Business Times*, and I'd like to talk with Jeff Downs for a story about his company."

"You'd like to . . . I'm sorry, who are you?" the receptionist said.

"I'm Iliana . . . Fisher," she said, trying to sound professional. Instinctively she used her maiden name, which had always been the name she used at work. "This is the blanket company Downs Textiles, correct? And Jeff Downs is president?"

"Yes, that's true, but the sales reps handle most media requests," the woman said. "What publication did you say you're writing for?"

Iliana hesitated. "*Business* . . . *Business Times* is where I'm targeting—but you see, I generally speak to company presidents—"

"*Times*? Oh, wait, oh, please. I didn't realize. Please hold on."

Iliana held her breath as she heard the line go silent. What had happened? Was there a problem? What had she said to get the woman so flustered?

A few seconds later, she returned to the line. "Ms. Fisher, Mr. Downs would love to speak with you," she said. "He's very sorry that he's with a customer right now, but he hopes you might come to the showroom next week. What day would be good?"

Iliana was sure she had heard wrong. "To come there . . . I mean, *there*?"

"Now let's see . . . how's Tuesday . . . I'm checking his calendar . . . ten thirty?"

"To meet Jeff Downs? Come there? On Tuesday?"

"Does that work for you?"

"Yes, sure," Iliana said. "Sure. That's fine."

"Great, we'll see you at ten thirty Tuesday."

"Yes, great, we'll see you then," said Iliana. "I mean, me. Me! *I'll* see you then."

Barbara Solomon Josselsohn

For the next two hours, Iliana tried to do some online research, hunting down information on blanket constructions and fabrics, and looking for background information on manufacturers that would compete with Downs Textiles. But mostly she wandered aimlessly around the house, unable to take anything but the shallowest of breaths. How was it that *Business Times* had as much clout today—or maybe even more—as it had back in her day? How was it that Jeff Downs would not simply take a call, but actually invite her *in*? She felt a little guilty—after all, she hadn't made it clear that she didn't have an actual assignment—but she could fix that later. The thing was, she was going to meet Jeff Downs and write a story about him. She was going to interview Jeff Downs for an article she would get published. What had Jodi said at breakfast? It was *so* exciting!

That evening as she was pulling out plates for dinner, she heard Marc's car pull up. Suddenly the name Jena Connors popped into her head. *Shit*, she thought—she had never gotten around to calling that woman, and the last thing she wanted was another fight. Setting the plates on the table, she went to the dining room and found the phone number on the invitation. An answering machine picked up.

"Mrs. Connors? This is Iliana Passing," she said in an amiable tone. "Thank you for inviting me to participate in the workshop. I'm delighted to attend, and I look forward to meeting you."

She put the phone down and looked toward the kitchen. Marc was watching from the doorway.

"So you're going," he said tentatively, as though he wasn't completely sure and needed confirmation.

She folded her arms across her chest. "You heard me."

"I think it's for the best."

"You made that point."

35

He sighed and put down his briefcase. "Look, Iliana, I'm sorry about how I came down on you last night, okay? I was tired and frustrated. The trip to Chicago really sucked. But I shouldn't take it out on you."

She let out a breath, releasing all the tension from her jaw and shoulders. It was nice that he apologized. "And I'm sorry I took so long to call," she said.

He held out his hand and she walked over to him, then wrapped her arms around his neck. He hugged her back and kissed her tenderly on the mouth.

"So how did everything go today?" she asked. "Was there any fallout from that contract?"

"Not too much yet," he said. "But there's still the off-site to deal with next week." He kissed her on the nose. "I'm going up to change."

"Can you let the kids know dinner's almost ready?" she asked.

He nodded and continued up the stairs, as she went to the kitchen to take the chicken from the oven. The whole fight, and even her resistance to going to New Jersey, was starting to seem a little irrelevant. She had scored an interview with someone who was notoriously press-shy, and she was going to write an article that Stuart would buy and readers would love. She was going to meet Jeff Downs. She had actually stepped up today and accomplished something she really wanted.

It was amazing how much that brightened her mood.

Chapter 4

The weekend was the usual blur of drop-offs, hand-offs, and pickups. Iliana started out on Saturday taking Dara to a friend's house, then stopped to purchase eight six-packs of Gatorade from Super Stop & Shop, where they were on sale. Next she went to the library, where she grabbed Matt after his study-group session and brought him back home to meet Marc, who had gone to the gym that morning. Marc then took Matt out for pizza for lunch and brought him to New Rochelle for his basketball game, while Iliana went to buy new ribbons at the craft store for Dara's hair, pick up Matt's skin cream from the drugstore, and sprint to the dry cleaner, sipping on cardboard containers of coffee to keep herself going. She crossed paths with Jodi in the drugstore parking lot and remembered to switch carpool days. She thought she'd be back from her appointment at Downs Textiles in time to do the Tuesday carpool as usual, but it couldn't hurt to be safe.

"Yeah, I can switch," Jodi said. "Whatcha doing on Tuesday?"

"Going into the city," Iliana said as she shifted into drive.

"Lucky you!" Jodi called from behind her. "Buy something pretty!"

Alone in the car, Iliana smiled that Jodi assumed she was going into the city to shop. Then she thought about where she was really going and immediately felt like a small bubble had burst in her stomach, sending warm juices up to her chest and out to her fingertips and toes. It was hard to believe that the whole thing had even happened. Who was this person who had mustered the courage to call?

The only thing that still troubled her was that the receptionist thought she had an actual assignment. She had tried to be honest, saying that she was "targeting" *Business Times*, but the woman had clearly misunderstood. Still, it wasn't so bad. What she had done was unintentional—not nearly as bad as all the manipulative tricks business-people often used to get their way. Even *she* had nudged the truth occasionally when she was at *Business Times*, saying "My deadline's tonight" to get someone to make time for her, or "I'm right around the corner," when she was way across town. It was so common in business that she could even tell Marc or Jodi about it, and they wouldn't see what the big deal was. And anyway, who wouldn't do anything to meet a celebrity? Marc himself had pretended to be having cell-phone trouble last summer when they found themselves at the same restaurant as Derek Jeter. He walked past Jeter's table and tried to listen in on his conversation, all the while shaking his phone and giving the worst performance of a frustrated cell-phone user that Iliana could imagine. She laughed with him about it on the ride home, as he good-naturedly defended himself: "Give me a break—it was *Jeter!*" It was cute, the way he had kept his eye on the ballplayer all through dinner.

Then she started thinking again about meeting Jeff Downs in his office, shaking hands with the guy whose face had set up camp in her imagination years ago, and before she knew it, she was back to hyper-ventilating. She would never share this with Marc or Jodi. They would never understand what she was doing. Marc would make her feel that she was being selfish and wasting time, while Jodi would probably just start to worry about her, the way she had outside of Chelsea's Home Details: *What's the matter with you, Iliana? I never see you like this.* Without intending to, they'd both end up making her rethink what she was doing, and she didn't want to second-guess herself. Thinking about Jeff Downs was diverting, just like it had been during those endless days in middle school, when she would stare out the window during class and choose a daydream about him to watch in her head, like a favorite book you pull off the shelf again and again. Often she'd imagine that she had graduated from high school and moved to Los Angeles, where she got a job arranging props on the *Guitar Dreams* set. She imagined that Terry would ask her out, while Jeff would hold back, intimidated by Terry's confidence. She'd turn Terry down, and finally Jeff would see that she liked *him*. And then one day he'd ask her to dinner.

And he'd look even more surprised than happy when she nodded. And at the end of their date, he'd tell her that he'd fallen in love with her the moment he met her. Then he'd hold her chin with one hand and kiss her, slowly and luxuriously, as though he was so in love that he wanted the kiss to last forever. He'd say she was the most incredible girl he'd ever known.

On Tuesday morning, after Marc left for work and the kids were in school, Iliana turned on the TV. Sitting on the edge of her bed, she flipped through the channels until she found a station airing an interview with the Dreamers. But Jeff wasn't paying attention to the interviewer. Instead, he looked straight into the camera, as though he were trying to catch her eye. How was that possible? It couldn't be. And yet he kept looking, the intensity of his stare forcing her to look back at him. When she did, he nodded ever so slightly, and she realized he didn't want the other boys to notice he had made contact. She waited. He nodded again. She pointed to herself and mouthed "Me?" Slowly, he lifted his arm and held it toward her, as though he intended to bring her into the TV with him.

"Good morning," she saw him mouth, and his hand started to emerge from the screen. She gasped. She could feel his fingers on her face. It was so close . . . it was that close . . .

"Whoa!" Marc said, looking down at her. "You okay?"

"Good morning!" the radio announcer repeated. "It's seven-oh-eight, time for traffic and weather together . . ."

"I just wanted to say good-bye," Marc said. "Man, you nearly hit the ceiling."

"I'm fine," Iliana said, her hands over her face. "I was sleeping. You scared me."

—⁂—

Back home after dropping the kids off at school—Matthew's violin was clearly visible in his hand—Iliana showered and put on the navy-blue suit she had worn to Marc's cousin's wedding last year. It was probably too formal for a business meeting, but it was the only professional-looking outfit she had. She hadn't needed to buy business clothes in a long time. She blew out her hair and put on more makeup than she usually wore—foundation, eyeliner, and blush, in addition to her everyday mascara and lip-gloss. She had fun pulling herself together in this way. It wasn't that she didn't normally care about her appearance, because she did. She liked to look nice. But casual clothes, little makeup, and air-dried, finger-combed hair had been the appearance she'd developed over the years. It was comfortable and it worked for her. It was sort of like her uniform.

In the kitchen, she put a pod into the Keurig and took out the milk. Her hands were so tingly that the carton nearly slipped from her fingers, and a few drops of milk landed on her suit. She wiped it down with a dish towel as she went to get a yogurt, but then changed her mind. She was way too nervous to eat; her stomach was bubbling so much, she could picture the acids rising in her chest. She took a few sips of coffee, then placed the mug in the sink and went to the hall closet for her shoes and coat. Now it wasn't just her hands that were clumsy, but her whole body. Her arms felt like they had no muscle tone, and her breaths were quick and shallow. She realized that if she kept imagining her morning—going to the station, getting on the train, walking into the Downs Textiles office, seeing Jeff Downs, meeting Jeff Downs, making conversation with Jeff Downs—her legs would give out completely. Would he look old? Could he be bald, or fat? Would he still be so cute she wanted to cry? Would seeing him still make her feel so good?

She decided that the only way to cope was to concentrate on the present. Grab her shoulder bag. Wallet and phone? Check. Slip a notebook and a pen into her shoulder bag. Anything else she had to do? No, all was set. She could go and come back with no one suspecting a thing. Marc was working, and she'd be home way before the kids were done with their sports and Jodi carpooled them home.

Nearly alone on the off-peak train, Iliana tried to close her eyes and relax. Moving vehicles usually put her to sleep in an instant, but today her eyes kept popping back open. Was she sure she knew where she was going? She took out her phone and googled Downs Textiles to recheck the address. Yes, she had it right—295 Fifth Avenue, between Thirtieth and Thirty-First Streets. She had spent many hours in that neighborhood back when she was at *Business Times*, interviewing retail executives who had their showrooms there. 295 Fifth Avenue, Suite 916, she said to herself. 295 Fifth Avenue, Suite 916. She forcefully let out another breath and shoved the notebook back into her bag. Then she rehearsed in her head what she planned to say: *I want to do a feature on your company because I've heard good things about your blankets . . .* She figured she'd start off talking about his business to get him to relax and open up, and then gradually talk about his life and former celebrity, which was what Stuart would most want to see.

In Grand Central Station, she walked down the platform, up the staircase, and through the huge main hall, joining the vast flow of people rushing in all directions. She felt powerful and energized, just as she had during her reporter days when she felt she was on the brink of unearthing a great story. Outside the station, she hailed a taxi, and a few minutes later, she emerged. Stepping onto the curb, she looked at the sky. It was cold, but the sun was shining, bright and warm on her face. She walked a few steps to a newsstand and bought a pack of peppermint Tic Tacs, just as she used to do before important interviews. She shoved a few in her mouth and stuffed the box in her bag. She chewed them up and swallowed. She looked at her phone. It was ten twenty. Time to head up.

Moving easily with the other people entering the building, she checked in with the security desk, found the elevator, and stepped inside. She saw herself in the mirrored doors of the car, one face among many faces, one person among many who were in the city today to make something happen. The elevator stopped on six. Eight. Nine. Murmuring "Excuse me," she stepped out and eyed the hallways to her left and right. Too wound up to focus on the posted floor directory, she turned left and peeked around the next corner. And there it was, straight ahead at the end of the hall.

Double glass doors with two words imprinted: Downs Textiles.

She took her hands out of her pockets and flexed her fingers to get the blood circulating. She took a deep breath and cleared her throat, then made a little "mmm" sound to make sure her voice was normal. It was. She looked at her phone—no messages—and then tucked it in her bag. She licked her lips and moved her jaw from side to side. Finally, turning the corner and walking forward, barely breathing, she reached the doors and pulled one open.

She entered a small reception area. Ahead was a large, open showroom, just like the photo on the company's home page, with several tall racks holding all styles of blankets. A few groups of people were sitting at tables scattered around the showroom. The largest group was sitting at the table closest to her, facing one of the racks. Their backs were toward her.

"May I help you?" came a gentle but authoritative voice. Iliana turned to her right and saw a very thin, older woman looking out at her from behind a long wooden reception desk.

"Iliana Fisher, for Jeff Downs? For a ten-thirty appointment?" She hated that she sounded as though she were asking permission.

"Oh, Ms. Fisher, welcome," the woman said. "I'm Rose, the person you spoke with on the phone." She got up and walked around the desk. "Let me take your coat. Jeff wanted me to apologize again for how I must have sounded. We get calls from the media from time to time, and usually the sales reps handle them. But I never meant to imply that Jeff wouldn't want—I mean, we're *all* so excited to see you."

She took Iliana's coat and went to a nearby closet, as Iliana watched stiffly. Suddenly it seemed that all the air was behind her, outside the double doors. This Rose person, and evidently all the people in the office, clearly thought Iliana had an actual *Business Times* assignment. It was going to be hard to admit otherwise.

"I'll let him know you're here," Rose said when she returned, putting up one finger to suggest that it would only take a moment. Iliana smiled and nodded. The woman walked into the showroom, and Iliana assumed she was heading toward an office in the back. Instead she went to the nearby table. She placed her hand on one man's shoulder as she leaned down and whispered into his ear. He stood. He was wearing a light-blue shirt, his sleeves neatly rolled up, and gray suit pants, and although Iliana could only see him from the back, she noticed that he had an attractive shape, with broad shoulders and a slim waist. Rose spoke a few more words, and the man raised his hands as though excusing himself from the meeting.

And suddenly it hit her: Oh my God, was that him?

The man turned toward her and came forward with confident strides. Iliana watched him, examining his face, his gait, searching for something familiar. Then she saw him smile, a shy, tight-lipped grin. But it was his familiar voice, mid-toned and smooth as Amaretto, that clinched it.

"Hi," he said, extending his hand. "I'm Jeff Downs."

Chapter 5

"Iliana . . . Fisher," she said, shaking his hand.

It was shocking to see him after all this time. He was the same person, that was clear, but his familiar features seemed superimposed on a completely different surface. His face was longer than it used to be; his once-full cheeks now led to his square chin in a sharper, more direct line. His brown eyes were small and close together—hadn't they once seemed huge? And his nose looked narrower, too. His hair was coarser, like the hair of a fox terrier. He wore it short all around, with the top slightly longer and casually parted to the side. It looked washed-out now, a dull taupe. Not the rich caramel-brown from way back.

And yet, he was still attractive, maybe even more so. The changes in his face made him look smarter than he had as a kid, while his bouncy stride and slim waist gave him an irresistible youthfulness. His familiar smile now produced a pair of deep double parentheses around his mouth and three prominent horizontal grooves just outside and below each eye. The parentheses pulled her into him, drawing her close with so much charisma that she felt she should take a step back or she might be too overwhelmed to speak.

"Nice to meet you, Ms. Fisher. Glad you could make time for us," he said. Then he looked over at Rose, who was standing a few steps away, and lifted his eyebrows mischievously. "So far so good, boss?"

Rose pressed her hand to her cheek and shook her head, and Iliana was sure she was blushing. "Oh, Jeff," the woman said. "You are just impossible."

He turned back to Iliana, his hands in his pants pockets, and rocked slightly on his heels. "Rose here has been coaching me on how to behave with a reporter—"

"Jeff, please, I think you know exactly how to do that—"

"—and she was sure I was going to muck it up. As a matter of fact, she insisted that I bring up Eureka. So how's it going? You think the changes will stick?"

Iliana looked at him blankly. "Eureka?"

"You know. The vacuum company."

She opened her mouth, but didn't know what to say. What was he talking about? He made blankets, not vacuums, didn't he? Did he think *she* was someone else?

Now he seemed confused. "Wasn't it Eureka—the management shake-up yesterday? It was the top story in the Business section this morning, wasn't it? We figured you and your colleagues over there at the *Times* must have worked late into the night to get that done. We were worried you might cancel our appointment so you could take the morning off and sleep in."

"Oh," she said. "Oh, Eureka. Yes." It hit her immediately: He didn't think she had an assignment in *Business Times*; he thought she was a reporter for the Business section of the *New York Times*! *Now* she understood why Rose hadn't handed her off to the sales reps, and had seemed so apologetic on the phone. *Now* it was clear why he had invited her in to meet him. He thought he was getting an article about his blankets in the *New York Times*—no wonder he'd been so happy to see her.

While she found his attempt to flatter her very sweet, it also terrified her. How could she admit that she was writing for *Business Times*—or actually just hoping to? It would be so embarrassing. Already she felt her cheeks grow hot. "Oh, no, you see, I didn't work on that," she said. "I don't actually write for the *Times* . . . Business section. I don't write for the Business section."

"No? What section do you write for?"

She looked at his sweet, youthful smile, at the double parentheses near his mouth, at the friendly look in his eyes that said that he liked her. "New York," she said. "I write for the New York section." Her cheeks suddenly felt hot. She put her hand against the one closest to him, so he wouldn't notice how red it probably was.

"Oh," he said agreeably. "Well, we'll have to pay more attention to that one." He clapped his fisted left hand into his open-palmed right. "So, how about if we go scrounge up some space in the back and talk? Sound good?"

She nodded and tried to discreetly breathe out through her mouth, hoping that her face would begin to cool down.

"Maybe some coffee first, Jeff?" Rose said.

Jeff knocked his forehead with his fingers. "Coffee, of course! Rose, you saved me again! Would you like some, Ms. Fisher? Or may I call you Iliana?"

Iliana smiled and nodded, starting to relax. Clearly he was a little full of himself, teasing his receptionist and making her blush, even though Rose was quite a bit older than he was. But he was cute and funny, and his charm was irresistible, just as it had been when he was young. "Iliana is fine. And I'd love coffee, thank you."

"Milk and sugar?" Rose asked.

"Just milk, thank you."

"Black for you, Jeff?"

"You got it, thanks."

The woman waved cheerfully, and Jeff extended his arm, inviting Iliana farther into the showroom. "We don't have any offices here, just tables," he told her. "I'm not really into the whole formal thing. You're probably used to interviewing people in big executive suites, right? Suited-up execs in their big, padded chairs?"

"I like all types—I mean, I interview all types," she said. It disarmed her, the way he was walking sideways so he could look directly in her eyes as they walked. She felt like she was twelve again.

"Well, we're pretty casual here, as you can see. But I'm sure I can find us somewhere quiet."

He turned and scrutinized the available tables, and as she followed him, her left foot caught the leg of a display rack. She felt her whole body start to propel forward but jammed her right foot down and found her balance just a few moments before she'd have landed on her face. Grateful that no one had seen her—and that the carpet had muffled the sound of her stumbling—she let out a shaky breath. She didn't know if she was nervous because she was pretending to be a *Times* reporter or simply because she was with Jeff Downs, but either way, she told herself, she had better calm down.

Jeff led her to a table, while Rose delivered the coffee. Iliana sat down and then Jeff did, leaning back in his chair and folding his hands on the table.

"So, Ms. Fisher—I mean, Iliana," he said. "We don't get many reporters here in the showroom, definitely not from the *Times*. Tell me about that. Have you been there long?"

She smiled as she started to formulate an answer. She hadn't expected him to start out questioning her, although it occurred to her now that many executives she'd interviewed had begun that way. Sometimes they were just breaking the ice, and sometimes they were trying to get a read on exactly who they were dealing with—how experienced she was, what other publishers she'd worked for—so they could determine whether she'd be throwing hardballs or softballs. She also knew it was possible that Jeff was suspicious about whether she was really with the *Times* or not, but she didn't think so. He didn't look suspicious. He looked like he truly found her interesting. She loved that—it was as though he recognized something special in her, the same way she had imagined he would back when she was in middle school. And yet it also made her uncomfortable. He was responding to her lies—and she was going to have to lie more to keep up this whole charade. She felt guilty, but she forced herself to ignore that so she could concentrate on her answer.

"I've . . . I've been writing for a long time," she answered. "But I don't work directly for the *Times*. I'm a freelancer. I work for myself." She nodded and relaxed a bit; calling herself a freelancer was at least somewhat more truthful than pretending to be an actual *Times* employee.

"Cool," he said. "That must be a great way to work. Gives you control over what you want to do. Gives you freedom, too. Have you always been a freelancer?"

"Before I . . . actually, I was on staff at a business magazine. I was there for a long time. But then I stopped writing for a while. To have my family."

"And now you write for the *Times*? Wow, you *must* be good."

She shook her head, embarrassed that his compliment was based on her lie. "Just trying . . . to do a job," she said.

"Hey, no need for modesty," he said. "My motto is, you gotta stand up for yourself in this world, because no one else is gonna do it." He drank some of his coffee, holding his cup around the rim and then putting it back down on the saucer. "So, I don't want to waste any more of your time," he said. "Tell me, Ms. Fisher—I mean, Iliana. What can I do for you?"

She took a deep breath and combined the words she'd rehearsed with some new ones the situation required her to improvise. "I'd like to do a piece on your company . . . for New Yorkers who read . . . the New York section," she said. "I heard about your blankets from . . . some of my sources, and I wanted to meet you and get the full story."

"Great," he said. "Who told you about us?"

"I'm afraid I can't answer that. When my sources talk about products, it's not for attribution." She was glad for that handy old *Business Times* line.

"Fair enough," he said. "Then I'll just get started, and feel free to interrupt if you have any questions. Let's see . . . the big picture is, we're a specialty blanket supplier with a full assortment of products. At the top end, we have our cashmeres and silk blends, and at the more affordable price points, we have our fleeces." He cupped his head with his hands and stretched out his legs, crossing them at the ankles. "Fleece, as you may know, is a perfect blanket fabric. It's warm but lightweight, it's strong but soft. It wears well, takes dye well, and it washes beautifully. We've been very successful with that line in particular."

"Yes, but fleece is a pretty basic product," Iliana said, and as she pulled out her notebook and started to take notes, she finally started to relax. It felt great, being back in the game again. She was a tennis player finding the sweet spot, a pitcher catching the edge of the strike zone. She was a dancer moving in perfect sync with her partner. She had always enjoyed the pas de deux she danced with the people she interviewed, especially the handsome male ones: both parties on their best behavior, looking their best and performing at their peak. "How do you compete with the cheaper imports coming in from China?" she said.

"Well, we've got a thicker construction and our color palette is unmatched," he answered. "In fact, our new spring colors are hitting the stores next month. Hey, Greg, throw me a couple of those fleeces."

A bearded young man who was adjusting some display racks pulled two blankets off a shelf and tossed them to Jeff, who spread them on the table. One was a pale sage, and the other was lavender. Iliana ran her finger along a fold.

"Very pretty," she said.

"Yeah," he agreed. "Our new colors are all great. We don't have the complete line here, but you can get an idea from the catalog—I'll show you." He jumped from his chair and opened the top drawer of a nearby file cabinet.

"Let's see, Rose was going to file them in here . . ." he said. As he shuffled through the folders, he started to whistle. Then he began to hum. Softly at first, and then a little louder.

Suddenly Iliana's shoulders rose and she gave a little gasp as her hands, her fingers froze. She leaned forward, watching his back, straining to hear what he was humming. And then she knew. It was "The Best of Times." At first it surprised her that he'd hum a song he had made famous decades ago. It seemed a little pitiful, like a guy who decorates his house with medals from his days as a high school athlete. But then she came to the conclusion that he wasn't doing it consciously. He seemed to be just humming a tune out of habit, the way other people might bite their lip or click their tongue to fill the silence.

"Hey, I know that song!" she said.

"What?" He looked up.

"The song you were humming," she explained quickly, regretting her outburst. She had meant to be subtler. Her thoughts started racing down a paranoid path: An actual *Times* reporter on assignment wouldn't exclaim like that over some old pop tune. What if he started to be suspicious of her, because she said she knew the song? What if he demanded proof that she was writing for the *Times*?

Jeff leaned against the filing cabinet and lifted his eyebrows in surprise. "I was humming?" he asked. "I didn't realize. What was I humming?"

She watched him, desperately hoping for a cue about how to respond. "You were humming 'The Best of Times,'" she finally said. Her voice cracked. She cleared her throat. "I used to watch your show."

He folded his arms across his chest. "So," he said with a Dracula-like accent. "I see you know about my past life."

The tension rolled down her body, the way it did when Dara used to run her fingers down her back after pretending to crack an egg on her head. "I'm afraid I do," she said, sounding flirtier than she intended.

"Come on, you must have been a baby when that show was on."

"No, but that's nice of you to say."

He grinned. "So a *New York Times* reporter remembers my song. What do you know about that?" He nodded, like he was considering the ramifications of this news and gradually finding them extremely appealing. "Yeah. I like that. I like it a lot." The lines around his mouth pulled her closer, until she was smiling, too. It was as though they were two people who had just shared a secret—a secret that changed them from acquaintances to something closer. Iliana felt as though it wasn't just *his* past they were talking about, but *their* past, a past that they had shared together.

He straightened up and clapped the fist of one hand into the palm of the other. "Sooooooo. Back to work. This catalog's gotta be some-where." He looked into the filing cabinet once more, and finally pulled out a glossy booklet. She could tell he still had plenty he wanted to share about his business, so she thought she'd let the interview continue in that vein for now. "Here we go, I knew it was here," he said. "Take a look. It's awesome."

He turned his chair backward and sat down, his chest against the chair back and his knees splayed, and he turned the catalog toward her on the table. She looked at the photos and nodded admiringly as he flipped a few pages, pointing out which were his best sellers. Then he closed the book and slid it toward her.

"What's next?" he said.

She asked him whether price fluctuations in cotton were having an effect on his bottom line and if he would have to pass any increases on to retailers for the fall selling season. He conceded that cotton prices were volatile, but said he had made a commitment to his retailers to hold prices steady this year, and he intended to keep it. She asked whether a small company like his could continue to be viable over the next five to ten years, considering the enormous cost of maintaining a Manhattan showroom and the greater efficiencies of larger companies that supplied the same products. He explained that he had moved his design and administration functions up to Westchester so he could continue to maintain a roomy showroom in Manhattan where retailers could see his product line in comfort. He added that bigger companies weren't as nimble in spotting trends and changing directions as a small company like his was.

She asked how "green" his products were and whether sustainable raw materials and environmentally sound manufacturing processes were a priority. He showed her some samples that his design team was working on, using new plant-based dyes, although he conceded that there were still color problems that needed to be ironed out. She asked if she could see the other products in his line, and he took her on a tour of the showroom so she could examine the high-end blankets that his company marketed.

Finally he looked at his watch and held up one hand. "Hey, I'm sorry, I didn't expect we'd go longer than an hour. I have a twelve o'clock with one of the merchandise managers at Bloomingdale's. I'd cancel but it's really important. Getting some tips for a meeting next week with the whole Bloomingdale's team."

"Oh," Iliana said. She didn't move. The time had passed so quickly! She hadn't asked any questions yet about *Guitar Dreams* or his life post-celebrity. She had been hoping the conversation would move there naturally, that he would tell an anecdote that would lead him to start talking about Hollywood. But that hadn't happened. The one time he had come close was when he hummed "The Best of Times"—but he had turned the conversation back to business pretty quickly after that.

"Hey, I don't want to cut this short," he added. "This article is important, too, and—wait, I have an idea! Why don't you sit in on that meeting? Those Bloomingdale's guys love reporters. It's next Tuesday at eleven. And when they leave, we'll wrap things up. I'll even buy you lunch."

She hesitated. She shouldn't be coming back here. She had let the misunderstanding about the *Times* go on too long, and it now felt too late to come clean. She didn't know how she'd tell Jeff the truth, and whatever she could possibly say, it would be too embarrassing to bear. The best thing would be to leave the office and never come back. She would have to come up with another idea for Stuart, but she could deal with that later. She should disappear from here, just consider this a fun meeting with her onetime crush and call it a day. After a few weeks of not seeing his company mentioned in the paper, Jeff might call the *Times* asking for her, but by then she'd be long gone and unreachable. She was glad that she hadn't yet gotten around to adjusting the settings on her cell phone, which came preprogrammed to keep her number hidden when she made calls. There'd be no way to trace her.

And yet, the chance to meet with Jeff again, to pursue this article further and see where it might take her, was too enticing to pass up. She wasn't ready to say good-bye.

"I would love that," she said.

"Then it's a date." He clapped his hands and stood. Iliana began to slip her notebook and the catalog into her bag, but feeling frazzled at this new turn of events, she couldn't get the pages to slide in smoothly. Her fingers felt huge and clumsy. After three attempts, she brought the books out, smoothed them on her lap, and finally succeeded. When she stood up, she saw Jeff looking at her, smiling sympathetically. She rolled her eyes and they both laughed as they started walking toward the showroom entrance.

"So do you work out of an office? Or from your home?" Jeff asked.

"My home," she said.

"Here in the city?"

"No, Westchester." She knew he was just making small talk, but she wished he'd stop with the questions. She didn't want to give out any more information about herself, at least not until she got home and had a chance to think this whole morning through.

"No kidding! I live in Westchester, too. What do you know about that? I'm in Mount Kisco."

He looked at her expectantly, clearly waiting for her to volunteer what town she lived in, but luckily Rose appeared just then with her coat. Jeff took it and held it up for her, and she slipped an arm through a sleeve, acutely aware that it was Jeff Downs—*Jeff Downs!*—supporting her coat's weight. She had daydreamed so many times when she was young about Jeff doing simple things—helping her with her coat, opening a door—that having him actually *do* one felt full of meaning. Suddenly her real life seemed unimaginably remote. If she had found a way to make Jeff Downs real, what else could she do?

"Well, Ms. Iliana Fisher, it's been a pleasure," Jeff said, taking her hand in both of his. She felt her face redden. She had expected a simple handshake. "Thanks for coming. See you next Tuesday at eleven."

Outside the double doors, Iliana turned and looked through the glass as Jeff jogged back through the showroom.

And then she was back in the elevator. She didn't remember pushing the button to call it. She sensed that the elevator was crowded, but she didn't see any faces. She was only aware of her black wool coat, which had been almost weightless as Jeff Downs helped her with it. She remembered the way the sleeves slipped on. She could feel how they glided up to her shoulders.

Gazing forward at the mirrored elevator doors, Iliana watched her face come into focus, peeking out between the shoulders of two men in front of her. It reminded her of when she was a teenager sitting in the backseat of her father's Ford Taurus, and could just make out her eyes in the small rearview mirror. Sometimes, particularly when her dad was driving her to a party, she couldn't believe how pretty her eyes were. Large and brown, a little almond-shaped, with huge black pupils, framed by the soft, brown waves of her hair. For the first time in a long time, she could see those pretty eyes again. Maybe it was because she had just come out of a very successful business meeting with a charming man who admired and respected her. She was feeling very good about herself.

She left the building and began walking, hearing Jeff's voice in her head: *"Wow, you must be good." "Ms. Iliana Fisher, it's been a pleasure."* Nearing the corner, she was vaguely aware of a man's voice calling out. It annoyed her because it was disrupting her thoughts, like an alarm clock that interrupts a delicious dream. She was trying to concentrate on the memory of Jeff's words, when suddenly she felt a harsh tug on her elbow. Alarmed, she pulled it back defensively, but then recognized the voice.

"What's going on? I've been chasing you for two blocks!"

"Marc!" she said. "Oh my God, Marc! I thought someone was trying to take my bag. God, you scared me. What are you doing here?"

"What am *I* doing here?" he said. "I've been working at the Affinia. I told you that this morning—Angers arranged the off-site for today. We just finished one meeting, and I was taking a walk to clear my head. What are *you* doing here?"

"I was . . . shopping at Macy's," she said, pointing toward Thirty-Fourth Street.

"You came all the way into the city for Macy's?"

"They have a wider selection here than the one in White Plains."

"Why, what are you buying?"

"I was going to look for something to wear to Jena Connors's." Looking over Marc's shoulder, she spotted Jeff Downs emerging from his building, wearing a black overcoat and holding the arm of a tall woman draped in a red sweater-coat. It dawned on her that the woman must be the Bloomingdale's executive he had been waiting for. She had assumed his meeting was with a man.

She grabbed Marc's elbow and pivoted to his other side, so her back was to the couple. "Marc, I really need to catch a train back so I'll be home for the kids," she said.

"Okay, fine, don't let me hold you up. But come to think of it, go ahead and buy something to wear for the workshop. You want to make a good impression. And maybe you should get something for next Wednesday, too—there's a cocktail party to celebrate the Cleveland office, wives invited." He kissed her cheek. "I'd better get back; I'll see you at home."

Iliana watched him proceed down the block, feeling guilty that she had lied to him. It was something she never did, other than to throw him off when she was shopping for his birthday presents. But she was also insulted that he had basically *instructed* her to buy new clothes. That was the kind of thing a parent did, not an equal partner in a marriage.

Backing up to the wall of the nearest building, Iliana peeked around the portico. She saw Jeff step off the curb and raise his hand. Meanwhile, the woman he was with swung her head toward Iliana, letting the wind sweep her mahogany-colored hair away from her face. A cab stopped in front of them, and Jeff opened the door. The woman laughed, pushed a strand of hair behind her ear, and slid inside. Iliana watched as the cab pulled away and disappeared into traffic. Their warm interaction made her question for a moment her own time with Jeff Downs. He had made her feel that he thought she was special—but was that simply the way he behaved with all women?

She pushed the thought from her mind. They had had a wonderful meeting that morning, and she wasn't going to let any insecurities change that. The bottom line was, she had loved being part of Jeff Downs's world, and loved being Iliana Fisher, *New York Times* reporter on assignment. It had satisfied a need she had been feeling a long time.

And she was going back next week to do it again. She could hardly wait.

Chapter 6

Where do ex–pop stars go when it's time
to leave the soundstage? Here's one who's
made the switch from rehearsal studio to
design studio, proving that a TV star's success can extend beyond reruns!

Later that day at the dining room table, Iliana finished typing and
leaned back in her chair. Not bad—it was a lively lead, and it focused on
celebrity, which was what Stuart wanted. She was pleased that after years
away from *Business Times*, she still could develop a solid business story.

She continued:

The ex–pop star in question is Jeff Downs,
one of the four teenage boys who made up
the Dreamers, the centerpiece of the one-
time hit sitcom *Guitar Dreams*. Back then,
Jeff Downs was a superstar. His slender frame
graced posters in teenage girls' bedrooms
across the country, and his modest smile

shone on magazine covers week after week after week.

But after a handful of years in the limelight, and many more out of it, Jeff has done an about-face. While once he filled the dreams of teenyboppers, now he covers their beds—with blankets that bear the name of his successful New York–based textiles firm.

How does it feel to go from pop stardom to business ownership? What does a former star miss—and what doesn't he miss? How did he come to land in New York? What did his years on TV teach him about making a go of it in the world of commerce?

Would you be interested in a 1,200-word profile about Jeff Downs and Downs Textiles? I'm ready to get started as soon as you give me the word. Thanks, and I look forward to hearing from you soon.

Iliana

She typed the last words and sat back, proud and satisfied. It was a good query, one she thought any shrewd business editor should find irresistible. Hell, if *she* were Stuart, she'd lock the piece up immediately with an assignment and a contract! She knew that Stuart had indicated in his email that he wanted to see a finished article and not a proposal, but as soon as she had gotten home from the city yesterday, she had decided to reach out to him this way. She would have felt too guilty otherwise to go back to Downs Textiles next week—especially when Jeff was including her in a client meeting and then taking her out to lunch. Jeff had been so generous and personable, and she figured that if she could at least get some interest from Stuart to hang her hat on, she would feel better about returning to be with him again. She could gradually nudge Jeff into seeing *Business Times* as a strong and significant publication—maybe even a preferred outlet for business coverage over the *Times* Business section—so that when she eventually told him she'd sold the piece to *Business Times*, he'd be fine with the switch.

It was a great story idea and would make a great article, she thought. Of course, she still needed Jeff to agree to share some thoughts about his past to give the story some color, but she felt confident that she could convince him to do so. He liked her, she could tell—he liked and admired her, and she thought he would trust her when she told him some anecdotes and personal comments would make her article better. And once it was published and out in the world, it could open up even more writing opportunities for her. Feeling that things were falling into place, she tapped "Send," and the email was on its way.

Then, just for good measure, she went to the *New York Times* website and found an email address for the New York section editor. Why not? If Stuart didn't like the idea, maybe the *Times* would, and if she somehow ended up with two acceptances, she could figure out then what to do. As an old journalism professor of hers used to say, *that* would be a high-quality problem.

She copied the text and pasted it into a new email and added some information about her past experience at *Business Times*. Then she signed off and sent it on its way. Two pitches in just over an hour. Two potential opportunities that didn't exist before.

She was feeling so good about all she had accomplished that day, so glad that things looked so promising, that later that night when the kids came downstairs—Dara to watch TV, Matt to get a snack—she blocked their way, pointing toward the kitchen table where she had set up the Scrabble board. She had realized while making dinner that often when she was with her kids, she was mostly in her own head—worrying about how fast the day was going, fretting over traffic, silently cursing drivers ahead of her who slowed down when the light turned yellow. Tonight, for the first time in a long time, she didn't feel compelled to throw in another load of laundry or sort through stacks of mail or write checks for pizza lunches and field trips and other assorted school events, in the hope that she could clear a few hours the next morning to accomplish something meaningful. Tonight she felt satisfied.

"Come on," she said to them. "Let's play."

They looked at her as though she had told them to scrub the toilet. "But I just *finished* thinking!" Dara complained. "I can't think anymore!"

"I'm so tired," Matt said. "Can't we do it this weekend?"

But Iliana wouldn't take no for an answer, and soon they were choosing letters and laying down words. At one point, Matthew found a perfect triple-letter spot for his "x" and celebrated his move by punching the air with his fists, shouting, "Yes!"

Iliana lifted her wrist to her forehead. "Oh, the humiliation!" she cried.

When Marc came home, there were just a few letters left in the bag. "Whose idea was this? I love Scrabble!" he said. He warmed the dinner plate Iliana had left for him and brought it to the table just as Matt won. Iliana suggested that they play again so Marc could join in, and the kids enthusiastically refilled the letter bag.

Later that evening, Marc was in bed reading *Wall Street Journal* updates on his iPad when she finished straightening the kitchen and went upstairs. He was in his boxers and his dress shirt was on, although the top few buttons were unbuttoned and his sleeves were rolled up. She could see his bare chest, the warm tone of his skin, the mass of pepper-and-salt hair. Closing their bedroom door, she climbed onto the bed and ran a finger gently from his ankle to his knee. Although they used to make love often, as the kids got older they gradually began waiting for weekend evenings when Matt and Dara were at the movies or friends' houses. The house wasn't that large, the kids' bedrooms were just down a short hall, and once both Matt and Dara had learned about sex, their presence in the house inhibited her. She assumed Marc felt the same way. But tonight she felt like making love anyway. Why not? The door was closed and the kids knew to knock if they needed anything, which they most likely wouldn't since they were both already in bed. She and Marc were creative and inventive, and surely they could make love in a quiet way. She didn't want to wait for the weekend and hope the kids would have plans. Why had she and Marc come up with that unspoken rule? Why hadn't either one of them questioned it before?

"By the way, they're changing the date," Marc mumbled, his eyes still on his iPad.

She looked up from his calf. "What date?"

"The cocktail party. For the Cleveland office. I told you about it when I saw you yesterday. It may not be Wednesday anymore, I'll have to let you know."

"Got it, change of date," Iliana said teasingly, as she leaned over and began planting kisses on his ankle, his knee, his thigh just below his boxers.

Marc twisted his leg away. "I mean it, Iliana, don't act like this is no big deal, because it is. It's coming up and I don't know when, so you're going to have to put Jodi or whoever on call—if there's driving to be done, she's going to have to cover for you."

"There's no driving to be done in the evenings."

"I'm just saying that all the exec wives will be there, so you can't start fighting with me about conflicts."

Iliana straightened her back and looked at him. On any other evening, this would be the time when she stormed into the bathroom, or went downstairs to the family room, just like she did last week when he came home from Chicago. This would be the time when she wrapped herself in the plaid throw and sulked, feeling rejected and sorry for herself. Now would be when she thought about how he was always telling her what to do, and then worried that maybe he was right and she was being selfish. Now would be the beginning of her passive-aggressive silence, which would gradually fade, only to start again after the next disagreement. But she decided right then that she wasn't going to follow that path. Not tonight. She was feeling too good about herself. She was feeling too excited about all the good things that were potentially in store for her.

"Okay, Marc," she said. "I understand this is important."

She pulled herself alongside him and kissed his waist, then ran her open palm over his chest. "Do you know that the way I most love seeing you is with your dress shirt unbuttoned?" she said.

He looked down at her. "What?" He laughed.

"No, I mean it," she said. "You've got your shirt buttoned up and a tie on all day, being the smart, serious lawyer you are. And then you come home and unbutton your shirt, and you're still that Marc but you're also the Marc who belongs to me. It's why when we were dating, I always liked to meet you right after work and go to your apartment. I didn't want you to change your clothes and then come to my place. I wanted to be there when you became my Marc."

He took off his glasses and closed the tablet. "And do you know what I love best about you?" he said. "It's the smile you give me when you know I'm about to kiss you. There's just a look you have that makes me think you feel really lucky to be with me. There—see? There it is."

Then he brought her face close to his and kissed her—a long, rich kiss that felt so good on her mouth. Their lovemaking was gentle, as they both explored how to be together with sleeping adolescents down the hall. It was a different kind of lovemaking than she was used to—stretchy and slow instead of intense and assertive—and it was wonderful. Her limbs felt like chocolate liqueur.

"Here she is, I see her walking in. Excuse me a moment."

Iliana could hear Jeff talking about her as she handed Rose her coat. When she turned, he was walking toward her, smiling that familiar Jeff smile. He had on a deep blue shirt and fanciful blue tie with gold and red saxophones.

"Hello, Ms. Fisher," he said, in a mock-formal tone. "Thank you for coming back."

"My pleasure, Mr. Downs," she responded, matching her tone to his.

"They're killing me out there," he whispered teasingly.

"Somehow I don't believe that," she teased back. He struck her as a winner, and his smile told her he liked that she thought that.

He stepped aside and she proceeded into the showroom. She was wearing a new outfit, a lavender sheath dress with a robin's-egg-blue cardigan, both of which she had bought on Saturday, in between drop-offs and pickups. It was unusual for her to wear colors—the other two professional-style dresses she owned were black—but she had thought that a *Times* reporter who wrote about home trends would definitely make bolder fashion choices, and once she tried the clothes on, she realized the colors made her brown eyes look bigger and the whites of her eyes, whiter. And because she planned to wear the outfit to Marc's cocktail party, she didn't feel guilty about buying it. It had been a nice surprise in the store to find that clothes seemed to fit her better than they used to. Apparently all her excitement about Jeff Downs had curbed her appetite, because it felt like she had dropped a few pounds. She had also decided to add some subtle highlights when she got her hair colored. She loved the way they looked.

Jeff led her to a round table where four people were already seated and made the introductions.

"Iliana Fisher. I've never heard that name," said the patriarch of the contingent, an elegant man with a long face and a mane of white hair. He rested his elbows on the table, and with his eyes closed, stroked his hair with one hand. "I thought I knew all the home furnishings reporters at the *Times*."

Reflexively she reached for her bag, anticipating a potentially quick exit. But Jeff saved her.

"Iliana's a freelancer, Paul," he said. "She works for the New York section."

Iliana nodded sheepishly. She knew she looked uncomfortable and hoped they would all think it was just because she was embarrassed at the attention. She felt bad that Jeff was now repeating her lie, but told herself that hopefully it wouldn't be a lie for long. She could soon be a writer for the New York section, she thought. She just had to get through these little bumpy spots until then.

"New York, huh? Never met those people. But they're good. They did an excellent article on commercial real estate a few weeks back. Two pages." He pointed a pencil at a young man with short, gelled hair and a body-hugging black turtleneck sweater. "See it?" he demanded.

The young man blinked. "Uh, yes, Mr. Charles," he said unconvincingly.

"I hope you did," Paul said dryly. "So, let's get started. And all money discussions are off the record, right, young lady?"

"Yes, sir," Iliana said.

"Greg?" Jeff motioned toward his salesman, who slid an easel close to the table and handed Jeff a pile of fleece blankets from a nearby shelf. Jeff held each one up, pointing out the neat stitching around the edge before draping it over the top of the easel. When he was done, the blankets formed a vibrant line of color, ranging from cream to berry to deep navy blue.

He folded his hands on the table. "So, how many millions can we put you down for?" he joked.

"Now hold on," Paul said, stroking his hair again. "There are a lot of great fleece products out there this season."

"I was impressed with the Modern Bedding line," a woman with thick black glasses put in. "They're doing some great things with microfibers."

"No, the Modern Bedding line isn't nearly as well made," said Jeff's lunch guest from last week, her voice polite but firm. "And please, the color range here is much more comprehensive."

"You've got a point, Shelly," Paul said. "But the one thing Modern Bedding has going for it are its prices. Jeff, you're way too high."

"Our blankets aren't cheap, you're right," Jeff said, nodding. "And that's because the quality is unmatched. And we're not going to change that. But if you go in for a big program, we can provide some volume discounts that will make the pricing very attractive."

"Let me see what you've got," Paul said. Greg handed over a sheet of paper. Everyone watched as Paul studied it. "I think you've got something here," he finally said.

"Great. Can I put you down for ten colors?"

"We'll start with four."

"You can't make any kind of impact on the sales floor with only four colors," Jeff said. "Come on, what'll it take to bring you to six?"

"Oh, maybe a few bars of 'The Best of Times,'" the man in the turtleneck said. "Or how about that catchphrase you used to say on the show—'Just start dreamin' to the max!'" He said it with a derisive edge and then glanced around tentatively, like a comedian testing new material. The women laughed a little, their eyes downward, as though they had heard an off-color joke.

Jeff nodded and waited for the laughter to stop, looking a little irritated. Then he stood and rubbed his hands. "Seriously, folks, six?"

"Six, but that's it," Paul said. "We're done."

Ten minutes later they were all shaking hands, Jeff holding a signed contract by his side. As they moved to the reception area, Iliana saw

Jeff's lunch friend give him a private nod, and he winked back. When he turned around, his eyes caught Iliana's, and he tilted his head questioningly. She quickly looked down and pulled an imaginary speck off her dress, angry with herself for watching their exchange. It was ridiculous that for a moment she'd felt jealous—she was here for a *business* meeting, after all. She certainly didn't want to give Jeff the idea she was there for any other reason.

He walked the group out the double doors, then jogged back into the showroom.

"Great job, Jeff," Greg said. "Boy, was I scared. Especially when he brought up the pricing. But you didn't even blink."

"Piece of cake," Jeff said. "Hey, I know how to handle guys like Paul."

"Congratulations, Jeff!" Rose called over, and a few other salespeople from the back echoed her sentiments.

"Yeah, but you got him to go for more colors than you even hoped," Greg continued, shaking his head. "And at a price that—"

"Hey, can you finish telling me how great I am after I get back?" Jeff said, handing Greg the contract. "Right now I've got a hungry reporter on my hands." He turned to Iliana. "Do you like Italian? I feel like celebrating. Rose, can you get us a table at Porto Aperto?"

Iliana looked at her watch. It was just after twelve. "Is it . . . close?" she asked.

"Two blocks south and a little west," Jeff said. "Why, is there a problem? Do you need to make a train?"

"No, I drove in today. But I just need to check in with my editor . . ."

"Sure." Jeff gestured toward the back. "Have a seat at one of the tables, and take your time. I'll wait by the front."

Iliana scooped up her shoulder bag and found the farthest table from the reception desk. She took out her cell phone and tapped in the number.

"Mr. Passing's office, may I help you?"

"Kelly, it's Iliana," she said quietly.

"Iliana? I can barely hear you."

"I'm sorry, it's my cell phone, I'll try to talk louder." She raised her voice a tiny bit. "Is Marc . . . is he in the office? They don't have meetings today in Midtown, do they?"

"No, he's here, but he's got a couple of other lawyers in with him, and they seem to be working on something pretty intense. Want me to interrupt him?"

"No, don't do that, but . . ." She paused. "So he's going to be there for a while?"

"I'd say they'll be here for at least a few hours," she said. "They just called in some sandwiches, so they're not going anywhere else. Want me to slip a note to him? I'm going out to lunch now, and I know he won't be picking up his phone anytime soon."

"No, that's okay," Iliana said.

"Are you sure I can't give him a message?"

"No, no need. I'll see him tonight."

She strolled through the showroom to the reception area, where Jeff was waiting. Marc was downtown for the next few hours, Dara had volleyball until five thirty, and it was Jodi's turn to drive the boys from school to basketball practice. She felt a little guilty—actually, more than a little—for sneaking around behind Marc's back and checking to make sure he wouldn't see her. But it would be confusing to him if he were to run into her and Jeff right now, and a confrontation could derail what she was working to accomplish. Once she got an assignment, she would tell him everything. Her new professional achievement would be cause to celebrate. And anyway, why wasn't she entitled to go out to a business lunch? Marc no doubt went out to business lunches with women all the time, and she knew nothing about them.

Of course, she also didn't feel great about the way she was continuing to deceive Jeff, as well as the multiple stories she had told Paul and his staff about herself. She was racking up quite a litany of lies. But she knew that she had to put the negative thoughts out of her mind. If things went according to her plan, everyone would be happy. Jeff would get his article, she would get her career boost, Paul would get his blankets, Marc would get a happy and fulfilled wife . . .

"Are you okay?" Jeff said. "You look a little worried."

"What?" She looked up, startled. "No, I'm fine. I'm good. All's good."

Chapter 7

The restaurant was airy and elegant, with high ceilings and polished wood floors. Iliana was seated on the banquette, with Jeff opposite her. Though the place was crowded, the walls absorbed the noise, and their table felt very private.

"How about a glass of wine?" Jeff said.

"Sure," she answered. She wanted to relax and let the conversation wander. She hoped to explore the side of Jeff that had hummed "The Best of Times" and then said he liked that she remembered it. She wanted to tell him how much a part of all her dreams he had been when she was young, and she wanted to know that in his own way, he had been searching back then for a girl like her—smart and full of promise, a girl who could become the successful professional sitting across from him now. She was entirely anonymous to him. He didn't know that she hadn't published a word in years, that her husband thought her top priority was *his* career, that the article ideas she had found time to pitch between carpools and errands had been rejected, that her closest friend was another stay-at-home mom who had accepted that no law firm would ever take her back. It felt freeing to reinvent herself as a lead actor in her own right, and not just a supporting player for others. It felt like taking off a layer of clothing.

She asked for a glass of pinot grigio, and Jeff said he'd have the same. They ordered their lunch, and when the wine had been served, Jeff held up his glass.

"Well, here's to a great day," he said. "And a wonderful new friendship and an awesome article."

She lifted her glass. "Thank you for that."

They both took a sip, and then Jeff leaned forward on the table. "You know, you're not like other reporters I've met. All pushy and ruthless, asking obnoxious questions, being cruel because they think it will make them seem clever. But you—you're different. You seem to really care about me. I like that."

She looked down, embarrassed but also thrilled by what he said. It felt good to be complimented. The things he was saying—they were almost exactly what she had imagined he would say when she daydreamed about him years ago. *All those other girls just care about jewelry and shoes. But you, Iliana—you're different from them.* He was right, she did care about him. And because he recognized that, she was optimistic that he'd be amenable when she told him she wanted to write about his life as well as his blankets.

"So tell me some more about yourself," he said. "Did you always want to be a writer?"

She nodded.

"From the time you were young? Like five or six?"

She laughed. "I don't know. Maybe seven or eight."

"Did you always want to work for a newspaper? Ever want to write anything else? A screenplay maybe? A book?"

She looked to the side, giving herself a moment to think. She wanted to keep up her *New York Times* cover, and she knew that talking about herself could be risky. And she wasn't sure why Jeff was questioning her this way—was he just trying to butter her up to make sure her article would be entirely complimentary? But no, he seemed genuinely interested in learning more about her, and she couldn't help but enjoy his attention. Nobody had asked her questions like this in a very long time.

"Actually, I did once want to write a book," she said. "I've always wanted to write about people—what makes them brave, what makes them scared, basically what makes them tick. So I thought I'd find four people who came to New York to follow some dream of theirs, and write about why they came, whether they stayed, how hard it was to keep pushing on, that sort of thing."

She smiled. "Maybe this is going to sound crazy, but one of the people I wanted to write about was Madonna. Do you know that she came to New York with almost nothing but the clothes she was wearing? She was just eighteen and wanted to study dancing. She did odd jobs to pay the rent. I love that. I love how driven she was."

"It's not crazy at all," he said. "I like brave people, too. So whatever happened to the book?" he asked.

She sighed. "I had to put it aside. Life was busy, and writing a book takes time. Who knows? Maybe I'll give it another shot someday."

"I think it sounds good," he said. "I'd read it."

"It's what I like, digging below the surface, finding the story beneath what everybody knows. I remember sitting at this writing desk my parents gave me when I was twelve, thinking of people to write about. I even once tried to write a story about—" She looked up and saw him smiling, which made her feel self-conscious. Maybe the wine was making her open up too much. "Forget it," she said.

"What?" Jeff said. "Tell me." He paused as the waiter served their lunch, then pressed some more. "Hey, you can tell me. We're friends now, remember?"

She rolled her eyes. "Okay, if you really want to hear it, but keep in mind I was only twelve. Do you remember the whole thing years ago about red M&M's—and how the company didn't make them for a long time because there was this controversy about whether or not the dye caused cancer? *I* set out to investigate. I went to the library with M&M wrappers in my hand to research the ingredients. Then I wrote to the president of Mars Candy, because I wanted to know what he was thinking. I wanted to know if he worried that he didn't eliminate the reds soon enough, and kids had gotten sick. I wanted to ask him if he was scared that other colors could be dangerous. I thought it would be a great interview and I'd be famous."

Jeff laughed out loud, and Iliana covered her face with her hand. "Oh, come on, don't be embarrassed, that's a great story," he said. "You were a determined reporter, even back then. Did you ever get a response?"

"No. I don't think I even had the right address. Anyway, it was a big nonissue. The reds have been back for a long time, in case you hadn't noticed."

"Oh, well. An early lesson that life can be harsh." He took a forkful of pasta. "Anyway, it's probably for the best that you never got famous."

"Oh?"

"You see, Ms. Fisher, take it from someone who knows." He wiped his mouth with his napkin. "Teen fame can be pretty complicated."

"You didn't like it?" she said, bolder now. He pretended to ignore her and kept eating. "Really, you didn't?" He looked up at her now with another amused smile, as though he planned not to answer but found her question flattering. "Come on, we're friends," she teased. "What it was like, being a Dreamer, having all those girls in love with you? How could that be bad?"

He put down his fork and leaned back, folding his arms across his chest. "That depends," he told her. "Is this just between us? Or is this for the article?"

"I don't know," she said. "Maybe both."

"Maybe *both*? I don't get it. Isn't your story about Downs Textiles? Aren't you just interviewing me about blankets?"

She forced herself to be strong and hold his gaze. After all, she wasn't Iliana Passing, chore doer and carpool driver, when she was with him; she was Iliana Fisher, the *Times* reporter who wasn't afraid to go after her story, who had been learning how to chase meaningful stories from the time she was twelve, and who had perfected her skills during eight years in business journalism. "Yes, of course," she said. "Of course that's why I'm here. But my instincts are telling me there's a much bigger story."

She saw his shoulders relax. "I'm listening."

"Here's the thing," she said, amazed at how she seemed to have suddenly developed the ability to be assertive. Or maybe she'd always had it; she had used it at *Business Times* and maybe she was discovering it anew now. She found herself drawing on arguments she once used to get reticent sources to talk, arguments she couldn't believe she remembered. "I'm curious about the Dreamers, and if I'm curious, I know other people are, too. My instincts are good that way. And if I can interview you about your past, I know I can make it a bigger and more significant article. That means more publicity for you and your blankets."

"And what's in it for you?" he asked.

"A bigger, meatier story is better for my career, too. Frankly, now that I've started working on this article, I think including some stories from your past is essential."

She watched him think for a minute, then scowl and shake his head. "Look, I don't think so. There's a reason I don't talk about all that stuff. Hey, I know about all those guys from old TV shows, signing autographs at those pathetic oldies events, trading wives on stupid reality shows. They look like idiots, all of them, but they do it because they need the money. I *don't* need the money. I'm a business owner, I've got a company and employees, and a great product line. I'm a success."

"That's what makes you so compelling," she said, putting her elbow on the table and extending her hand, palm up. "You're *not* like those others. And *Business* . . . I mean the *Times* . . . you know, any of the business publications in the city—they're not pathetic events or stupid reality shows. What I'm talking about is *different*."

He studied her, his chin forward. "Other reporters haven't been this convincing. Why are you? What is just so special about the past, Ms. Iliana Fisher, that makes you want to write about it so much? You, the *Times* reporter, with the house in the suburbs, kids, husband who's a . . ."

"Lawyer," she admitted.

"Lawyer, very good, proves my point. The present is what matters. Why do you care about the past? What do you miss about the past? Being a kid? Being a *teenager*?" He shivered dramatically.

She smiled. "I miss . . ." She stopped. How could she tell him that she missed who he used to be—and how she used to feel when she watched him? "I miss starting out," she finally said. "When you didn't know where things might lead."

"You mean your career?"

"That, and other things, too. Going to college. Getting married. Having babies."

"You miss *that*? The only thing I remember about babies is no sleep and dirty diapers."

"You have children?" she said. It was surprising to think of Jeff Downs as a father. The memory of him as a nineteen-year-old heart-throb was just so vivid.

He nodded. "Three teenage girls."

She was curious to know if he was married, but she didn't want to ask. It felt like far too personal a question. "Then you have to agree there was more than just dirty diapers. I mean, what I remember . . ." She paused, feeling slightly dreamy from the wine. "I remember the summer when my oldest was a baby, and we lived here in the city. We'd go out early in the morning, and I'd stroll him down Second Avenue and look at the store windows. And I'd stop at this coffee shop and get a blueberry muffin and coffee to go, and then we'd head over to Central

Park. And I'd give him a bottle and I'd eat my muffin as we watched the bigger children in the playground. And that muffin always tasted so good."

She stopped talking, hypnotized by the memory. She remembered the sun on her shoulders, and the sound of Matthew sucking rhythmically on his bottle. She remembered seeing the children playing, framed by the tall, green trees in the park and the high-rise buildings on Fifth Avenue. She remembered going home and giving Matthew a bath and then closing the blinds and watching him fall asleep in her arms. Later, when he woke up, she would put on a CD with children's songs by artists like James Taylor, Nicolette Larson, and Kenny Loggins, and dance around the living room, holding him. That's how Marc would find them when he got home—dancing in the living room. And he'd take off his suit jacket and tie, roll up his sleeves and unbutton the top buttons of his shirt, and join them. She loved that he didn't take the time to change his clothes. He had missed them that much.

"We spent every day like that," she said. "And on those long summer days . . . I felt like I found the meaning of life." She smiled, enjoying how wistful she felt. She'd never expressed these feelings before to anyone, not even Marc. Maybe she'd been too scared of missing it all too much. She had seen many things drift away in her life: her dreams of becoming a famous writer; her excitement at being a newly minted reporter; the warm pleasure of falling in love with Marc; their wedding; the birth of their first baby, Matthew; and the birth of their daughter, Dara. She had relished their babyhoods completely. But they were over. What was there now to look forward to? Teenage rebellions? More fights with Marc? An empty nest? Illness? Old age?

"Yeah, well," Jeff said, looking a bit unnerved at how personal the conversation had become. "I guess you wouldn't want them to stay babies forever. How old are they now?"

"Fourteen and twelve."

"So you must know that watching them grow up is fun, too. I mean, yeah, the teenage years can be rough. Our oldest, Katie, she was dating this real loser for a while, but thankfully that's over. And these days I really like my daughters. I like the people they've become. So does Catherine, my wife."

Iliana looked up. Now that he had mentioned his wife, she wanted to know more about her. She was curious: Who was the woman who had married the guy thousands of teenage girls across the country adored?

"Tell me about your wife," she said.

"She's a dancer," he answered, no longer reticent. In fact, it looked like now *he* was the one who was enjoying being questioned. "She teaches ballet at Purchase College, when she's not managing the back-office stuff for Downs Textiles. That's how we met. She danced on *Guitar Dreams* sometimes, for the party scenes. Those scenes were a blast."

"Aha!" she said playfully. "So you *did* enjoy being a star."

"It's like I said, it was complicated. It had its ups and downs. Although most of the downs came after the whole thing was over." He paused, looking at her. "You really want to interview me about the Dreamers? You really think it's essential for the article?"

She nodded.

He leaned forward, putting his elbows on the table. "The reason I don't often talk about those days is because to a lot of people it's a joke. Four talentless guys who got paid to smile at the camera—that's what they think. Like that idiot today who brought up the 'dreamin' to the max' line. Barely old enough to drink and he tries to look clever by making me the butt of his joke.

"Look," he said, leaning in closer. "I stopped doing media interviews a while ago because no matter what I said, the reporters always ended up talking about pretty-boy looks and bubblegum music. And the only reason I said yes to you was because I could really use the publicity about my blankets in the *Times*. But I saw the look on your face when I hummed my song—I didn't do it to test you or anything, I was just humming. And the way you lit right up makes me think I can trust you with my past. You won't trivialize my life, will you?"

She looked at him, at his beautiful brown eyes set deep in his appealingly weathered face. She would never have guessed that he carried so much resentment. She would never have guessed that his casual charm was a kind of self-protection. Now more than ever, she wanted to know his story. She wanted to uncover all that had made him who he was, and develop a portrait of him that was honest and profound.

"Of course not," she said.

He looked at her, then smiled his charming, tight-lipped smile. "Okay then. I'll do it. I'll talk about the Dreamers. Hey, it'll be fun."

They agreed that they didn't have enough time to continue the interview now, so they'd schedule another meeting. "I've got an idea," Jeff added. "Why don't we continue this up in Mount Kisco? You can see where we do our product development, and you'll get a better feel for the business. And then we can talk some more." He took his phone out of his breast pocket and made a few taps. "Except I have some meetings here in Manhattan coming up. Can we schedule it for . . . next Thursday? Or is that too late for your deadline?"

Things were moving so fast that Iliana felt as though she were racing to keep up with her life. Another meeting . . . and this time up in Westchester? She needed a moment to stop and think. The waiter returned and Jeff ordered coffee for them. Iliana excused herself to go to the ladies' room.

Weaving among the tables, she felt wobbly on her legs. Clearly the wine had gotten to her. At the sink, she rummaged in her bag to find her lipstick. That was when she spied her cell phone, buried deep inside, and discovered that she had missed six calls and had two new voicemails.

She hadn't heard the phone ring. Not once. Snapping to attention, she forced her shaking fingers to tap the right numbers. She hoped that Dara's orthodontist had called to confirm an appointment, or some stranger had reached her by mistake. But then she heard the voice. The tipsy sensation she'd been feeling immediately drained out of her, like an air mattress that had been unplugged.

"Iliana, it's Jodi. I have Dara here at my house. I ran into her when I picked up the boys. She felt too sick to stay for volleyball, and I think she has a fever. Where the hell are you? Call us."

The second, earlier voicemail was from Dara. "Mom, why aren't you answering your phone? My throat hurts and my head, and I think I'm gonna throw up. I just wanna go home. Where are you?"

Her heart racing, Iliana tried to call Jodi's house, but her fingers were shaking and she couldn't concentrate. Shit, how long ago had these calls come? Finally she finished dialing. "Jo, it's Iliana. Is Dara okay?"

"She's okay, she's sleeping. Are you all right?"

"I'm in the city—"

"In the city?"

"I'm on my way home, I'll be there in forty-five minutes, an hour max. Jo, thanks so much, I'll be there soon, I'll be right there."

Grabbing her bag, she left the ladies' room. Her palms and face were sweaty. Poor Dara, waiting for her, feeling so sick and scared. It hadn't even occurred to her that either one of her kids would be looking for her, would need her while she was gallivanting with Jeff Downs. What was wrong with her? She was a jerk to have come here. She was a jerk to have started all this.

Jeff smiled as she returned. "Hey, I was just about to go in there and find you," he joked. But as he looked at her, his expression changed. "Something wrong?"

"Just something at work. A problem . . . I'm going to have to get home right away." She wiped the corner of one eye with her finger so she didn't have to look at him.

"Wouldn't it be faster to go to the *Times* office? It's just a few blocks away, isn't it?"

"Yes, but . . . I need to look at my notes. Jeff, I've really got to go," she said, heading to the door.

He called to the waiter to put the check on his house account, and quickly they were out on the street. He held her arm lightly as they walked. Almost in a complete state of panic, she showed him her garage ticket and let him lead her up the right block. As they waited for her car, she tapped her toes inside her shoes and gritted her teeth.

"Guess this really has you worried," he said. "Hey, it's just a job."

She nodded. Her head was pounding. Finally her car arrived.

"Look, this was a great conversation—before, you know, all this happened," he said, offering his hand. She put hers into it, and he gave it an affectionate pat with his other one. "Call me when this is all over, okay?"

"Thanks for lunch," she said, pulling away and sliding into the car. She didn't even want to look at him.

"I hope we'll get together again. I hope you'll come to Mount Kisco next Thursday."

"Yeah, thanks," she said. She put the car in gear and was stepping on the gas before her door was even completely closed.

Chapter 8

"Relax. She's sleeping," Jodi said, pointing toward the family room. "I think I was as freaked out as she was. Seriously, what were you doing in the city again?"

Iliana rushed past Jodi and into the family room, where Dara was asleep on the sofa. She kneeled down and gently shook her daughter's shoulder, warm beneath her volleyball shirt.

"Mom, where were you?" Dara said, her eyes squinting open. "I called you like a million times."

"I think my phone's broken. I'm sorry. Let's get you home."

Jodi walked into the room with Dara's coat and backpack. "Your phone isn't working? Is it the battery?"

"I don't know," Iliana said as she helped Dara up.

"Or probably not, since you eventually got our messages. That's so strange—it stopped working but then it started again?"

"I don't know, Jo," Iliana said. "I'll look at it later." She took Dara's coat and held it out.

"It was so weird, Mom, because you're *always* around," Dara said, putting an arm through the sleeve. "And then you weren't home and you weren't answering your cell phone. I was so scared."

"But I told you there was nothing to worry about, didn't I?" Jodi said, playfully tugging Dara's ponytail. "I told you that by the time we dropped the boys off at basketball and got back here, we'd hear from her. Didn't I tell you that?" She turned to Iliana. "I didn't give her Tylenol or anything because I wanted to check with you first. And then by the time I heard from you, she was already sleeping."

Iliana walked Dara out to the car and helped her climb in, then came back up the front walk, where Jodi was standing, holding the backpack. "Thanks, Jodi, I really appreciate this," she said, taking it from her. "Go back inside, it's cold and you don't even have a coat on."

Jodi shivered and crossed her arms over her chest. "What were you doing in the city anyway?" she asked.

"It was for a job. A possible job . . . that I was thinking of doing," Iliana said.

"A job in the city? I thought you liked freelancing. You're going to leave your kids to commute to the city?"

"No, no, it's over. I'm not going to do it. I mean, I'm not even going to get the job. But I wouldn't take it anyway. It's over. No more."

Jodi smiled. "Well, that's a relief. I kept picturing you in some horrible car accident. I couldn't imagine why else you weren't answering. I almost called Marc—"

"You called Marc?"

"I was about to, but I didn't have his number. I thought about waking Dara to ask her for it, but then you called and everything was fine."

Iliana let out a breath. "Good. I wouldn't have wanted . . . you know, to scare him."

"Yeah, well, you scared *me*."

"I know, and I'm sorry. It won't happen again." She looked at the car. "I should get her home."

"Yeah, go ahead. And don't worry, I'll bring Matt home after practice today."

Iliana nodded and climbed into the car.

"And go get your phone fixed!" Jodi called. "I *never* want to go through this again!"

Later that night, Iliana came downstairs and curled her body against Marc's on the family room sofa, pulling his arm around her shoulder. She wanted to be held and comforted, reassured that she wasn't a bad mom for not being right there when her daughter needed her. There was a time early in their marriage when she knew Marc would have done exactly that. He wouldn't have even had to know precisely what was bothering her; he would have sensed that she needed his love, and he would have given it to her easily. But that had been a long time ago. Tonight he just kept watching the market wrap-up on the Bloomberg TV channel.

"Is she asleep?" he finally asked, switching to CNBC.

She nodded. "They both are."

"Then why do you look so jumpy? You're not getting sick, too, are you?"

"No," she said. "Just having a hard time calming down. Long day."

"You think your phone's broken?"

"I don't know. Maybe it was just buried in my bag so I didn't hear it. I'll take it to the phone store tomorrow if it acts up again." She snuggled in closer.

"You think it's a virus?"

"My phone? Oh, you mean Dara. Yeah, probably. There's a lot going around at school. I'll keep her home tomorrow and see if the fever goes down. If not, I'll take her over to the doctor."

"Good thing the cocktail party got changed to next Tuesday. You probably wouldn't want to leave the kids alone tomorrow night."

"Cocktail party?"

He looked at her. "The one to celebrate the new Cleveland office. I told you about it when I saw you in Midtown. We talked about it the other night, too. What, did you forget?"

"No, it just slipped my mind for a second. I'm thinking about Dara. Relax, okay?"

Marc settled back on the couch. "It's also a send-off for Keith Rein, he's moving to Cleveland to run things. His fiancée's going with him. It's a huge promotion—they threw a ton of money at him to get them to relocate." He looked at her sideways. "What do you think we'd do if I got an offer to relocate?"

Iliana caught her breath. "Why? Do they want you to relocate?"

"No, no. I'm just wondering. What do you think? What would we do?"

She looked down at her hands in her lap. She wanted to say she would go wherever his career took them. She wanted to say the kids were resilient and would adjust, and that she'd adjust, too. She knew that's what he wanted to hear. He wanted to know she was behind him, and he could count on her no matter what. But the words wouldn't come out of her mouth. She just couldn't mindlessly agree to follow him anywhere. She would want to know where they were going and for how long, and what the move might mean for her. She'd want to know that she could be happy in her own right, and not be expected to be happy simply because he was. She was a person, too. She wasn't his employee, she was his partner. She had to have an equal voice.

She looked down. "It's hard, you know, to talk in hypotheticals . . ."

"You mean you wouldn't go?"

"I don't know—"

"You wouldn't jump at the opportunity to make our kids' future more secure?"

"Marc, why are you attacking me? I forget about the cocktail party for one second and you act like it's a federal offense, and now we're fighting about a job you never even had."

"Forget it, okay? I was just asking," he said, turning off the TV and going upstairs.

Later that night, she climbed into bed and soon found herself stroking Marc's chest and kissing his neck. She desperately wanted to connect with him. She felt bad that they had fought once again. She couldn't shake the feeling that by pursuing Jeff Downs and neglecting Dara in the process, she had played Russian roulette with her marriage and family. It made her feel like a stranger in her own home, something she had never felt before. She thought that being close—even just physically close—with Marc tonight would make her feel safe again. She desperately wanted to feel safe.

"Of course I'd go with you no matter what," she whispered, even though it was a lie.

He rolled toward her and lifted her T-shirt, and she took his face and kissed his mouth, deeply and forcefully. She wanted the lovemaking to be as tender as it was last week, but something had changed in her, causing her body to betray her. She was restless and aggressive, pressing her legs against him, shifting and turning, and when he tried to kiss her arms or her neck, she kept pulling his face back up to hers.

Finally he pushed himself up on an elbow. "*What* is going on with you?" he said.

"Nothing," she whispered.

"Then why are you acting like this?"

She rolled away from him, onto her side. "I don't know," she said. "I just feel so bad that my phone didn't work."

—m—

Dara's fever was down the next morning, but her throat was sore and her nose stuffed, so Iliana devoted every ounce of her being to taking care of her daughter, trying to make up for being unreachable the day before. She carried Dara's comforter and pillow—as well as Fluffy, the worn-out plush kitten she'd been sleeping with since she was three—down to the family room sofa, and happily studied the movies available on demand, renting *Frozen* when Dara saw it on the list and nodded. She brought over a big cup of apple juice with a bendy straw, and gently covered Dara's pink-pajama-clad body with the comforter when she fell asleep. She scooted out for a quick trip to school to drop off Matthew's forgotten violin again, enduring another scolding from the school secretary. She was annoyed that she had been too distracted that morning to check that Matthew was carrying it—but more than that, she was glad that she had been available to answer the phone when he called and to bring him what he needed.

At lunchtime, she made a pot of Lipton noodle soup and called Dara into the kitchen. Watching her daughter crumble two saltines into the bowl and then slowly sip from a wide spoon, she thought about the day before. She was lucky it hadn't all been worse. Dara—or Matthew, for that matter—could have been really sick, appendicitis- or pneumonia-type sick. There could have been a bus accident or a school emergency—a gas leak or a power outage—and her kids would have been abandoned. Dara could have tried to walk home if Jodi hadn't been there to get her, in the freezing cold through busy intersections that she had no experience crossing by herself. She could have been hit by a car, she could have been killed or seriously hurt, and there Iliana was, giggling over some stupid M&M's idea she had when she was twelve. Gushing over this little private baby-world she made for Matt when he was an infant, gushing that Matt had taught her the meaning of life. Was this how she treated the people who gave meaning to her life—abandoning them just when they might need her most?

And she had betrayed Marc, too. He had told her on their first real date, after they met on the train, that he wasn't sure he wanted children, because he was scared of screwing them up the way his parents screwed up him and his brother. They never knew what they'd come home to—broken dishes on the kitchen floor, a telephone ripped out of the wall, evenings waiting for a dinner that never got made. "Our children will always have dinner," she assured him months later, when they started to talk about marriage. "Meat loaf or baked chicken and broccoli, rice on the side, a tall glass of milk, ice cream for dessert. Our kids will always know what to expect," she promised.

And they *would*, from now on, Iliana told herself as she picked up Dara's soup bowl and wiped away the cracker crumbs. The pretending and the sneaking around were over. She was not going to visit Jeff in Mount Kisco, she was not going to even get in touch with him, and he had no way to reach her either. She would no longer tell Jodi lies about phones breaking and jobs that didn't exist. Her life would be an open book. They could talk about the kids, the laundry, the upcoming orchestra concert, Chelsea's annoying favors. Regular stuff like that.

Dara went upstairs to take a nap, and Iliana followed behind, carrying up her bedding and Fluffy. She tucked Dara in and made sure she was comfortable. Then she went back downstairs and sat at the dining room table, looking at the dark computer screen. She knew what she had to do. It was the one thing that would confirm she had broken completely with her crazy pursuit of the past two weeks, the one thing that would show she was truly sorry for taking her family for granted.

She woke up the computer and typed:

Hi, Stuart,

Unfortunately, the article I emailed you about isn't going to work out. Sorry for the inconvenience.

Iliana

She took in a deep breath and pressed the "Send" button. Off it went.

Lacing her fingers together, she rested her chin on them, her elbows on the table. The thing was, she knew the article would have been extraordinary—far better than any article about mattress or appliance stores. It had been evolving in her head for the last week or so, simmering on the back burner while Jeff Downs displayed his blankets and Jodi reviewed Chelsea's lease, while Dara played volleyball and Matthew ran out of the car without his violin, while Marc envied his colleague's promotion and obsessed about the Seattle contract. And ultimately she knew it could be something far more important than a profile of a man who found a second career peddling blankets. It was a story about promise and disillusionment, about growing up and believing in dreams, and getting hurt and getting smart. It was about a guy who soared to the stratosphere, and the millions of girls like her who found a way to navigate the agony of adolescence by hitching a ride. And she was on the brink of learning and of telling the world what it means—what you gain and what you lose and what you're left with—when you rise so quickly and fall so far.

It would have been a story that people read and thought about and talked about. It would have been a story that people loved. It would have been a story with impact. It would have been a story that only a true writer could write.

She got up and loaded the lunch dishes into the dishwasher, then straightened the cushions on the sofa where Dara had been resting. She gathered some used tissues that were on the coffee table and took them to the trashcan in the kitchen. She sprayed some Lysol in the family room. No need for all of them to catch Dara's virus.

As she was going to put the Lysol back under the sink, she heard the beep that signaled an email. She went back to her computer. It was from Stuart:

Just as well. He's pretty much a lightweight.
It wasn't right for us anyway.

A piece of her wanted to cry. But she told herself it was all for the best. It would be good to put this whole strange chapter behind her. She wasn't a sneak or conniver by nature, and she wasn't up for all the stress and guilt that the pursuit of a major story would entail for a stay-at-home mom like her.

She hoped that at some point soon, she would actually believe it.

Chapter 9

Dara recovered, Matthew apologized about the violin, and the week flew by. Iliana threw herself into her routines, planning her schedule extra carefully for Tuesday so she would have plenty of time to shower, dress, and arrive at Marc's office promptly at seven thirty for the cocktail party. But that afternoon the tailor in Tarrytown gave her some other kid's orchestra tuxedo, which she didn't realize until she got home, so she had to go all the way back to get Matt's. That made her late to pick up Dara from school, so they missed her orthodontist appointment and had to wait in the office an extra half-hour until they could be slotted in. Then she had to run across the library parking lot in a downpour to track down Matt inside, since the cell service in the building was weak and he didn't get her text that she was waiting.

Soaking wet and slightly carsick from the stop-and-go traffic, Iliana rushed upstairs as soon as they got home. Fearing that the bad weather would make the trip into the city slow, she decided to forgo the shower and just dried her hair and threw on some makeup and her blue suit. She had thought about wearing the dress she'd worn to the Bloomingdale's meeting, but just looking at it made her feel guilty again about missing Dara's call. Running downstairs, she kissed the kids and gave them money to call in a pizza, reminding Matt that he was in charge and should call Jodi if there were any problems. She didn't have time to eat anything, and she didn't have much of an appetite anyway, so she grabbed a packet of nuts from the snack drawer. She figured she and Marc could stop somewhere for dinner on the way home.

"Great, you're on time!" Marc said as she walked into his office. "I heard Dan's wife is going to be late. This will give us some time alone with Angers before they show up. I can really use the extra face time with him." He got up from his desk and kissed her on the cheek. "You look great. I don't remember that suit."

"No?" she asked. It was dark outside, and the tinted windows worked as mirrors. Peering at herself across the room, she adjusted the jacket. Somehow it didn't look as good as it had that day in Jeff Downs's office. "I wore it to your cousin's wedding," she said.

"Don't remember it. I don't know, maybe I do."

He went to get his own suit jacket off a hook on the back of his door, which gave Iliana a moment to glance around the office. On the credenza was a photo of her taken many years ago, to accompany her *Business Times* column. The photographer, while setting up the lighting, had entertained her with observations about a male colleague who was smitten with him, and Iliana had found the story charmingly off-color. He snapped her at the precise moment when she was most enjoying his recollections, and the contrast between her business clothes and her amused expression made the photograph sexy. Marc saw it in the magazine while they were dating and asked for an eight-by-ten print, which he had framed and kept on display ever since.

She picked up the picture, remembering how much fun the photo session had been, how much fun just being in Manhattan had been. The city was crowded and diverse, and everyone she met—from the photographers and designers who lived in the Village to the corporate executives who worked in Midtown office towers and even the Russian drivers who answered her call for a car service when she had to work late at night—had stories to tell that surprised her or enlightened her or made her laugh out loud, and she sometimes regretted that she had to leave it behind to go back to her apartment each night and sleep.

"Come on," Marc said. "I hear the elevator opening." He took her hand, and they rushed down the hall. "Now remember to talk about how glad you are to be going to the Jena Connors thing," he said. "And try not to mention that you were a reporter. Angers was annoyed with the financial coverage from the Seattle deal, and that would just remind him about it."

The cocktail party was on the twentieth floor, in the circular lobby near the executive suites. There was a high ceiling, and the light from the enormous crystal chandelier made the silvery marble floor shine. Across from the elevator was a long mahogany bar, behind which bartenders in crisp white shirts and red bow ties mixed drinks. Iliana had frequently gone to cocktail parties when she was at *Business Times*, at cool downtown lofts or showy Midtown hotels. It was at these venues that she heard about and talked about businesses opening or dissolving, ideas being launched, and deals taking off or sometimes falling apart. She had been an integral part of the commerce that powered the city. And nobody had ever scripted her in a hallway, she thought ruefully, as she and Marc stepped out of the elevator.

Marc looked around, then took her elbow and led her toward an older couple, a hefty man with curly gray hair and a slender, blond woman. "Richard," he said. "The place looks great."

"Marc, right on time as always," the man answered. Then he turned to Iliana and extended his hand. "Nice to see you again, Iliana. Glad you could make it."

"Nice to see you, too," Iliana said. "What a lovely party."

"Do you remember my wife?" he asked.

"Of course," she said. "Hi, Karen." The women shook hands.

A waiter carrying a tray of cosmopolitans approached, and Iliana nodded and took one. Richard took one and handed it to his wife.

Karen took a sip, and the enormous diamond ring on her finger glimmered. "How old are your children now, Iliana?" she asked.

"Fourteen and twelve." She felt Marc's eyes on her. "Oh, and I should tell you, I'm so pleased to be included in Jena Connors's program. I'm looking forward to it." It was hard to get the words out—she really hated that Marc had told her what to say—but she reminded herself she was there to support him. She took a sip of her drink and immediately coughed, pressing her fingers to her mouth. Boy, was it strong! She told herself she'd better take it slow. There wasn't that much food around, and she'd only had that pack of nuts to eat in the car.

"It's always quite an event," Karen was saying. "The women are so interesting, and the speaker sounds wonderful. I love fresh floral arrangements in the house. Not that I have any time to make them lately—we're in the middle of this major renovation, enlarging the front entranceway and adding a second patio behind the dining room and a gazebo near the pool—"

"Karen, can you come here for a moment?" Richard called. He and Marc had moved a few steps away, and now Richard was talking to some other people.

Karen touched Iliana's hand. "Anyway, it should be wonderful. Will you excuse me?" She stepped away and joined her husband, as Iliana breathed a sigh of relief. She truly had no idea how to talk to women like Karen Angers, who were so rich and lived in such luxury. Giving her empty glass to a waiter, she took a full one from his tray. She didn't want to drink too much, but the cosmo tasted delicious, and she hoped a little more liquor could help her feel less awkward around any other Karen Angers types she might meet.

Turning to her left, she saw that Dan and his wife had arrived and were talking with Marc and the Angerses. She wondered if Marc was stressed because he hadn't had as much time alone with Richard as he had wanted. She looked around for him so she could make sure he was okay, but then she saw him approaching two women in business suits.

She recognized them from past company functions; one was a lawyer who worked in Marc's department and the other was in finance or something. They were both in their late 30s and looked as though they jogged eight miles each day before going to work. Marc began talking, gesturing comfortably as he spoke, and the two women listened attentively and nodded. At one point Marc seemed to have said something funny. The two women laughed, the one on the left grasping his elbow and dropping her chin, her silky dark hair spilling down around her face.

Iliana watched Marc take in the laughter, rocking back on his heels and putting his hands in pants pockets. He looked like he was enjoying himself, and suddenly she found herself wondering how happy *he* was with his stay-at-home wife. Sure, she made his life easy by taking care of the house and kids, but did he find the women he worked with more exciting? Was he disappointed that she had not made more of herself? She remembered how interesting he had found her that day they met on the train. He thought it was so cool that she wrote for a living, and he wanted to hear all about her job. Later, when he moved from the law firm to Connors Holdings, they found it serendipitous that she wrote about retailing and his company bought and sold retail chains. They often talked shop at home, and he liked to hear her thoughts about how different sectors of the retail industry were doing. Was apparel going soft? Were home furnishings picking up? Sure, they both had agreed that she should stay home with the kids; but was he now a little let down by the woman she'd become—just as she was?

Shaken, she turned in the other direction and slowly walked around the perimeter of the room. She didn't want to go over to Marc just now; she didn't want to be the kind of wife who takes her husband's hand when she sees him talking to attractive women. The place had become crowded in the last few minutes, so no one really noticed her, and the few who did nodded and stepped out of the way, as though they assumed she was heading somewhere intentionally. She stopped near a small table with a fruit platter and took a few grapes, snacking on them as she continued to saunter. Ultimately she ended up at the bar and put down her glass, which was already nearly empty.

"May I take this?" the bartender asked.

She nodded and the waiter placed another cosmopolitan in front of her. Before she could say, "No, thank you," he went on to serve two women to her left. She didn't want the drink; she typically never finished one mixed drink, let alone two. But Marc was still talking to the other women, and she felt uncomfortable standing there by herself, doing nothing. She needed something to do with her hands.

"So, are you all packed?" one of the women was asking.

"Almost," answered the other, a round-faced redhead. "Our furniture left this morning. I have a few boxes still to pack, just some really fragile things I didn't want to give to the movers, and we're driving out for good on Sunday."

"And how about the wedding? Everything set?"

"Pretty much. My mother can handle most of the details, and I'll fly out in the spring, you know, to get my dress fitted, finalize the menu, things like that."

Iliana took a sip of the drink, wishing there were some stools around so she could sit. She lifted one foot to rest it on a ledge at the bottom of the bar, but the ledge was much narrower than she realized, and her foot ended up sliding to the floor. The rest of her body lurched forward, and some of her drink spilled onto the bar's glossy surface. The redhead and her friend looked over.

"Oh, excuse me. Clumsy," Iliana said, accepting a napkin from the bartender, who quickly mopped up the mess. She knew she was getting tipsy. She could feel herself slightly swaying. The room was starting to seem slightly out of focus.

"It's so hard not to spill with this kind of glass," the redhead said amiably.

"That's true," Iliana said. "Hi, I'm Iliana Passing, Marc Passing's wife."

"This is Rosanne Green, Bruce Green's wife, and I'm Gwen Freelander, Keith Rein's fiancée," the redhead said.

"Oh, Keith Rein—he's going to be running the new Cleveland office," Iliana said. "Marc told me all about it." The bartender put a fresh drink in front of her. She vowed not to touch it. She could hear herself starting to slur her words. "Congratulations. When's the wedding?"

"In June. But we're moving this weekend."

"How are they taking it at work?" the other woman asked.

"It's been hard, but I think they appreciate that I'm tying up all the loose ends," Gwen answered. "Just have a few more things to take care of with the new play."

"Play?" Iliana said, curious. "What do you do?"

"I'm an intern with a Broadway casting office, Telesido Brothers. They're really successful. They're working on a new show that may have Meryl Streep in it."

"Really?" Iliana said. "What an exciting job."

"And Hugh Jackman is coming in next month to have lunch and talk about a new project. I was hoping I'd be made an assistant casting director by then. Kills me to be leaving now," she said, wrinkling her nose.

"Then, why are you?" Iliana asked seriously, leaning toward her.

The woman moved back a step. "Because I *love* my fiancé," she said, sounding affronted. "And because I'm building a life with him."

"Of course you are," her friend said. "And if you don't meet Hugh Jackman this time, you'll meet him the next. Don't worry, a woman with your skills—there'll always be a way back, whenever you decide to return."

"I don't know about that," Iliana said under her breath. She raised her glass, and her drink sloshed over the side.

"Excuse me?" Gwen said.

"I'm just saying it's not so easy. Trust me, I know. I have a lawyer friend who left her job to raise her kids. She says no law firm would ever want her now."

"So what are you saying? I should break off my engagement?"

"No, but couldn't you stay here anyway? I mean, there's no guarantee *his* job is going to work out. Why give up yours?"

"Come on, Gwen, I think we should go," her friend said.

"No, I want to answer that," Gwen said. Then she looked at Iliana. "I worked hard to get the job I have, and no, I'm not thrilled about leaving. But I'm smart enough to know that marriage is about compromise. I'm smart enough to know that life isn't always perfect, so you examine your options and you make the best decisions you can."

"I don't mean to be a jerk, I'm just being honest," Iliana said, grasping the woman's wrist. "You may think you can always go back to work, but the sad truth is, it's a myth. When you're ready to go back, they don't want you, and besides, with a family, it's too complicated—" She raised her foot to place it on the ledge again, forgetting how narrow it was. When it slipped down this time, she fell forward with such force that her drink flew into the air.

She squeezed her eyes shut just before the glass shattered on the bar, spewing shards and fruity liquid in all directions. When she opened them, Marc was behind her, his hands on her shoulders.

"I think it's time to go home," he hissed coldly in her ear.

In the car, she looked at the wad of wet paper towels wrapped around her middle finger. A faint, dark circle had formed where blood had seeped through.

"I think the bleeding is stopping," she said. Marc continued to drive, both hands on the steering wheel. "Hope I got all the glass out. I'll check again at home."

She watched the glittering lights of the approaching Triboro Bridge. "Those glasses were awfully thin," she said. "You know. To shatter like that."

"Huh," Marc said.

"You mad at me?"

He didn't answer.

"I'm sorry if I caused a scene," she said. "I didn't mean to. I'm sorry."

They drove a little farther in silence.

"Come on, Marc, I said I was sorry," she said. "It was an accident. A drink got spilled. Angers didn't even see it, and neither did his wife."

"Oh, Angers's wife saw. She saw the whole thing."

"Okay, great, she saw the whole thing, and she'll tell her husband about it. And you can blame me for the rest of your life, and make sure the kids blame me, too. You didn't get promoted because I dropped a glass. The kids won't go to college because I dropped a glass."

"No, I won't get promoted because you got drunk—"

"I did not get drunk—"

"You got drunk and started harassing Keith's fiancée—"

"What, were you spying on me?"

"No, I came over because I thought you might want some company. And before I could shut you up, you were carrying on, the great champion of women, telling her to keep her job and to hell with her fiancé."

"I didn't say that—"

"Is that what you think she should do, Iliana? Is that what you wish *you* did?"

"No, Marc! I don't think that at all!"

She turned and looked through the car window up at the sky. Planes were lined up as far as she could see, brilliant white lights lined up in the night sky as they made their way to LaGuardia. "I mean, sometimes I think it would be easier if I had never left the magazine," she added quietly.

"I *knew* it!" Marc shouted. "I knew that was where we were going. I made you leave your job, I ruined your life—"

"Can't I tell you how I feel without your jumping down my throat?"

"Because let me refresh your memory, Iliana. Your career wasn't exactly skyrocketing when you left."

"Excuse me, my career was—"

"Oh, come on, you worked for a marginal magazine, you got one promotion in eight years, and you were going nowhere."

"What?"

"Face the facts, Iliana," Marc continued. "The new guy was the rising star. You had plateaued, and it was just as well that you left."

"No, you face the facts, you son of a bitch," she said, turning to look at him. "I worked my hardest to do a good job at *Business Times*, and if I didn't move up the editorial ranks fast enough for you . . . if I wasn't successful enough because I fell in love with you and took my eye off the ball, it doesn't mean . . . it isn't . . . it's not okay . . ." She was so upset she couldn't even continue. How could Marc, of all people, sit there and denigrate her entire professional career? She had never felt so stupid and worthless in her life. She pressed her fist against her mouth and turned back to the window.

"I'm sorry," he muttered. "I didn't mean it that way."

When they arrived home, she followed Marc into the house, wiping her wet cheeks with her hands. Matthew was asleep on the family room couch, a half-filled milkshake on the table next to him. She gently woke him and walked with him upstairs, then reminded him to put his violin where he'd remember it in the morning. She peeked in on Dara, who was fast asleep in her bed.

Coming back downstairs, she picked up Matthew's cup and brought it to the kitchen sink. Marc was staring into the refrigerator, one hand holding a slice of bread with cheese and the other on the door, as though he were waiting for more satisfying food to make itself known. He often did this when they came home from somewhere; it usually meant that he wanted her to step in and make him a sandwich or warm up some leftovers. In the early years of their marriage, she thought it was sweet that he wanted her to take care of him, that she could show her love by supplying domestic things, like comfort food, fluffy new bed pillows, or a medicine chest stocked with his favorite body wash and shaving lotion. But tonight she found it repulsive. How could he hurt her so badly and still be in this posture, clearly expecting her to walk over and fix him a bite?

Turning away, she wandered into the dining room. Yes, she knew that just last week, she had promised to commit herself entirely to her husband and kids. The situation with Dara had convinced her that wanting anything more was dangerous. She hadn't intended to trash-talk marriage at the cocktail party, and she hadn't intended to get into a fight with Marc in the car. But she couldn't keep her mouth shut, and Marc couldn't either, and now they were fighting again. Wasn't it Einstein who said that insanity was doing the same thing over and over and hoping for a different outcome? How could she continue to tamp down her dreams and hope things with Marc would get better, when tamping down her dreams was exactly what kept making them get worse? What was she doing wrong? What could she be doing better?

Sitting down at the table, she woke up the computer. An icon appeared that indicated she had an email. She opened it. It was from someone at the *New York Times*:

Dear Ms. Passing:

Great idea, love that this successful guy was an old teen heartthrob, but a little too feature-ish for us. Why don't you try the

magazine section? They eat up stuff like this.
Try Julius Criss. Use my name. Good luck!

Allie Paulson
Senior Editor, New York section
The New York Times

Iliana sat back in her chair and stared at the screen until the words blurred. She had completely forgotten that she had sent an email to the *Times* proposing a Jeff Downs story—but here was a pretty exciting response. Allie Paulson hadn't ignored her query or rejected it. Allie Paulson of the *New York Times* had liked her pitch! *Why don't you try the magazine section? Use my name!* Iliana smiled as she realized that she had believed in her story enough to send it out to the *Times* and not just to Stuart, and as a result, she had a link to the editor of the *Times* magazine. And eventually she might actually get an article about Jeff Downs into the *New York Times* after all. Then Marc would have to see her in an entirely new light.

In a flash, the email changed everything. *Thank you, Allie Paulson!* she whispered to herself. She could hardly wait until the next morning. She could hardly wait to call Jeff's office and confirm a trip to Mount Kisco on Thursday.

Chapter 10

"Well, if it isn't my old friend Iliana."

He was sitting in a booth in the narrow coffee shop where Rose had said he'd be. He was reading the newspaper, his chin tilted up to keep his glasses from sliding down. At first she didn't recognize him. The sunlight easing through the window blinds in long, hazy stripes made his hair look gray and seemed to add lines to his face, and her eyes passed right over him as she surveyed the restaurant. She blinked when he stood, wondering why a stranger was approaching her. Although she had met with him twice, she still had been looking for someone much younger.

"What's wrong?" he asked, holding her shoulders and bending his knees so they were eye to eye. "Cold? Hungry?"

"I could use some coffee," she said.

"Jim, could you get my reporter friend some coffee?" he called to a short, elderly man behind the counter, then looked back at her as he added, "Just milk, no sugar." He remembered how she liked her coffee. She smiled.

He took her coat and hung it at the back of the shop. She was wearing a blue V-neck sweater over tan pants, with a wide black belt.

She loved that she now looked good in belts. She thought the last time she'd worn one was before she was pregnant with Matthew.

"I hope you don't mind meeting here," Jeff said as they sat. He looked as good in a black crew-neck sweater and jeans as he had in a shirt and tie. "It seemed a good idea, since it's right off the highway, and they've got the best coffee in Westchester. And look!" He held up his newspaper, and she saw it was the *Times*. "They sell your paper. The good old-fashioned print variety. I forked over cold hard cash today in honor of your visit."

"I appreciate it," she said, nodding. Hopefully it really *would* be her paper. She had whipped out an email to Julius Criss right before she left for Mount Kisco that morning:

> Allie Paulson from the New York section
> suggested I get in touch with you. She and
> I have been in contact about an article idea
> that she thinks might work in the magazine
> section . . .

"You know, I've been looking for your byline," he added, more seriously.

"Freelancers . . . don't always get bylines because they tend to write shorter pieces," she said smoothly, after a beat. "And I'm still getting to know the editors, since I took all that time off to be home with my kids. So I'm not the first one they call for assignments."

"Oh," he said, nodding. "Makes sense." She wondered why he accepted her explanation so easily. If their roles were reversed, she thought she'd probably have questioned him more.

"But *this* piece will be a bylined piece," she added. "In fact, they are taking a look at it for the magazine section."

"The magazine? That means it will be fairly long, right?"

She nodded. "I think so!"

"And I guess that's quite disappointing, considering the look on your face," he teased.

Iliana laughed as she realized that yes—she *was* happy. She was pleased that Allie Paulson had liked her query and suggested she send it to Julius Criss.

"The New York editor thinks the story may work in the magazine," she said. "She loves the idea of bringing in your past. 'Love that he was an old teen heartthrob,' that's what she said."

"*Old* heartthrob, huh?" he said, as he pantomimed taking a bullet to the chest. "Boy, you sure know how to hurt a guy."

"No—I mean, it sounded better coming from her—"

"And here I thought we were friends! Let's change the subject. What else is doing in the big world of journalism? Interview anyone interesting lately?"

"I did go to a cocktail party recently," she answered. It was the only out-of-the-ordinary thing she had done. She realized that in answering his question, she was back to twisting the truth. She knew the magazine was still a long shot, but she desperately hoped it would work out and she'd soon be able to stop all the lying. "Spoke to someone from one of the big Broadway casting offices. I thought I might get a scoop about Hugh Jackman in talks about a new Broadway show. But she wouldn't confirm it."

"That's too bad. But don't be discouraged. Go back and butter her up. Or better yet, hound her until you get what you want. That's what I do."

"Somehow I don't buy that. You were quite smooth with the Bloomingdale's crowd, as I remember," she said.

He grinned. "Guess you're right about that."

"But it wouldn't help anyway," she said. "She's leaving her job. To move with her fiancé. To Cleveland."

"Sounds like you don't approve," he said. "Got something against Cleveland?"

"What I've got something against is her abandoning this great career. Women always think they have plenty of time and they can switch things up later, but it's not always so easy. They get caught up in the day-to-day, letting their calendar get filled up with chores, knowing the months and years are passing by but not doing anything to . . ." She looked up and saw him watching her. "What? Did I say something stupid?"

He leaned back in the booth, clapped his hands, and laughed. "Just burst my bubble is all. Never again will I think of journalists as open-minded and nonjudgmental."

"I didn't insult you, did I? I mean, your wife works; you told me that, didn't you?"

"Catherine? She's practically my boss. I wouldn't have a business without her. But don't worry, I like that you have strong feelings. Hey, I have lots to show you today. I'll be crushed if I don't get at least a few strong reactions."

He got up, took his wallet from his back pocket, and pushed her shoulder playfully as he walked toward the cash register. "Come on, stop being embarrassed and let's get going. We've got a lot of ground to cover."

Outside, he zipped his jacket all the way up, bracing himself against the cold. "That's my car," he said, nodding toward a blue, older-model BMW in the parking lot. "The house is only about ten minutes away, but there are a lot of turns. So you can follow me.

"Oh, and one more thing," he said, reaching into his jacket pocket. "Here's something to inspire you. Or make you curious. Either one."

He took out a small photograph and extended his arm to give it to her. The wind suddenly kicked in, blasting against her back, but she grabbed the picture just before it could blow away, and took a long look. It was a picture of the Dreamers, one of the earliest, if not the earliest, she had ever seen. The boys all looked young, not much older than Matthew, and their heads were tilted upward, as though they were watching someone on a high platform right in front of them. Terry was sitting on a stool, his curls falling into his eyes, and Jeff and the other two boys stood behind him. They all looked somber, as though they had gotten mixed up in something they weren't sure they wanted. Jeff's mouth was open, with the bottom tip of one of his top teeth showing.

"You look scared," she said.

Jeff looked over her shoulder, blocking her from the wind, hands in the front pockets of his jeans. "No, not scared," he said. "Just full of . . . astonishment, I guess. It was our first day on the set. And I was about to take off on the ride of a lifetime. See how we're all looking up?"

She nodded, looking behind her at him.

"We were looking at the crew. They were all around, on ladders, on scaffolds. There were literally dozens of them. And their only job was to make us soar."

—⁂—

In the car, Iliana followed Jeff out of the parking lot and onto a long, two-lane stretch of road. Eventually he made a few turns that led through a small town, and then they came to a residential neighborhood with split-level houses and a concrete sidewalk. Iliana assumed they were just passing through, but soon Jeff slowed and parked near the curb. Iliana pulled in behind him and watched him get out of his car, wondering why they were stopping. Did he need to tell her something?

She rolled down her window and he leaned down toward her. "Welcome to the headquarters of Downs Textiles," he said with a laugh. His breath came out as steam. "Pretty corporate, huh?"

She turned from him and dipped her head to see the whole house through the opposite window. Was it some kind of a joke? She knew there were some very expensive areas in this part of the county, and she'd been expecting something much more impressive—a sprawling estate with a tennis court and a pool, maybe a round marble fountain with cascading jets of water, a huge front portico. After all, he had to have made a ton of money from the TV show, hadn't he? Instead, they were parked beside the kind of modest house she saw advertised in the paper every day: four bedrooms, eat-in kitchen, family room, maybe a fireplace. He had never described his home, but she had come here with expectations she hadn't even realized she had.

"Surprised?" he said. "I know. Pretty small and basic. But I gotta tell you, after all the glitz of Hollywood, Catherine and I wanted something scaled way back. And we've never regretted it. I was tired of the high life."

She opened her door and stepped out of the car, wondering if it could be true that he really preferred a basic split-level. Or did he just want her to think that? Suddenly she wondered if he had been working all along to manipulate her impressions of him. How badly did he want this article she was hoping to publish? All his reluctance to talk about the Dreamers, and there he was waiting for her at the coffee shop, holding a photo to whet her appetite. Had he always been hoping for a full-length feature about himself? Had he been waiting to find a reporter he could charm into telling his story the way he wanted it told—and was that why he was always so nice and friendly to her?

"I just need to check the mail real fast," he said, and she followed him up two concrete steps, through the front door, and into a small, red-tiled entranceway. There was a stairway to the right, with a basic tan carpet. To her left was the living room, with a white leather sofa, a square glass coffee table, and two club chairs. Ahead she could see one wall of the kitchen. The white countertop held the normal supplies of suburban living, a coffeemaker, a toaster, a mixer. It didn't seem that anyone else was around, and she started to feel uncomfortable. Where were his employees? She didn't think she'd been alone in a house with a man other than Marc since she was single. It made her wonder if maybe she had misjudged his intentions when he invited her here. Had he actually brought her here to try to sleep with her?

He picked up some envelopes on a small glass table and shuffled through them, and she instinctively moved several steps away from him and closer to the door. To her right was a ledge with a few framed photographs, and she leaned in to examine them. The one in front, a five-by-seven, showed three teenage girls leaning back on a wooden fence, a turquoise ocean behind them. Iliana assumed they were the daughters he had told her about at the restaurant. The older two, in halter tops and shorts that couldn't have been any tinier, looked bored, their long hair in their faces, their shoulders slumped, their mouths slightly smirking. The youngest, a chubby girl with a large, fleshy face, was in a black midriff with spaghetti straps, her baby fat flopping over the waist of her too-tight jeans. She looked defiantly into the camera, as if daring the photographer to go ahead and shoot.

More relaxed now that Jeff was paying attention to the mail, Iliana thought about why Jeff and his wife had put this picture in the front hallway. Was this the best vacation picture they had? Was their perception so warped by years of living with sullen, moody teenagers that they actually thought the girls looked *happy*? She had imagined Jeff's life so differently. Maybe she had idealized him too much. After all, she had spent years knowing only what she saw on TV—an incredibly cute guy with great hair and a winning smile, playing the role of a boy who is liked by everyone and always gets the girl. She was the one who liked to figure out what made people tick. Maybe she should have realized that his real life would be more complicated than his on-screen one.

It made her wonder even more what else she might learn today.

Jeff tapped the stack of mail on the palm of one hand. Iliana could tell he was uncomfortable, too. "Okay, done. Now we can get started. The office is behind the house. This way."

She followed him outside and down a path on the side of the house. Beyond the back lawn was a structure that looked like a small barn. "This whole area used to be one big estate, and when they subdivided it, they left some carriage houses," he said. "We were lucky our property came with one. We thought it was a good idea to decentralize our operation—you know, focus the showroom completely on sales and marketing, without all the distracting administrative functions in the way."

He led her up two small wooden steps and held open a painted green door. There was a small, dark entranceway that led directly to a steep wooden stairway. He gestured ahead, and she began climbing, aware of how closely her pants hugged her body. She wished Jeff would turn around and go back downstairs so she could, too, because it felt wrong to be alone in this dark stairwell with him. But she could hear his footsteps, clop, clop, clop, closing in on her.

She reached the top step and felt a tingle of relief trickle through her body. The large attic room was entirely businesslike. It reminded her of the small lofts in old buildings in Soho where graphic artists she had sometimes hired for *Business Times* worked. There was a wood floor and slanting wood beams on the ceiling, with tall, old windows lining the walls. Two tables with computer monitors were in the center of the room. A man and a woman were staring at one.

Jeff seemed more at ease now, too. "Hey, guys, here's the reporter I told you about," he called as he took her coat. "You online with Stefano?"

The two nodded, the man holding up a finger to indicate that they were in the middle of a critical step. "We're waiting to hear if he'll do it."

Jeff kept his eyes on his employees as he explained to her what was going on. "We're creating this whole new category," he said. "A lightweight, real upscale comforter—organic cotton, super-high thread count, all the bells and whistles. Perfect for expensive beach homes— the Hamptons, Fire Island, those kinds of places. We got a lead on this amazing Italian designer and we're hoping to convince him to do some ultra-sophisticated prints for us. We've got a small shop in East Hampton that would do the launch, and if it takes off, we'll roll it out to other high-end markets."

The two people pulled back from the computer, smiling. "Perfect!" the man said. "He'll do it. Man, this product's going to be awesome."

Jeff congratulated his employees for locking Stefano in and then introduced them to Iliana.

"We're going to overnight some fabric samples to the factory and get something to eat," the woman said. "See you later, Jeff. Nice meeting you, Iliana."

The two of them headed downstairs, and she and Jeff were now alone again. The room was quiet—as quiet as the house had been when they were alone there together. Iliana started to feel nervous again, but Jeff looked totally relaxed as he sat down in a modern, leather office chair behind a large executive desk made of dark wood.

He motioned to Iliana to sit opposite him. "Okay, Ms. Fisher," he said, leaning back and putting his hands behind his head. "The ball's in your court. What exactly would you like from me?"

They were words she would have given her right arm to hear when she was in middle school. And back then, she would have answered *Love me! Be with me! Make me special!* Today she had a different answer. But in a way, she realized, it was still the same.

She reached in her bag and double-checked that her phone's volume was turned up, so she'd hear it if Matthew or Dara called. Then she took out the small digital recorder she used for her local stories, flipped it on, and set it on his desk. She didn't know if she'd actually get an assignment and need his quotes, but she wanted to record them anyway. She wanted to hold on to his story forever.

"Are you okay with this?" she asked.

He shrugged good-naturedly. "You're the boss."

"Then tell me your story," she said. "I want to know everything. I want to know how you became a star, and how it felt to be one. I want to know what you liked, and what you didn't like, and how being a star was better or worse than what people would expect it to be. And I want to know how it felt when everything ended, and how it feels now, when it's all behind you. I want to hear it all. "

Her interest clearly delighted him, as he looked like a man who had just drawn a winning poker hand. "Okay," he said. "Here we go."

Chapter 11

"It all comes down to the music," he began. "The first day on the set, they told me they didn't need me to play. They had studio musicians lined up. But I took out my guitar and started performing this song I wrote, and their mouths dropped open. Even the top guy, Stan Shore, did a double take. 'Waddayaknow?' he said. 'The kid's got a sound.' And then—"

"Wait, wait," Iliana said. "Start at the beginning. The very beginning. How did it all happen, how did they find you?"

"From the jeans commercial."

"And how did you get that? Did you go to an audition?"

"Yes. Well, no. No, what happened is . . ." He sighed and rolled his eyes. "Okay, if you must know, Ms. Fisher, it starts a year earlier with this community theater thing that is just too embarrassing to talk about."

"Oh, come on," she said. "You promised me great stories. And remember, I told you my M&M's story. As you said, we're friends now."

He folded his arms on his desk. "Pretty shrewd, to use my own words against me. Okay, if that's what you want, that's what I'll give you. But I reserve the right to cut this part out of the finished article, got it?"

She laughed. "We'll discuss what goes in and out of the article later," she said. "Let's just start. No holding back."

He leaned his chin on the palm of his hand. "Okay, then I guess I'd have to say that it really starts when I'm sixteen," he said. "Living at home, bored at school, hating my parents, desperate to lose my virginity—a typical teenage boy, right? But then everything changes when this new family moves next door. The guy, he's nice and all, but it's his wife, Wendy, who gets me *crazy*. Man, she was hot. Long, honey-colored hair and pink lipstick, golden-tanned legs that go on forever. And they had these two little kids, and I just loved that. It meant that she actually had sex! Yes!"

He pumped his fist, and Iliana forced a smile. She didn't like to think of Jeff examining Wendy's legs or imagining Wendy in bed. Her daydreams of him when she was young had always been G-rated.

"And she's part of this community theater group, and one day she tells my mom they need a teenage boy to play one of the roles," he said. "All this kid has to do is sit on the couch pretending to watch TV, and at one point say, 'Hey, shut up, I'm trying to watch!' So my mom asks me, and Wendy tells me she's in the cast, too, and I say, 'Oh, yeah!' You see, I didn't have much to do with girls before then. My friends and I, we just hung around at the mall or behind the school, getting high. But now, I'm spending all this time in rehearsals with Wendy—and even though the play sucks, I'm in goddamned heaven."

Again, Iliana found herself slightly put off. She hated to think that Jeff was just like all the potheads she remembered from school who gathered in the afternoons, swarming the building like termites. "So was it only about this woman?" she said. "Or did you like being onstage? What did you want to come of this? Were you thinking the play could lead to something big?"

He shook his head. "Wish I could say I had big, important goals for myself, but hey, it was all about Wendy. What can I tell you? I was just a kid. So opening night comes, and I'm backstage, and suddenly I notice a couple in a corner, in this intense lip-lock—yup—it's Wendy, with one of the idiot lighting guys. I don't know if I was more upset for myself or the poor schmuck she was married to, but I just want to punch someone. And then the stage manager yells, 'Places!' So I'm onstage and I have nothing to do but watch an imaginary television and listen to the other actors say these stupid words I've heard a million times, and you can tell that the audience hates the show, they're coughing and talking and barely paying attention. But me, I keep seeing that damn kiss over and over in my head, and it's killing me. And finally it's time for me to speak and I shout, 'SHUT UP ALREADY, I'M TRYING TO WATCH!'

"And don't you know, I brought the house down! I stole the show. I guess the audience recognized in me every teenager they had ever encountered, and they thought it was hysterical. They laughed and clapped for almost a full minute!"

"That's wild," Iliana said. *This* was the story she wanted to hear. She loved the chance meeting of passion and good timing. Of course, she didn't like the hints of egotism emerging as he told his story. She hoped they were simply an indication of inexperience. As he told her, he hadn't talked about himself to a reporter in a long time. Maybe he didn't remember how easy it was to sound arrogant.

"And as it turns out, there's this casting agent in the audience—a chunky lady with electric-blue eye makeup, and she tells my parents that she could get me work. I had never even thought about doing more acting, but Wendy walks over and I scream, 'Yes!' as if this is my life's dream. And Wendy looks disappointed, I guess because she was hoping this would be *her* big break. But the agent barely acknowledges her. So much for Wendy—she could have her husband and her babies and her little backstage indulgences. *This* whiny teenage boy was going to be a star!"

Iliana sat forward. "So this agent got you the jeans commercial?"

"Yeah, and my mom, she's not too keen on the whole thing. She wants me to be a doctor. She's always saying I'm a science whiz—and she was right, I was pretty smart in school."

"And what about you? Did you want to be a doctor?"

He thought for a minute. "I don't know. Maybe. I know I wanted to please my mom. But it wasn't in the cards. I was moving in a whole new direction. Anyway, the commercial. Turns out there are two boy parts. One is this romantic type and the other only wants to play basketball. So I'm hoping I'm a shoo-in for the romantic one, but for some reason they give that part to this short, dorky guy. He never went anywhere after that, no surprise."

Iliana tried to remember what that other boy looked like—was he really so bad? She couldn't conjure an image of him in her mind. Like millions of other girls back then, she had only really seen Jeff. And yet, it was strange to hear Jeff talk about people so disparagingly—the chunky agent, the dorky other kid. The person he had appeared to be, first in the commercial and then in the series, was so different. Always kind and sympathetic, always looking out for others and taking the high road. Had she been expecting too much of the real-life Jeff? Because when you came right down to it, nobody could be as perfect as that on-screen persona. Maybe she was being too hard on him—about his house, about his daughters, about his pretty typical adolescence. Maybe it was unreasonable to expect him to live up to all her childish expectations.

"So they start the rehearsal by working with the 'romantic'"—he made air quotes around the word—"guy and the girl, and I'm bored and insulted, and finally I just wander over to the basketball hoop they've got on the set, and I pick up a ball and start dribbling. And the director calls, 'That's great, keep going!' and they start filming me. Now, I'm no

LeBron James, and basically my shots keep missing, but they still keep the camera rolling."

"So you were *actually* missing all those shots on the commercial?" Iliana teased.

"Ooooh, the press can be cruel," Jeff teased back. "Well, once I got used to the surroundings, I did make several shots. At least that's my story, and I'm sticking to it. But as you know, since you obviously watched it, they ended up keeping only my misses and cutting all my lines except for one word—'Basketball.' Which became my nickname on the Dreamers set. Basketball."

"Basketball," Iliana repeated. "I never knew that." She had read so many issues of *Teen* magazine when she was young, she'd been sure she knew every teeny morsel about the show. But now she was getting more juicy tidbits to savor, the behind-the-scenes stuff she had never been privy to as a girl, no matter how many magazines she bought. Now she was an insider.

"The commercial airs, and pretty soon people start recognizing me," he continued. "I'm in the mall, and girls are pointing at me and whispering. And at the pizza place, a girl asks, 'Aren't you the Reese Jeans guy?' The Reese Jeans guy! And other girls ask for my autograph! All for whining about basketball."

"You know it wasn't just for whining."

"No? Then what was it for?" he asked.

She laughed, shaking her head. Was he being coy, or did he really not know? It wasn't the whining that girls loved. It was that he was cute and helpless and nonthreatening, missing all those shots. They wanted to meet him. They wanted to be his girlfriend.

"I think you know," she said. "But continue. What did you make of your sudden popularity?"

"Well, life is never the same after that commercial," he said. "Girls are always following me now. My friends think I'm king of the world. No surprise, I finally lost my virginity. Actually, I slept around a lot."

She looked down. She wondered how many girls were in love with him and got their hearts broken by his selfishness. But maybe she was being naive. Surely this was the way any teenage boy in his situation would behave.

"Then one day my agent tells us about some TV show they want to build around me. By now, my mother's all into it, but my dad, he was a classical musician, and he thinks I'm selling out. Like TV is bullshit. I remind him that it's a show about a band, and I'll be playing guitar and singing, too, but he doesn't buy it. And one day he gives up trying to get me to turn it down. He just says, 'Jeff, if you're going to take this ride, I hope it's the best time in the world.' A sentiment that eventually became the title of our biggest hit."

Iliana smiled at the reference. She remembered sitting in her bedroom, listening to "The Best of Times." Listening and imagining he was singing about her. "So how did it feel to be on a TV show?" she asked.

Jeff stretched his arms above his head. "It was like nothing you can imagine," he told her. "Before I know it, it's the first day of rehearsal, and I'm meeting the other guys in the cast. Terry had been on TV all his life. He was funny, man. The morning we did our first read-through, he grabs my arm and says, 'Basketball,'—he was the first to call me that—'Basketball, in six months your face is gonna be on a lunchbox.' And he was right."

"I remember Terry," Iliana said. His character was the one who usually had the girl problems—girls chasing him down the halls at school or fighting over him in the lunchroom. Iliana always felt smug when the teen magazines ran articles about Jeff instead of him. *Take that, Terry!* she wanted to say. *Girls want sincere boys like Jeff.*

"Then there was Bruce, he was the surfer dude. And the fourth, the drummer, was Peter. He grew up on a dairy farm near Scranton. They found him in some catalog for a local clothes store."

Jeff laughed and shook his head. "You know, it all happened in a heartbeat. The show aired, and the next day we were famous. Can you imagine?"

"I think so," Iliana said. The fact was, she *could* imagine, more than she wanted him to realize. She had spent almost all of middle school imagining what it would be like to be Jeff Downs's girlfriend as his star ascended to the sky.

"I couldn't live at home anymore—it was too dangerous, with all the girls and the mobs, the photographers," he said. "The studio ended up moving us all into this building for VIPs. Man, what a place! We each got an apartment with a huge sunken living room and a serious stereo system, a huge master bathroom with a Jacuzzi, daily maid service, and gourmet meals whenever we wanted. And there was twenty-four-hour security, with cameras and intercoms. I loved it. At first.

"But then, you know, it got frustrating. We were so isolated. I mean, it's understandable. If one of us got a girl pregnant or were caught with drugs, it would have destroyed the show. But we were kids! We wanted to go to rock concerts and stay out all night, drive down the coast in a convertible and camp out on the beach. Terry liked Las Vegas, and all Bruce wanted was to drive into Mexico and drink tequila. So the studio kept us working all the time, and if we did go out, we had to do it their way—drivers and bodyguards."

"So what did you do?" Iliana asked.

"We rebelled. Hey, we were kids. One night Terry and I put on baseball caps and snuck out of the building. Freedom! The next week we got braver, and went to a convenience store for potato chips and Twinkies. Nobody recognized us. It was a crazy thrill ride. So a few months later we're on tour, staying at this big hotel in Detroit, and Terry and I decide to do it again, and Peter and Bruce come, too. Only this time it's different. There are a billion girls behind police barricades, and they recognize us immediately, and they just come charging. We race back through the revolving doors, but Bruce doesn't make it. The girls jam the revolving door so he can't get in, and they're pushing his head into the glass and ripping his shirt.

"Well, finally the police tear everyone off, but boy, is he beaten up. He's got this big cut on his cheek, and his wrist is fractured and his ribs are bruised and he's got scrapes all over. You can bet we *never* went out alone again."

"My God," Iliana said. "How scary. Did you ever want to quit?"

Jeff shook his head. "Never," he said. "Not then. Because most of the time it was fun. And the acting—I was really good. Do you remember the episode where my character's dad has a heart attack? I actually cried real tears for that show. Wait, I'll show you." He looked straight at her and squeezed his eyes shut four or five times, as though trying to wring water from them. It was bizarre to watch, and she had to stop herself from laughing.

He pressed his fingers on his eyelids, then squeezed again. "There we go. See?" he said. "I'm thinking about the heart attack, and I can feel I'm starting to cry. I can do it, see?"

Iliana didn't want to make him feel bad, so she nodded, even though she didn't see any change at all. He was clearly a little deluded about his acting ability. After all, he hadn't been performing Shakespeare. Still, the show was a long time ago. Maybe he was remembering how he saw things back then.

"And when we were touring, man, we were treated like kings!" he continued. "We rode in limos, we had huge hotel rooms, and if we were hungry all we had to do was pick up a phone and they'd send up anything—steak, a bottle of champagne, tanks of ice cream. And companies were always giving us stuff. I got a Porsche one year. I got cases of Dom Pérignon each New Year's. I got VIP tickets to any ball game I wanted. One day Terry tells some interviewer how we could all use time away on a deserted island, and the next day a big travel company calls: No deserted island available, but would two weeks on a private beach in Tahiti do? We went to the White House. We were on the *Tonight Show*.

"And then there was the money," he said, looking as though he barely remembered she was there. "We didn't make much when we started the series, but once we had concerts, that's when we raked it in. I didn't even know how much I got, that's what I had a business manager for. All I knew was that I was loaded. I bought a house. I owned three cars. I built my dad this acoustically perfect music studio. I sent my mom to the Riviera.

"Needless to say, I didn't do much saving. So the money didn't last long. I lost a ton on some hotel venture in Texas that my business manager talked me into. I lost a ton to agents and managers I trusted, who are now living the high life because I never read my contracts. All those Jeff Downs posters that hung in millions of teenage girls' bedrooms? I never saw a dime. We signed away all our merchandising rights."

"So what made it worth it?" she asked. "Tell me—what was the best time you had, the best thing you remember from those years?"

Jeff lowered his voice and folded his arms on his desk. "The best time was when it was all starting—those first weeks of rehearsing, when we were so stoked about what would happen," he told her. "There was this place we'd go, Nate's, before we got too big to go out on our own. It had the best burgers, and it was on the beach and smelled of beer and ocean. So the day comes when our show will be on the air for the first time, and we're there eating lunch, and Terry notices a row of those old newspaper machines, where you put in a coin to open the door and get a paper? Well, he gets one and turns to the TV page and sees our names listed, and he's got this big smile on his face. And suddenly he puts in another coin and this time takes the whole pile, fifteen of them. He's standing there, smiling and holding this stack of papers.

"Well, Peter goes to the next machine and pulls out all the papers, and then Bruce and I do it, too. So now we've got around forty newspapers, and Terry jumps into his car and takes off, and the rest of us get into my car and follow him. And a few blocks later, we see Terry at another row of machines, taking more papers, so we do the same. At some point Terry heads back to the studio, but I keep driving the others, and we keep emptying newspaper machines and laughing our heads off.

"Yeah, we got yelled at when we showed up at the studio nearly two hours late," he said. "But it was so great. I swear, I think it was the best afternoon I ever had."

He got up and went over to a half-size refrigerator against the wall. He pulled out two bottles of water and placed one on the desk in front of Iliana. She twisted the top off and took a sip. He sat back down.

"What's on your agenda this afternoon, Ms. Fisher?"

"Just have to pick up my kids at two thirty," she answered. She looked at her watch. It was almost eleven. She hadn't heard her phone ring, but she reached in her bag and double-checked anyway. No missed calls.

"And I take it you want me to continue."

"I want to know what happened next," she said. "How did it end? Will you tell me that?"

"Ahh, the painful part," he said, still smiling but also sounding a little melancholy. "I guess I promised you the whole story, didn't I? Okay, onward. So the first season it's all beginning and the second season we're on a roll, but then things change. Did you know teen idols have a shelf life of two years?"

She shook her head. It was strange to think of Jeff as having a shelf life, like bread or cereal. But by the time the Dreamers started their third season, she was in high school, writing for the school literary magazine, covering the debate team for the school newspaper, getting to know the president of the debate team, who would become her first boyfriend. After the second season, she couldn't even remember any episodes.

"It happens slowly so you don't even realize it," Jeff was saying. "Our fourth album didn't sell as well as the other three, then the TV ratings started to drop, then one week we didn't even make it into the top ten. That's when the fighting began. We were animals, trying to protect our hides. Terry complained that he wasn't getting enough close-ups. And Peter was married by then, he threatened to quit if he had to keep touring. There should never have been a fourth season. Nobody was watching anymore. The reporters were calling us 'The Bad Dreams,' 'The Nightmares.' Same guys we used to slip bottles of liquor to or bring into our hotel suites when we were touring. Now they made fun of us. We were a joke."

He opened the desk drawer and took out another old photograph, which he offered to her. She took it. It showed the four Dreamers sitting on the wood railing of a boardwalk, with the ocean behind them. They were shirtless and tan, with blue Levis and bare feet. There were four girls in the photo as well, two standing on either side of the boys. They were in bikinis, although the one on the far left was wearing a long, unbuttoned denim shirt over it. Everyone was smiling, except for this fourth girl, who stared into the camera, her lips a short, straight line. She reminded Iliana of the youngest girl in the family picture down-stairs. The photo looked faded and felt thin and worn in her hand. She knew it was old, but she also guessed it had been handled a lot. Did he show it often to others? Or look at it a lot when he was here alone?

"That's Catherine, my wife, the serious one. Did I tell you she was in the show?"

"You did," Iliana said. "Were you dating back then? What did you like about her?" She was curious as to how Catherine ended up with Jeff. What had it taken to date this adored teen idol, let alone to become his girlfriend and later his wife?

"It was mostly that she wasn't like the other girls," he said. "She was smart, always doing something brainy. She was getting a degree in dance, and she would read these biographies of famous choreographers—Balachee or something. Once she spent two hours on the phone with her father, helping him with his taxes! How does a twenty-year-old know how to do taxes?

"But there was this thing about her, this tiny little piece of her that was a risk taker," he continued. "I mean, she came all the way from New York and auditioned for our show—you've got to have some adventure in you to do that. And I was always chasing that little piece of her. And it was so sexy when I found it. Once I convinced her to spend an entire weekend in my apartment without getting dressed. Just to go back and forth from the bedroom to the kitchen, eating and making love for two days straight. This was so not like her, she always had to study or clean out a cabinet or something. I got such a charge, being the guy who got her to go against her nature. What an incredible weekend."

The mention of Catherine's decision to travel from New York to California was like a knife jab. Why hadn't *she* ever had the courage to do something like that, something gutsy and bold and risky? Why had she played life so safe?

"But at the end of the third season, Catherine decides to leave LA," Jeff said. "I don't know, maybe I wasn't such a great boyfriend. But I was so mad when she abandoned me. She thought the show didn't have a future, and she was right. After the fourth season, we're canceled. Nobody likes the Dreamers. Nobody will admit *ever* liking us. And it's every man for himself. I tried a solo singing tour. Do you remember that?"

Iliana shook her head guiltily.

"Don't worry, no one does. Nobody bought tickets. I could barely fill half an auditorium. So I cancel the last few cities and go home. Except now, home is on the East Coast. My parents have moved with my brother to New York, so I move in with them. But I can't stop thinking about what it was like at the beginning. When the commercial came out, and those girls asked for my autograph, or the day we drove around, grabbing newspapers. I would have given anything to do it again. I felt like an old man. I was twenty-three years old."

Iliana looked down. She knew just how he felt. Going to college, getting her first job, meeting Marc, getting married, giving birth—all the important firsts of life, why did they have to come so early, so close together, bam-bam-bam? Why couldn't they be spread out over a lifetime? What was a person supposed to do when all the good firsts were over and the only ones left were bad firsts that you didn't want anyway? The first irreparable fight. The first promotion lost to someone younger. The first spouse to get sick. The first funeral to plan. And yet Jeff was wrong. He hadn't been washed up at twenty-three. He went on to get married, have a family, start a business, create a product line. Life gave a person a lot of chances.

"I registered for a couple of classes at Columbia," Jeff said. "But it didn't work out. I was older than everyone, and people kept their distance, like they didn't know what to make of me. But then my brother calls me up. He became a skier when my family moved east, and he wants to start his own outerwear business. So he gets his business degree at the University of Maine in Portland and begins working at L.L.Bean to learn the ropes. He starts out entry-level, but then he gets promoted, and he bugs me to come work for him so in a few years we can go into business together. At first I say, no way. Working for my baby brother? Living in Maine? I was a Dreamer! But after a while I gave in. I wasn't doing much, just sleeping late and writing bad music and driving my parents nuts. So I pack up and head north. I stayed there fourteen years."

He tilted his head. "Ever been to Maine?"

"During the summer, with the kids," Iliana answered, picturing water parks, traffic, and countless kids-eat-free restaurants.

"No, I mean the winter Maine. I rented a small house set back off a main road and started calling myself Jay. Jay Downs. I grew my hair long and I grew a beard, and I gained some weight, too. Nobody recognized me. I joined a bowling league. My teammates were big, hairy guys, plumbers and builders. I never watched TV, I hardly dated. Just worked, bowled, and slept.

"But then there comes a day I need a new coat, so I drive to the big L.L.Bean store in Freeport to use my employee discount," said Jeff. "And it's fall, and families are shopping for parkas, parents trying hats and snow pants on their kids. And I start to think it might be nice to get back into circulation. And right about this time Jack, my brother, he wants to leave Bean and start developing sports apparel made with polyester fleece. He's been saving money, and I've got a little saved, too. We signed a good designer and hooked up with a small, hungry factory in South Carolina. We called our business Hats and All That.

"At first, we had two products—a ski hat and a set of knee-high socks with separate pockets for each toe. Bean picked both items up for the catalog, and we also started selling them locally, to sports and ski shops. Then one day I'm in a coffee shop and I see this guy and I blurt out, 'That's my hat!' Of course, he nearly socked me until I told him what I meant, but then he said he loved that hat. And it was a hoot, listening to him."

"Why did that mean so much to you?" Iliana asked.

"Because I had created this thing, do you see? I liked making a product instead of being one. So after a few years I'm ready to expand into another category, and Jack doesn't want to, so we shake hands, and I start Downs Textiles. I spend some time in Europe and Asia, checking out factories that can give me a good price on raw materials. Then I arrange with the factory to begin blanket production, and I start calling on buyers in New York. Pretty soon it's clear that I need a New York showroom. So I move to Manhattan, get a showroom, and hire a receptionist. I'm in business."

"Back to New York," Iliana said. Lucky for her.

"Yeah, but what I haven't mentioned is that Catherine's kept up with me," Jeff said. He tilted his head, the way he always seemed to when he wanted to gauge her reaction. She thought that maybe he wanted to see how she reacted to the mention of Catherine again. Maybe he wanted to see if she looked jealous. Maybe he wanted her to *be* jealous. She looked away, not sure what expression she wanted him to see.

He chuckled. "Catherine had been sending me Christmas cards each year," he said. "She's married and divorced by now, has a couple of daughters. So I invite her to Manhattan. Hey, I've got a business, a product line, employees. I've got things to be proud of now. Well, she walks in the door, and she's changed so much. Her face is even thinner, and she looks so tired. And all she can talk about is how much she admires what I've put together from nothing. It makes me so happy to hear her go on. Not that I'm a narcissist, at least I don't think I am. But it's nice when someone you care about thinks you're hot stuff, don't you think?"

Iliana nodded. She knew, especially from the last few weeks, how very good that felt.

"And so, Ms. Fisher, six months later we were married. Eventually we moved up here and had our daughter. And then there's our older two girls from Catherine's first marriage. And maybe once in a while I wonder if I did the right thing, leaving Hollywood behind. Especially when someone recognizes me, or tells me they used to love my songs. Someone pretty and important like, I don't know, a newspaper reporter?" He winked at her, something she had never seen him do, not even on TV. Iliana blushed.

"And then a few weeks ago, I get a call," he said, reaching a crescendo. "And one morning, to my great delight, Iliana Fisher walks through my door."

There were voices downstairs. Iliana had been aware of them for about ten minutes, but now they were coming closer. Iliana was sorry that Jeff's employees were coming back. She had enjoyed hearing him tell his story. It was what she had always wanted when she was young—to be close to him, to know exactly what was going on behind that one-of-a-kind, tight-lipped smile. She only wished there was more to hear.

Jeff seemed reluctant for the morning to end as well. He stood and smoothed out his pant legs with his hands. "Hey, I should let you go," he said.

She shrugged. "I guess it's getting to be that time."

"Okay then," he said resignedly. "Let me get you to the highway."

Chapter 12

Iliana took one last look before she went to the stairs. The sun threw a splash of light from one of the windows onto the floor, and it lit up like a stage. Jeff greeted his two employees when they reached the landing, and they waved to Iliana before sitting at their computers. Then Jeff gestured to Iliana that they should continue down, and she started to descend.

She knew it was time to go. She clearly had all the material any reporter could need for an article. She had spent a lot of time with Jeff, much more than she used to spend with a subject she was profiling. She had met some employees and customers, viewed his product line, heard him make a sales pitch, and even spent some relaxed time talking openly over lunch. And now she had heard him recount his past as well. She knew that he could sometimes be self-serving—his claim that he had demonstrated great acting skill was almost laughable—and yet she realized how strong his need to protect his ego must be. She recognized that the first part of his life was a mix, with thrills as exciting as a lottery win, followed by defeats and misgivings. And she understood his decision to patch what he could and embrace a future with fewer ascents but fewer crashes as well.

And yet, it wasn't enough. There was something unsatisfying about this moment, like a diet meal, a salad without a roll. She didn't know if the *New York Times*—or any magazine, for that matter—would think she had a story worth publishing, but in a way it didn't matter. She had loved being Iliana Fisher, *New York Times* reporter, and she had loved interviewing Jeff Downs. She didn't want it to end.

The thing was, when Jeff was talking, there were times when she felt she was there. She could see him running from girls at the Detroit hotel; she felt breathless, as though she had run, too. She could feel the waist of his frayed jeans as he leaned against the boardwalk railing with his pals. It was just like when she was young and would sit in front of the TV, feeling Jeff's charm shoot out and envelop her. Just like in her dream on the day she first met him, when he reached through the TV screen to draw her in. *This* was what she loved about reporting. She had peeled away layers and explored all the nooks and crannies she found underneath, doing exactly what she had told Jeff she always loved to do, from the time her parents bought her a writing desk for her birthday, or even before.

And yet, now that it was over, she couldn't feel or see or hear any of it anymore—why was that? Why were feelings and sensations so hard to hang on to? She had given birth to two babies, had been a full-time mom to each of them, and even now, not all that much later, she couldn't feel what it was like to hold them. She *remembered* holding them, but her arms no longer carried the sensation. She couldn't feel Matthew's solid infant body in her arms; she couldn't see Dara raise her diapered bottom in the air as she tried to stand. She couldn't even hear the sound of her father's voice anymore, even though he had called weekly after her parents moved to Florida, ending each conversation with "Goodnight, my sweetheart." It didn't matter that she could remember those things; if she couldn't feel them, hear them, if her senses didn't kick in, what good were her memories?

When they got close to the front of the house, they saw Catherine walking toward them.

Iliana knew it was Catherine immediately. She was thin and taut, with brown hair styled in a short, precise haircut. Her appearance was neat, her posture erect, her face serious and composed. She looked to Iliana like a person who liked to be in control, the kind of person who counted every calorie, kept track of every detail, meticulously cleaned the lint out of the dryer after every cycle. She was wearing a thick red sweater and jeans tucked into laced-up, calf-high leather boots.

"Hey, you're home," Jeff said, kissing her on the cheek. He seemed to be trying to appear casual, but he looked surprised and a little scared, like a teenager who had snuck his girlfriend into the house, not expecting his mother to return. "This is the reporter I told you about, Iliana Fisher," he said. "Iliana, this is my wife, Catherine."

"Nice to meet you," Iliana said, extending her hand.

"Likewise," Catherine answered, shaking Iliana's hand. "Did you get everything you needed?" She didn't come across as particularly warm, but her smile was pleasant.

"I did," Iliana said. Nobody spoke for a moment. Iliana sensed tension between husband and wife, and it made her uncomfortable. She wondered if Catherine thought she was romantically interested in Jeff. Whatever the problem, Iliana wanted desperately to take the stress level down. "It's a great space here, and the showroom in the city is beautiful, too," she said. "You've got a wonderful business. You both should be very proud."

"Jeff, did you tell her about the new product?" Catherine asked, sounding more relaxed. "It would be nice to get a little advance publicity on that. I ran into Melly and Charles on their way back. They said Stefano is on board."

"Yes, I heard about the new product, and it's very exciting," Iliana said. "And I heard some great stories about your earlier life, too, how you met Jeff when you were on the show."

Barbara Solomon Josselsohn

"Jeff talked about the show?" Catherine said, her eyebrows raised.

Iliana immediately knew she'd said something wrong. "A little about it, yes. Some about the business and some about the show."

"I think I'd better get Iliana on her way," Jeff jumped in, gesturing toward the street. "I'll be right back and we can go over Stefano's contract."

He walked down to where the cars were parked and waited by hers. Iliana followed, feeling concerned that she had created a problem between the couple. "Look, you don't have to do this," she said. "I can find my way back to the highway by myself."

"No, the GPS takes you miles out of the way," he said. "No need to put you through that. It won't take long for me to get back here."

She unlocked her door and he opened it for her. Then he went to his own car, looking anxious and distracted. Watching him pull away from the curb, she couldn't help but feel sorry for him. Why had Catherine been so disturbed by her presence, and then even more so when she brought up the show? Did she have a problem with that aspect of the article? Did she not want Iliana to write about the Dreamers?

Ultimately, Iliana realized, it didn't matter. She was done asking questions, of Jeff and about him. And yet, the more she had learned about him that morning, the more she had come to empathize with him. Jeff, with his cheery exterior and his complicated past, trying to hold on to the dream that he still had an exceptional life, when what he really had was a middling business and a sour-faced family. What had he said when he talked about the day right before the TV show debuted— that the afternoon the guys spent taking newspapers out of the vending machines was the best afternoon of his life? She knew exactly what he meant. Being on the verge of something big—that was what made life thrilling. She had felt just the same way in the days and hours before she first met him. And now that it was ending, she felt horrible. Because it was all a fantasy. It was foolish to pretend you were something you no longer were or never had been, because at the end of the day you

131

had nothing. It was true of Jeff, and it was true of her, too. She wasn't a writer if she was spending all her time writing a pretend article. She'd be a writer when she actually *wrote*.

She sighed. She liked Jeff Downs. She liked the person she was when she was with him. She would miss that feeling. She *had* to figure out how to get it back.

Jeff's car traveled through the small town and then onto the long, two-lane stretch of road, and Iliana followed behind. Soon the coffee shop was visible, and Jeff turned into the parking lot and pulled into a space. She pulled in alongside him, figuring she probably should use the restroom inside. And she wanted to say good-bye to him. She didn't really know if she would ever talk to him again.

She got out of her car, and he got out, too, looking at her with his palms up. "What's up?"

"I just thought I'd stop inside for a moment before heading home," she said.

"Oh. Well, as long as you've stopped, let me buy you a cup of coffee for the road. It's cold—couldn't hurt to have something warm to drink in the car."

Inside, Jim pointed toward the back of the shop, and Iliana made her way down the narrow aisle to the restroom. When she emerged, Jeff was standing near the front, his coat unbuttoned and his elbows on the long counter.

"Here you go," he said, and slid a Greek-style cardboard coffee cup in her direction.

"Thanks." She took it from him.

"So when does this great epic run?"

"I'll be in touch when I know." She figured that if she sold the story, she would call him, but if she didn't, she would just disappear.

He rubbed his chin. "You know, Catherine's not too crazy about your story. Oh, publicity for the company, she's all for that, but I mean the rest of it. The stuff about the past."

"Oh," she said. That was the problem.

"I guess it's because she saw me getting all pumped to talk to you today," he continued. "She feels all that stuff should be buried. Dead and gone."

Iliana nodded. She felt bad for Jeff. It was painful, she knew, to bury something that you really enjoyed. Just saying good-bye to him now was hard.

He looked at her. "You know, you're a really good writer," he said. "We googled you, Rose and I, after you left the showroom that first day. There wasn't anything from the *Times*—although like you said earlier, I guess freelancers don't always get bylines for short articles."

She nodded. It was hard to believe that he totally bought this line she had come up with earlier that morning. He must really want this article, she thought, to have accepted her lame explanation with no questions. The realization made her feel especially guilty. More than ever, she wanted to get an article about him published, so she would feel that his faith in her was well placed.

"But we found a ton of stuff from before, from when you were at *Business Times*, and also some articles you wrote locally," he said. "Hey, we even found your Facebook page. It was a little hard to find. I didn't realize that Fisher was your maiden name. Nice picture, though. Nice-looking family."

Iliana felt all the blood drain from her face—he had found her online?

"But there wasn't much on your public page," he said. "I guess you're a private kind of person."

She nodded. "It's my husband. He . . . he's obsessed with privacy." It was true. Marc thought the more personal information you had online, the more you risked identity theft. He didn't have a Facebook page and had convinced her to use the highest possible privacy settings. But then she relaxed, realizing that even if her privacy settings had been lower, it wouldn't have mattered. So what if Jeff saw where she went to high school or what town she lived in? The only lie she had actually told was that she wrote for the *Times*. As long as he didn't go calling there and asking about her, she was safe.

"I even thought about friending you," he said. "But I didn't want you to think I was a stalker."

If she didn't have so much adrenaline pouring through her veins, she thought, she actually might have found that last comment funny. *He* was worried about looking like a stalker?

He looked at his watch. "I guess I should be heading back. But the reason I brought all this up is because I wanted you to know . . . that since I met you, I've been thinking a lot about the past. Like . . . like maybe it would be fun to sing again. Play some gigs, maybe get in touch with the guys again."

It was a complete surprise, this train of thought. "Singing?" she asked. "With the Dreamers?"

"I haven't spoken to any of them since we broke up. There were all these bad feelings, we all blamed each other when the show failed. But I'm sure I can find them. And maybe we can bring back some of the old music, write some new songs even. I'm not a kid now, I won't be pushed around. I can do it the right way this time, the way *I* want to do it."

"But you didn't even want to talk about the past until I pulled it out of you," she said. "You liked that you were a success in business. You didn't want to be like one of those reality-show guys."

"I'm *not* like them, just like you told me. Look, I know it's crazy. But I see everything differently now. It's because of talking to you. You're the one who made me realize how much I miss it all."

She felt herself withdraw from him, actually lean toward the back of the shop. She didn't want this responsibility. She didn't want to be the cause of any problems in his marriage. "I never . . . I never meant to do that," she said.

"Well, it happened. One way or another, it did," he said. "And at this point, there's no going back. See, I have business meetings in LA on

March tenth and eleventh, trying to get our line into more West Coast stores, and I've been thinking of staying on for a few days. I thought I'd try to track down the guys, get the ball rolling for the next act of the Dreamers. Maybe visit some of the old places we used to go, get some inspiration for new songs."

He looked at her. "Hey, you said you always liked the Dreamers. Why don't you come along?" he teased.

She laughed. "Very funny. You know, you shouldn't tease a New Yorker about trips to California in February."

They were quiet for a moment. Jeff folded his hands on the counter, his eyes focused ahead at the bulletin board on the wall, which held posters with information on hand-washing regulations and ways to help a choking victim. Looking at his profile, with the sun coming in from the windows, Iliana could make out old acne scars on his cheek, ridges he surely once covered up with makeup. She could tell that he was concerned, and she figured he was thinking about Catherine, who probably knew nothing of these plans and would be furious if she were here right now. She was clearly the strong one of the two. Iliana truly felt sorry for him. Life had thrown him a huge curveball when he was sixteen by making him famous, and then another when he was twenty-three by taking it all away, and to this day he was still trying to figure out what to make of it all. He was still trying to reclaim his past glory, even though that glory now only existed in the inflated memories he held.

"I just think it would be awesome to go back there and give it another shot," he said. "We were these four young guys, all thrown into this crazy situation, and it made us who we are, and to go back now and see how we each turned out and how maybe we can move on and make it even better . . ."

He dropped his head. "Listen to me. I'm starting to sound like you. Seeing stories everywhere, huh?" He looked up at her and grinned. "But it does sound like a good story, doesn't it?"

"It sounds like a great story," she told him. "Actually, it sounds sort of like that book I wanted to write. I told you about it in the restaurant—about the four people living in New York and how they got there, what became of them, who they thought they could be and what ultimately became of them . . ."

Her smile slowly disappeared, as her eyes widened. "It sounds like that book I always wanted to write . . ."

God, she wanted to go to California. Driving home, she realized that she wanted to go and start working on that book idea as much as she had ever wanted anything. Even the tiniest muscles in her fingers tensed with excitement when she thought about doing that research and writing. It would be a book about who the Dreamers once were and who they were now, and about all the teenage girls like her, who had loved them. It would be a look back in time, but also a larger story of what it meant to be young and on top of the world. It would be a book about the phenomenon of the teen idol, told through the story of Jeff and his fellow Dreamers. Maybe she would interview some cultural historians or media experts who would comment on the power of TV back in the pre-Internet days. After all, girls back then could only see *Guitar Dreams* once a week, while girls today saw stars anytime they wanted, simply by googling them or going on Instagram or Netflix. Did that change the experience of falling in love with a teen celebrity? And why did preteen girls fall in love with teen idols anyway? Why was that experience so common? Maybe she would speak with an expert in adolescent psychology who could offer some thoughtful perspective.

And along the way, she would be spending time with Jeff Downs, visiting all the places he had talked about that morning. He could take her to that burger joint, Nate's, if it still existed, and to the boardwalk where the cast took that ocean photo. They could see if those newspaper vending machines were still there. Maybe he would even introduce her to the Dreamers when he found them: *This is my friend Iliana.*

It was decades after she had imagined such an experience, but it didn't matter. It was his chance to make a comeback, but it was her chance too—her chance to make up for those horrible middle school years when Lizzie dumped her and no one cared. Her chance to step out of the self-pity she had been feeling for so long. Forget about Stuart blowing her off, forget about Jodi insisting that her professional life was over, which made Iliana feel discouraged and helpless. Forget about that horrible evening when she had meandered around the Connors's cocktail party alone, watching Marc converse with women who were actually doing work that had an impact on the world. Now *she* would be putting herself out into the world and creating something that didn't exist before. Now *she* would be in a position to make an impact.

Just before she had left for home, Jeff again raised the possibility of her meeting him in LA for a day or two to spend some time in the old Dreamers environment and get a closer feel for what his life had been like.

"I don't know, Jeff," she said. "I mean, my kids, my family. It's hard to just pick up and go on a trip like this—"

"But you're a writer. They know you're a writer. Think how proud they'll be when they see your name on a book cover."

"There's no guarantee this book will ever get published—"

"But you're already writing an article about me. And once it's published, it will be a hop, skip, and a jump to the next step. I bet the book publishers will be pounding at your door."

"It doesn't work like that—"

"Don't you want to write a book?"

"Of course I do."

"But how can you, if you don't give yourself a shot?"

She shook her head as she picked up her coffee, and they walked out the door. She lifted the tab on the cup, and the steam rose in a soft, fragile trail.

"Think about it," he told her as she climbed into her car. "Just do me that favor. Think about it for a little while before you say no. Okay? I think it would be awesome for both of us."

Turning off the highway back in Scarsdale, Iliana knew she agreed with him. It would be good for her to go, to spend just two little days doing some research. Then she could come home in the best position possible to write a book that could sell. And yet, how could she possibly pull it off? What would she tell Marc—that she was flying to California to spend two days with a married ex-TV star who somehow believed she was a *Times* star reporter? Sure, she told herself sarcastically, that would work. And she hadn't forgotten the big mess that occurred when she went to lunch with Jeff and missed Dara's phone call. She could hear all the promises she had made to herself that she would never, *never* put her children second again. She couldn't go back on that.

And then she remembered something else—March 13 was when that Connors workshop was set to start. She wasn't free; she had to be in New Jersey that day. She had promised Marc she'd go, and he was annoyed with her already for getting drunk and mouthing off at the cocktail party. And she was still mad at him, too. They had both been walking on eggshells, scared to do or say something that might send the other one out the door. If she changed her plans and went to California instead of participating in the workshop with those flower-arranging women, it could be the last straw.

But going to New Jersey instead of being with Jeff sounded unbearable. Choosing colors and filling vases instead of walking on the beach, having burgers near the ocean, hearing more stories, imagining a fabulous book that couldn't be written without *her*. She was a great reporter, according to him. She was the writer he wanted to work with, and his confidence in her made her ego soar. Who knew where this book idea

Barbara Solomon Josselsohn

could lead? Who knew how many women might read it and feel that in telling the story of Jeff Downs from her own perspective, she had captured the story of their own lives: the confusion of being an adolescent girl trying to fit in, the sweet escape of a fantasy life with a cute boy whose sweet smile made your problems go away, the eventual ability to look back on those days with insight and affection? Who knew what this could mean for her? How could she say no?

Round and round the arguments went—go, don't go, go, don't go—with no resolution, until she got home and made her way to the computer. There in her in-box was an email from Julius Criss of the *Times* magazine. She wasn't surprised it had come relatively soon—she knew that editors tended to get back to writers quickly when another editor on staff had suggested their name—and she decided right then that his response would be the deciding factor. If he liked the idea and he gave her a green light, she'd be able to truthfully tell Marc that she had a real, paid writing assignment. The prospective publication of her work in the *Times* would add legitimacy to her plans, and she would bow out of the workshop and go to California with a clear conscience. Even though Jeff had no experience in publishing, he was right that her byline in the *New York Times* could possibly open doors for a book deal. It would be a whole new ball game for her.

On the other hand, if Criss turned her down, the trip was off. There was no way she could truthfully make the case to Marc that she needed to withdraw from the Connors program and travel to California instead. She'd have to lie about an assignment, or lie about a possible book deal, or figure out some other fake reason to go, and that was a level of deceit she just couldn't stomach. Her fate was in Julius Criss's hands.

Trembling, she opened the email:

139

Dear Ms. Fisher:

Wish I could say yes, but it's a little too light
for our readership. Still, it's worth pursuing.
Have you thought about one of the women's
magazines—*More, Self*, maybe even Oprah's
magazine? Or if you like the business angle,
how about *Entrepreneur, Fast Company,
Forbes*? Online maybe—Slate.com or Salon.
com? I think there's a home for it somewhere!
Good luck,

Julius

She read the email a second time and ultimately accepted the fact that no matter how nicely it was stated, a no was a no. And a deal was a deal. She had told herself that if the *Times* gave her a thumbs-down, she would abandon any thought of going to California—and sure enough, that was what happened. Enough was enough. It was time to disappear from Jeff's life and move on to other things. The middle school orchestra concert was a week away and Matthew would be playing, that was something to look forward to. And Dara had upcoming volleyball games and probably needed new hair ribbons. She was always losing them. Plus, Iliana could come up with other article ideas and send some more queries out, and she could take on a few more local writing assignments in the meantime. That was still writing, wasn't it? And of course, there was Jena Connors's event to get ready for. She probably could use another outfit.

Sitting at the dining room table, she sank her forehead into her hands. The thing was, she really wanted to go to California. She really wanted just one more chance to explore that life she had yearned to have when she was young. Just one chance to enjoy those dreams for real, out in California with Jeff Downs and not just sitting in front of the TV on a Thursday night. But it was not going to happen. It was finally over. Without getting even the slightest shred of actual interest in her work, that was the only reasonable choice. After all, she had given the idea of writing about Jeff Downs her best shot. Hadn't she?

Chapter 13

"Hey, stranger!" Jodi waved to her from the back booth. "Staying in town these days, I hope? No more abandoned children?"

It was a week after Iliana's trip to Mount Kisco. She had tried hard during that time not to think about that day, because it made her feel so discouraged. She had tried hard to convince herself that she was better off forgetting about Jeff and pulling the plug on his whole story. What other choice did she have? She had received no outside endorsement that an article about Jeff Downs had merit, so it seemed unwise to pursue it, let alone begin a book. It would likely be a waste of time, and she'd end up disappointing them both. The fact was, publishing was a tough business. Magazines were shutting down left and right, and book publishers were consolidating all over the place. Traditional media companies were getting rid of staff, and tons of editors were joining the ranks of freelancers. There were too few publishers and too many writers hawking their projects.

Sliding into the booth, she shook off her coat and slid a mug along the table so the waitress could fill it. "No more abandoned children. Actually, I'm giving up the hunt for work."

"No! You wanted it so much."

"There's nothing out there for me. It's like you said, nobody hires women like us, who've been out of the workforce since forever. You were right. I give up." She looked up at the waitress. "Whole-wheat toast, please."

"Same for me," Jodi said, pushing her menu to the edge of the table. She turned back to Iliana. "I'm sorry to hear you say that—"

"No bacon? What's going on?"

"What I was trying to say is that I'm sorry to hear you say that because—you'll never believe it—I got a job. Aaaah!" She raised her hands and jiggled her fingers with excitement, then tossed back the hair that cascaded forward.

Iliana felt her upper body collapse. "You got a job? You weren't even looking!"

"I know, it's insane! It's because of Chelsea's thing. I ended up talking to the lawyer for the landlord who's renting Chelsea the new space because I had some questions. We got to chatting and the next thing I know, he's asking me if I'd be interested in talking with him about joining his firm. It's a great job, not partner, but I'm heading up my own section and I have two other lawyers reporting to me."

"He's giving you a *department*? When you haven't worked anywhere in ten years?"

"He said my experience is strong and I'll quickly pick up what I don't know. I start in two weeks, can you believe it? And I still have to hire some help around the house and buy work clothes. More spin classes, too, gotta get back in shape. So I think this is it, pal. Our last breakfast."

"That's really something," Iliana said. "Congratulations, Jo. It's great news." She pushed away the plate that the waitress set before her. She no longer had an appetite.

"And I owe it all to you," Jodi said. "I never would have even considered going back if you hadn't brought it up. You've always been the motivated one, always trying to do something different. And don't worry; something will come along for you, too."

"No, I don't think so. But thanks."

"And I gotta give up the PTA stuff, too! No more volunteering, I won't have time. Which reminds me—I said I'd pick up refreshments for the hospitality table at the concert tonight, but there's no way I'm going to get to it. Can you possibly do it for me?"

Iliana turned away, feeling her breath get heavy. She told herself she was not going to cry right here at the coffee shop. If she had to cry, it would wait until she got home.

"What, you're upset because I got a job?" Jodi asked.

"No, of course not. I'm happy for you. I'm just tired."

"Look, the boys are having dinner at the school before their final rehearsal, and doesn't Dara's team have an away game today? She won't get back to the school until right around the time of the concert. You have the whole day. Go home and take a nap and then go back out to the store and do me this little favor. Please?"

Iliana nodded. After all, Jodi had been there for her when Dara got sick. "Fine. I'll take care of it."

"Great, Iliana, thanks. You're the best."

They paid the check and headed toward their cars, passing by Chelsea's. Through the window, Iliana could see the corner of the desk that reminded her of her father, the one that Jodi had called a sentimental knockoff.

"See you later, and for God's sake, cheer up," Jodi said. "Something will come through for you. You never know what's coming around the bend."

The desk beckoned. Iliana turned away.

In the car, she decided to head right over to Super Stop & Shop and get the shopping done. A half hour later, she emerged from the store wheeling a cart holding four bags filled with packages of Chips Ahoy! cookies and six bags with gallon jugs of apple juice. As she started to haul the stash to her trunk, the cart rolled forward, and when she reached out to grab it she lost her grip on one of the bags sending a jug crashing to the ground. It exploded, splashing juice all over her pants, shoes, and coat. She went back into the store to get a replacement, and was just loading it into her trunk when a text from Jodi showed up: Don't forget the new allergy policy! You can only get cookies that aren't made in a factory that processes nuts—read the labels!

So for the third time that morning she went back into the store and began searching for the right type of cookies. It took her nearly forty minutes to examine the packages along the entire cookie aisle, until she finally found a brand of sugar cookies that was safe. Then she had to argue with the store manager, who refused to take back any of the Chips Ahoy! packages because they were all at least slightly wet from the juice spill.

"It's your cashier's fault, for making the bags too heavy," she told him. "You're going to lose the PTA as a customer. We'll never shop from your store again!" He looked over her shoulder and asked to help the next person in line. He wasn't even listening.

She drove to the school building and parked in the rear near the loading dock, before a custodian came running out to tell her she had to get a pass from security first. Obediently she drove around to the front of the building and parked in the lot, made her way to the security desk, and returned to the loading dock with a big, white "Visitor" sticker affixed to her coat. It took another twenty minutes for the custodian to show up again with a trolley so she could begin to unload.

When she had pulled the last bag out, she discovered Dara's hair ribbons, squished into a corner of the trunk. She looked at her watch. It was twelve thirty, right in the middle of the sixth grade's lunch period. She knew Dara wouldn't be allowed to play in her volleyball game that afternoon without her team hair ribbons, so she decided to go inside and deliver them. No doubt Dara didn't even yet realize that she didn't have them.

Making her way through the school hallways and into the cafeteria, she surveyed the round and rectangular tables arranged on the huge floor. All the girls looked practically the same from the back, with their long, straight hair. Then she spotted Dara's brown sweater, and she walked across the room to where Dara and her friends sat. She heard them talking as she approached the table.

"My cousin in Chicago met Brandon Ryde! Of that new band Amplify!"

"Awesome! How?"

"He was at a mall signing autographs."

"Oh my God, when is he coming to New York?"

"I love him!" Dara said. "I have to go to their concert, and— *Mom!*" she exclaimed when one of her friends pointed in Iliana's direction. She climbed off the bench and rushed over, obviously trying to put as much distance between her mother and the girls as possible. "What are you *doing* here?"

"I brought your ribbons," Iliana said. "You left them in the car."

"I know! It doesn't matter. I was going to borrow."

"Maybe no one has extras."

"There's always extras."

"I thought that maybe—"

"Mom, I'm going to lose my spot if I don't sit down. I'll meet you in the lobby after my game, okay?" Dara snatched the ribbons and went back to the table.

Iliana turned and dragged herself back to the car. What was wrong with her, thinking that Dara would be happy to see her? Girls in sixth grade didn't want their mothers at school. It wasn't like when Dara was eight and would beg Iliana to help out in the lunchroom, serving pizza, or in the school library, checking out books. Iliana realized that when *she* was in middle school, the one thing that definitely would have made lunch worse would have been if her mother had shown up to give her something. That would have made her even more of an outcast. She was lucky Dara had even gotten up and talked to her at all.

She drove back home and entered the house just as her cell phone rang. The caller ID showed the school's number. What now?

It was Matthew. "Mom, I forgot my violin again. Can you bring it over?"

Iliana leaned over the kitchen counter, her forehead in her palm, her eyes closed. "Matthew, I can't. I was just there. I'm not coming back again, you'll have to borrow."

"But Mom—"

"I can't, do you get it? You've forgotten that thing too many times."

"But Mom—"

"I don't feel well, Matt. I think I'm sick."

"But Mom—"

"Find a way to borrow one. I'll see you at the concert tonight."

She hung up the phone and walked up to her bedroom. She pulled back the covers and climbed into bed.

—⟐—

Later that afternoon, she took a shower, made sandwiches for Marc and Dara since there'd be no time for a real dinner, and went to pick up Marc at the train station. She gave him his sandwich, and he wolfed it down as they headed to the school for the concert. It had been a horrible day. She hoped the evening would be better. She liked Matt's concerts. It was fun seeing the orchestra improve year after year.

They parked and found Dara in the school lobby, then walked into the auditorium and found seats. Iliana handed Dara her sandwich and then scanned the stage, looking for Matthew. He usually sat on the left side, but tonight he wasn't there. Had they moved the violins? But no, she saw Jodi's son, Zach, and the other violin players, right where they always were.

"Where's Matt?" she asked Dara. "Do you see him?"

Dara pointed to the front row of the auditorium, all the way on the left. Matt was sitting by himself, wearing his concert tuxedo and looking straight ahead at the orchestra onstage.

"Why's he there?" Marc said, leaning over Iliana. "Why isn't he playing?"

"Because Mom wouldn't bring his violin to school. Mr. Finn said anyone without an instrument couldn't play in the concert."

"*What?*" Iliana turned to Dara. "How do you know that?"

"I saw him when our bus got back from the game."

"But it can't be true. When he told me he forgot it, I told him to borrow a school one."

"They weren't tuned."

"Mr. Finn was supposed to have them tuned for concert week."

"I guess he didn't. And he's taking a letter grade off from anyone who wasn't prepared."

"Why didn't Matt call me back, then?"

"Maybe he didn't have a chance."

"If you knew all this, why didn't *you* call?"

She shrugged. "I don't know, I was with my team. Don't blame me; it's not my fault."

Iliana pressed her fingertips to her head. She had put Jeff Downs out of her mind, she had decided to commit herself fully to her kids and her husband—but even then, even after deciding to do just that, she was still screwing up. And her kids were still suffering. Because she was their mom. She turned to Marc, her heart racing, her eyes filling. "Oh my God, what did I do? What did I do to him?"

Marc raised his arms and then dropped them into his lap. "Nothing you can do about it now."

"I feel terrible. He wanted to play."

"Then why didn't you drop off the violin?"

"I didn't feel well. I had apple juice all over me, and the smell was making me sick. It's hard for me to be there for all of you all the time. We talk about what I can do to make things easier for you, but we never talk about what you can do for me."

"What, was I supposed to run home from the city to drop off his violin?"

"Mom, Dad," Dara murmured. "Stop already, *please?*"

Iliana looked at her daughter, who had sunk down in her seat. People must have been looking their way. She had once again embarrassed Dara.

Marc reached into her lap and took her hand. "Look, it's no big deal," he said. "He's a big kid, he should be responsible for remembering his own violin. He'll get over it. Don't feel so bad."

"But I *do* feel bad," she said, pulling her hand away. "I can't feel better just because you tell me to."

He shrugged and crossed his arms over his chest. "I was only trying to help," he said.

The lights went down, and the music started, but Iliana didn't take in any of it. She didn't hear one note the orchestra played, not one clap of applause from the audience or one whistle of approval at the end of a piece. She didn't see one bow slide or one finger press, didn't see one wave of Mr. Finn's baton. All she saw was Matt, his face visible from the stage lights bouncing off the instruments, as he sat straight up in his seat, watching his friends play.

In the lobby of the auditorium, Matt assured her that she didn't have to be sorry. "I don't care that much about playing," he said. "And Mr. Finn said he won't take away the letter grade since I stayed and watched the whole thing." But Iliana didn't think she'd ever stop feeling guilty. While her family went to get some cookies, she headed outside. The last thing she saw before she left the building was a team of PTA moms serving refreshments, grimacing from how sticky the juice bottles were. They must have gotten wet when she carried them after the first bottles had broken and splashed juice all over her. Another mess she made.

That night, after Marc and the kids had put the evening behind them and were fast asleep, Iliana tiptoed downstairs. She turned on her computer and began composing a note to the PTA president:

> Dear Mrs. Berwich,
>
> This evening, my eighth-grade son, Matthew, was supposed to perform in the orchestra concert, but he didn't have his violin. I had hoped to drop it off at school, but I wasn't feeling well and was unable to do so. My understanding was that Mr. Finn has school violins that the children could borrow, so you can imagine how upset I was when I came to the auditorium and discovered that Matthew had been forbidden to play . . .

Sighing, she stopped typing and sat back in her chair. What was she doing? The concert was finished, there was nothing that could be changed now, and Matt had gotten over the whole incident hours earlier. Still, the memory of him in his tuxedo, sitting in the audience when he should have been performing, haunted her, and she was sure it would continue to haunt her for days. Rubbing her forehead, she closed the email, and her computer screen returned to the school's website, where she had found the PTA president's email address. On the home page was a picture of kids in a science lab watching a heated beaker, presumably of water. A lid was on the beaker, and the steam was frantically trying to escape.

Going back to her browser, Iliana searched for Jeff Downs and *Guitar Dreams* and clicked on a link to a YouTube video. Seeing him on TV used to make her feel better; maybe watching now would have the same effect. She waited for the video to load and leaned her chin on her hands to watch. It was an interview the Dreamers did with Jerry Lewis the one time they appeared on the muscular dystrophy telethon:

Jerry: So, what does the future hold? What are you guys gonna do when you're no longer the biggest stars on TV?

Terry: Sleep!

Peter: Probably go back to my family's farm. Bruce, here, he'll be in Hawaii.

Bruce: Right on! Or Fiji. Australia. Anywhere there's surfing. Chasing the biggest wave of my life.

Jerry: And you, Mr. Quiet? You're the deep one, that's what they say. What will you do?

Jeff: I think I'll be a doctor. Really, you guys, don't laugh. My mom always thought I'd be a doctor. Maybe I'll do it for her.

The video ended, and Iliana stared at the screen, feeling tears start to run down her face. She cried for the dreams people had and the way they so often let those dreams die. She cried for parents like her father and Jeff's mother, who expect their kids to soar, and for parents like her and Marc, who believed that school concerts and volleyball games mattered, when their kids would likely grow up as frustrated and disillusioned as they were. She cried because if Jeff really wanted to be a doctor, then he should have been one, instead of just talking about it. She cried for Jeff, who looked so young and earnest and happy in this video, not realizing that a pretty face was only going to take him so far.

And that was when she realized that she had to go to California. It had nothing to do with getting or not getting the *Times* assignment. She had to give herself a chance to make something amazing happen—a book, Jeff's comeback, *something*. Just like Catherine when she went out to California, *she* had to go. There was still a lot of life ahead of her, and it had to begin now. If she didn't go, she was resigning herself to an existence without surprises, without adventure, without dreams. And she'd continue to be miserable, which would make her family miserable, too. Hadn't she urged Dara to be confident and try out for the volleyball team? Wasn't she going to encourage Matt to audition for all-county orchestra in ninth grade, despite his absence from this latest concert? How could she expect them to try for new things if she wasn't willing to? And okay, there'd be a couple of days of inconvenience with her gone, but Marc could make a few sacrifices, and Jodi would help out. She would ask them to make it work, and she wouldn't take no for an answer. Because writing this book had become her dream—and she absolutely intended to do whatever she needed to chase it down.

The thing was, she *had* to go, because while taking care of her family—to the exclusion of all else—had been fine when her children were young, it was no longer enough. By traveling to California to write Jeff's story, she was writing the next chapter of her own story, too. And it needed to be a good one.

Chapter 14

And so it was set. She called Rose the next morning to say that she'd accepted Jeff's invitation to join him in California, and to get his itinerary. Rose read it to her, and she and realized that the Connors workshop would be no problem. She could fly out to California on Tuesday and stay through Wednesday, then take the red-eye home Wednesday night and make it to the estate in New Jersey for the workshop Thursday morning in plenty of time. And because Jodi would not start her job for another couple of weeks, she'd be available to drive Matt and Dara to school and their activities. Iliana was sure Jodi would be willing, since this was probably the last time she could help Iliana out during the day. All she needed was an explanation, a work-related scenario that both Marc and Jodi could understand and accept.

But what could it be? She thought briefly about saying she had an actual assignment that required her to go to California, but that would be a difficult story for her to pull off, since she hadn't mentioned any upcoming assignments to either one of them lately. But then she realized it would make more sense to them if she said she was *hoping* to get an assignment. She could say she was developing an article, or a series of articles, about blankets—no, broader—home furnishings to pitch to some business magazines or maybe some local publications, and she needed to do some West Coast research. It was almost the truth—just minus a few details, which she could fill in later, if things worked out as she and Jeff hoped.

Sitting down at the kitchen table with a hot cup of coffee, she thought the situation through. Jodi, she knew, would be easy to talk to; the hard part would be discussing the trip with Marc. She decided it was best to call him at the office, since she didn't want to spend the whole day worrying about his reaction. And more important, she knew that he'd be too distracted by problems and colleagues to come up with objections. By the time he came home and was ready to protest, she could say she'd already booked her flight and the trip was a done deal.

Picking up the phone, she silently rehearsed some possibilities. She could do annoyed—*You're not going to believe it, I can't even get a magazine assignment until I do all the research*—in the hope that Marc would try to console her: *It's worth a shot, you want to put your best foot forward.* Or she could be ho-hum—*Hey, goin' out to California to do some research, lined up Jodi*—but scheduling a business trip for the first time in nearly fifteen years when she didn't even have a job wasn't a ho-hum event, and Marc would definitely be confused. The best approach, she decided, was to be excited—no, thrilled—at the prospect of business traveling, and relieved to be coming home in time for the Connors workshop. If she were strong enough in her conviction to carry out these plans, maybe he wouldn't see the point in objecting.

"Guess what?" she said when he came to the phone, concentrating on keeping her pitch high and her breathing shallow. "I've made a decision, and I hope you'll think it's as exciting as I do. I've decided I really want to get a magazine assignment from a local magazine about home furnishings. So I'm going to California to do some research. My pitch will really stand out, don't you think?"

"What are you talking about?" Marc said flatly, as though he had been inoculated against enthusiasm. She could picture him at his desk, his glasses on and his hands still at work on the keyboard.

"I want to write for a magazine, remember? I said that when I told you a few weeks ago about contacting Stuart at my old job. But it's harder than I thought. I'm never going to get an assignment unless I show some initiative."

"Okay."

"And that means going to California."

"How do you figure—what are you *talking* about?"

"Are you even listening, or are you working while I'm here on the phone?"

"I'm listening. It's an absurd conversation, but I'm listening."

"Look, if I go to California to check out some stores, I can write a story about home furnishings trends on the West Coast, which I bet some local magazines would buy."

"Can't you find trends on the Internet?"

"Anyone can read stuff online. If I want to stand out, I have to do things firsthand."

"Who do you want to stand out for?"

"Editors. *Westchester Magazine, Journal News, Hudson Valley Home.*" She grimaced. The lies were just pouring out of her mouth, and they were making her feel horrible. This was her husband, after all. She had to stop and take a different tack. "Marc, I really want to get my career off the ground. Jodi's got a job, and I can get one, too—and this could be a start for me."

"And who would pay for this trip?"

"I would . . . I mean, we would have to pay up front. But if my career gets back on track, I would start making money again."

"It's going to cost a thousand dollars."

"It won't be that much. I can take a red-eye back, they're cheaper."

"And when does this epic journey take place?"

"Very funny. It's next Tuesday, and I'll be back on Thursday morning in time to get to Jena Connors's house."

"That's the same week? You'll never be able to function."

"I'll be fine. I used to take night flights sometimes when I was working. And Jodi will do all the driving for the kids. All you have to do is come home at a reasonable time so you can have dinner with them. This barely affects you."

He paused. "Hang on a minute," he said, and she heard him put the phone down. She made out the sound of a door closing. "Look, Iliana," he said stiffly when he returned. "I know things haven't been so great between us lately, but I don't know what you're doing. I don't know if you're testing me, I don't know if you're mocking me, I don't know if you're *trying* to get me angry, but whatever it is, stop, because you sound like a lunatic."

"Marc—"

"You can't just drop a thousand dollars and run off on a whim. Look, I understand that you want to do something with your life besides just running the house. You're no Karen Angers, I get that. But I just think there are better ways than doing something so ludicrous."

"Marc, it may sound ludicrous to you, and maybe I'd agree if circumstances were different. But for the story and the situation we're talking about now, I have to take this trip. I guess I'm just asking you to accept this for no other reason than it's very, very important to me. Can you do that this one time? Because if you had to take a trip and pay for it out of your pocket to help your career, I think I'd go along with it. I really think I would."

"Kelly, who's that?" she heard him yell out in the other direction. She had no idea if he had heard what she'd just said. "I gotta take this call," he told her when he got back on the phone. "We'll talk later."

He hung up, and she stared at the kitchen countertop. Suddenly the trip that had been so breathtaking less than an hour ago felt inane, frivolous. Why did Marc always have to be so damn oppositional? This was so typical, she thought, these calm, biting questions—*Can't you find trends on the Internet? Who would pay for this trip? You can't drop a thousand dollars and run off on a whim*—that made her feel foolish. What had he asked—was she mocking him, was she testing him? How was he so good at making himself the center of every conversation?

But then she folded her arms across her chest and lowered herself into a kitchen chair. She was deluding herself. Maybe Marc could be a little harsh sometimes, but his questions weren't biting, and they weren't self-centered. They were reasonable. After all, there were plenty of other ways to do research that didn't involve unreimbursed travel. Even for a book on teen idols, or Jeff's experience as a teen idol, she could go online and browse videos of Dreamer concerts or episodes of his *Guitar Dreams* on YouTube. She had already found that snippet from the Jerry Lewis telethon with no trouble at all. And she could interview Jeff and the other guys he located by phone or email. She didn't have to go to California. Marc was right—the plan was ludicrous. She should just forget it, just call Jeff's office and tell him she couldn't get away.

She got up to make the call, but paused midway to the kitchen. No, she thought—*no*, she wasn't going to cave. Wouldn't that be just like her, like the miserable Iliana she had become over these past several years? Sure, there were other ways to research a book on teen idols. But the truth was, the trip was what felt essential. She had spent years sitting at her dining room table in front of her laptop, researching article ideas and writing up queries, only to watch them fail and then seek to distract herself through an endless parade of chores. What had all that effort gotten her? Disappointment and frustration. She couldn't keep doing things the same way over and over. It was time to be bold and try something very different. Okay, she liked Jeff Downs. There was no getting around that fact. She liked how charming he was, and she liked the banter between them. She liked how much he seemed to like her. But she wasn't going out there just to be with him. She didn't want to have an affair. She loved her husband! What she wanted was to get out of her life for a while, to go back and live out the youthful dreams she once had. It was thrilling to think that she had actually engineered a way to meet the person she had dreamed about when she was young, and that he thought she was smart and talented. Who knew what other dreams she could recapture if she just stayed strong? She wanted to go to LA She wanted so badly to be just that adventurous.

Taking a deep breath, she went to the computer to find the cheapest possible round-trip flight to Los Angeles. Then she called Rose with her flight information.

"I've made a reservation for you, Iliana, at the Grand Somerset, where Jeff is staying," Rose said. "He has some appointments late Tuesday, so he said that if it's okay with you, he'll meet you in the lobby at nine on Wednesday morning."

"Thank you, Rose," she said. "Thanks for everything."

With her plans set, she drafted queries to all of the magazines and websites Julius Criss had suggested, and she added a few of the cool women's websites she had been following recently: BlogHer.com, HerStories.com, and even ScaryMommy.com, which ran quirky personal-experience stories. She hoped that one editor—one was all she needed—would see the value in her ideas and give her an assignment.

Over the weekend, Iliana casually mentioned her trip to Marc a few times—"I'm freezing a lasagna for you, just defrost it in the microwave when you get home," and "I'll take your shirts in tomorrow, since I won't be around on Wednesday"—but Marc only shrugged and nodded in response. She knew he was thinking, or hoping, that if he ignored the trip, it would just go away.

On Sunday evening after dinner, Iliana went upstairs and opened her closet. She knew some working mothers from the kids' school who traveled on business to the West Coast or even to Europe every month or so and considered it as routine as a trip to the grocery store. She figured that if she were one of these women, she would probably use a quiet night like this to get an early start on packing. She took out her overnight case, which she thought was big enough for what she needed, and was folding her clothes when Marc walked in.

"So you're really going?" he asked, sitting on the bed.

"Yes, I'm going." She put in a pair of shoes.

"Which credit card did you use for the flight?"

"Amex."

"Which card are you going to use when you're out there?"

"Which do you want me to use?"

"I don't know." He stood up. "My commuter ticket goes on the Amex automatically, but the quarterly bill for train station parking goes on the Visa. You don't pay the bills, Iliana. You don't have a clue where we stand with our money."

She turned him. "You're right, I don't. I guess I abandoned my role in all that when I stopped working. And that's absurd, I'm not a child. Let's talk about it when I get home."

"That's not the point—"

"Then let's not fight about it," she said. "Marc, the point is that I'm going to California. I know you don't understand it, but I have to go. And I know you're mad, but that's just the way it has to be. I'm not going to change my mind. It's *that* important. And I'm sorry to be putting you through this. But I hope that when I get back, we can both move on and be happy."

He shook his head and walked out of the room, but came back in a moment later. "So you're not happy now, is that it?" he said. "So I'm still ruining your life? Well, let me tell you something, Iliana. Life hasn't been so great for me either. You know that Cleveland position, the one that Keith Rein got? *I* got the offer first. And if I had just taken that job, I wouldn't be dealing with this contract mess I'm in now."

"You were offered that job?" she asked. "Why didn't you tell me?"

"Because you'd have given me the silent treatment. You'd have made me feel all over again that I was making you miserable. You'd have told me I was making you a second-class citizen, by dragging you to a new city just for my job. I heard you in my head and I quashed the whole thing."

She threw up her hands in exasperation. "So I ruined your life and you ruined mine. So what's left for us now?"

She went to the bed and zipped up her overnight bag, then placed it on the floor. "I'm leaving," she said.

She walked out of the room and went downstairs. When she got to the bottom, she sank down on the bottom step. She had meant that she was leaving the room. But for one split second she thought she was telling him that she was leaving for good.

In the hallway, she reached over to the wall and raised the temperature on the thermostat three degrees. Then she sat back down. The weather had been warmer that weekend. But suddenly she was freezing.

Chapter 15

Tuesday morning found her in a cab heading toward LaGuardia Airport. She had barely slept all night, worrying about the trip: Was the cab coming early enough? Would there be traffic? Or long lines at security that would make her miss her flight? Had she allowed herself enough time? But now that the cab was sailing over the Whitestone Bridge in the gray of morning, and the digital traffic boards indicated a quick shot to the airport despite the wet and slushy roadways, she realized that her nerves had nothing to do with travel at all. Her stomach felt like an elevator that was stuck several inches above the uppermost floor of the building. She felt unsafe, but because she couldn't pinpoint what exactly the threat was, the sense of physical danger was even more acute. She tried to reassure herself that all was fine. She was in a cab, with her seat belt fastened, driving to LaGuardia, taking a flight to LAX—things that millions of people safely did every day. The only threat, she told herself wryly, was a massive coronary because of how fast her heart was beating.

At the airport, she pulled herself out of the car. The adrenaline pouring into her bloodstream made her legs feel warm and the bones soft, like they might not support her, so she squeezed her fists twice and began to silently and methodically direct herself through the next steps in her trip. Pay the driver. Grasp the handle of her overnight bag and begin wheeling. Find her gate number. Take off her shoes. Proceed through security. Reclaim her stuff. For a moment she wished it were Thursday morning and the trip was over, that she was arriving home instead of taking off. She felt guilty for leaving her kids, guilty for walking out on Marc to spend two days with another man, guilty for not appreciating the good life she had at home. But then she angrily told herself to get a grip. She had put a lot on the line for this trip, and the last thing in the world she wanted to do was wish it over. Had she forgotten already how difficult the last few months had been? This trip was the best way she had of reclaiming the identity that she longed for, of making some kind of meaningful impact.

Her seat was next to the window. Opening her shoulder bag, she dug inside for her iPad so she could find something to read. But the sight of the notebooks and pens she had raided from Matthew's and Dara's desks made her eyes fill. She had kissed them both on their heads before heading out of the house, and she now pictured the way Dara looked, warm and cozy under her pink comforter. For a moment she wished she were still home, so she could take off her shoes and climb into bed with her, like she used to do when Dara was little. But then she decided there was no way she was going to spend the whole flight missing her kids and crying about it. So she ordered a screwdriver from the flight attendant and let the alcohol put her to sleep.

At LAX, however, it was a different story. Refreshed from her nap and invigorated by the energy of a busy airport, she wheeled her bag purposefully through the secured area and into the terminal. She had traveled often for *Business Times* to visit the corporate headquarters of retailers or check out trade shows and preview new product lines in apparel or home furnishings. It had made her feel smart and important, that the magazine thought enough of her to spend a couple of thousand dollars each month sending her to press conferences or product launches, wanting only her written observations and impressions in return. She recalled that feeling now, and it added a confident rhythm to her walk. Looking around at the other business fliers in the terminal, she felt part of an important club—each person a success story who had flown across the country to transform someone or create something. She was excited about seeing Jeff here in LA, about what they would talk about, what he would reveal, what she would discover, and how she could shape it all into something new and salable and irresistible.

She followed the signs for ground transportation and before long was in a taxi, marveling at how sprawling and powerful the freeway looked, with its green overhead signs and its lanes aligned like racehorse gates, its gray cement barriers and bridges. The New York she had left behind had cramped highways broken up by potholes, and commercial roads that looked narrower than usual because of patches of old, dirty snow along the sides. She had been in LA only once before, when she and her college roommate had traveled here for a vacation after graduation, and they'd been confused by the freeways, the way the exits came on both the left and the right. They frequently ended up in the wrong lanes, getting off the freeway when they didn't mean to and having to drive around until they found a way back on, and they'd laugh hysterically each time it happened.

She took off her blazer, straightening out her sleeveless black blouse. She was glad she had decided not to take her winter coat with her. The sky was blue and cloudless, and the sun was strong. She tilted her face to the sun and shook her head. The breeze from the open window mingled with her hair.

"Hey, California agrees with you."

It was finally the next morning, and when she stepped out of the elevator, Jeff was right there in the lobby. He was leaning against a marble column, his legs crossed at the ankles, smiling his trademark smile.

He strolled over leisurely, his hands in the front pockets of his jeans, and she savored the last few moments of anticipation until he reached her. It had been a rough night. She had felt lonely and misplaced. To make the time go faster, she had meandered around the hotel bar and gift shop and had run on the treadmill in the fitness center. When it was finally dinnertime, she called for a salad from room service and ate it while watching *Breakfast at Tiffany's* on one of the cable networks. She called the house to say a quick goodnight. Marc had barely said hello before giving the phone to the kids. The time change worked in her favor, so she was exhausted by eight o'clock. She fell into a restless sleep.

But this morning when she woke up, she was excited for what the day held. She realized with a smile that it was just like she used to be every Thursday in middle school, when math class and science class weren't a bore but a delicious tease, a sweet obstacle she could easily overcome. The periodic tingling in her arms and chest would grow more and more intense as she drew closer to evening and a brand-new episode of *Guitar Dreams*. It was fun to have that feeling again.

They stood before each other, and she hesitated, not quite knowing what to do. They were out of the office, out of New York, away from spouses with their own agendas. It was as though they were standing without a script on an empty stage. What were they right now? Business partners, friends, something else? It felt silly to extend her arm for a handshake, as she would to a business colleague she was meeting for the first time or hadn't seen in a while. She felt paralyzed. Finally, Jeff shook his head, as though willing the awkwardness away. He reached over to hug her.

She closed her eyes, slipped her arms beneath his, and hugged him back. She could smell the cleanness of his aftershave. She could feel the warmth of his body, a little bit of stubble touching the side of her face, his plaid shirt against the palm of her hand. So many things to take in, and she knew it would be over in an instant. She held on to him for a moment longer than she thought she should, and she felt him holding on, too. She told herself she was trying to seal the perceptions into her memory so she would have them if she needed to use them in her writing, but the truth was, it felt good to hug him.

Then they separated. He looked more relaxed. "How was your flight?" he asked.

"Fine. Long," she answered. "How were your meetings?"

"Good. Even better than the Bloomingdale's meeting in New York. Seems there'll be lots of fleece blankets in Southern California soon. I hear the nights can be bitter cold." He pretended to shiver.

"They don't really need them here, do they?" she asked, as though she had finally gotten a joke.

"Oh, come on, everyone can use a good blanket." He gave her a playful push on the shoulder. "I didn't know you were all into the investigative reporter thing already. You have to give a guy some warning."

She smiled. "Got my notepads right in here." She patted her shoulder bag.

"Very impressive. Very prepared. But then, I'm prepared, too." He pointed to a white bag on the concierge counter. "Two coffees, one with milk only. And I was taking a chance here—blueberry muffin?.I seem to remember that you ate blueberry muffins when you took your son to the park years ago."

"That's right," she said. "I love blueberry muffins." And she loved that he remembered the story she told him at the restaurant, about taking Matthew to Central Park when he was a baby. It felt rare to have someone pay such close attention to her.

"Well then, we're ready to go—oh, except for one more thing." He leaned in closer. She felt herself instinctively pull back. "You're flying home tonight, right?"

"That's right, the red-eye."

He sighed. "I thought so. Look, I was able to arrange a surprise for you, but it's not going to happen until tonight. Any chance you can stay until tomorrow?"

Iliana felt her mouth drop open. "I wish I could, I really do—"

"Come on, if you take a late flight, you're not going to get home until tomorrow anyway. What's a few more hours?"

"It's just—there's a meeting I'm supposed to be at tomorrow."

"Can't you cancel it?"

She had promised Marc she'd be back for the Connors session. It was the linchpin in her case that her trip to Los Angeles wouldn't inconvenience him or hurt him in any way. But it killed her to say no to Jeff. What kind of a surprise could he have for her? She couldn't even imagine, and the suspense was as strong as if she were a kid looking at a wrapped birthday present.

"Come on, Ms. Fisher," Jeff said. "Say you'll stay. I've made an eight o'clock dinner reservation at one of the best Italian restaurants in the city, and I've got this incredible surprise for you."

She knew she shouldn't do it. She had given Marc her word. And yet here Jeff was, looking at her with his beautiful brown eyes. He was smiling at her with that shy, tight-lipped smile that she had always loved, that was seared in her head as the smile of a guy who thought she was smart and special and always wanted to hear what she had to say. *"I want to know what Iliana's thinking."* At the moment New York and Marc and Jena Connors seemed a world away. Would it be so terrible if she missed the first Connors session and went to the other two?

"I . . . I'll have to make a phone call," she said tentatively, looking at her watch. It was late morning in New York.

"No problem," Jeff said. "Give me your plane ticket, and while you make the phone call, I'll get the concierge to change your flight."

"It's a nonrefundable fare—"

"Don't worry, the hotel has ways of working this out. If there's a fee, it's on me."

She opened her bag, found her ticket, and handed it to him. He took it and went to the concierge desk. She walked a few steps farther into the lobby and pulled out her cell phone. She hoped Marc would be away from his desk and she could just leave a message on his voice-mail or with his secretary—but no, she thought. He deserved a direct conversation. At any rate, she didn't have to decide. There he was, on the phone.

"Marc Passing," he said.

"Hi, it's me."

"Oh. What?"

He was still mad. And, she knew, he was about to get madder—with good reason. She would be letting him down, and she hated doing that. He had been counting on her. But she would make it up to him when she got home! She would go to the next two workshop sessions, and she would be enthusiastic about them. People often had to cancel their plans, didn't they? Surely she wouldn't be the only one who had to miss a session. Jena Connors probably wouldn't even think twice about it. And it was probably better to miss the first session than either of the other two. By the time the third session came around, nobody would remember she had missed the first.

"Marc, I have to talk to you," she said calmly. "I'm going to stay in California an extra day. I'm changing my flight to tomorrow morning. I'm sorry, but I won't be home in time for the first session with Jena Connors. I'll make every other session, I promise."

There was silence on the other end. "Tell me I didn't just hear that," he finally said.

"Marc, I'm sorry. I'll make it up to you."

"No. No way. You're coming home tonight, understand?"

He sounded like he was talking to one of the kids, but rather than getting defensive, she felt herself grow more assertive. "I'm not," she said. "I already changed my ticket."

"You promised you'd be back—"

"But now I have to stay. I'll apologize to her, and I'll make it fine."

"It won't be fine. I told you already. If you don't go, it will hurt my chances of making exec."

"I'll be there for two of the sessions, and I'm sure other women will need to miss one, too. It's not that terrible. Things come up. But Marc . . ." She hesitated, then went ahead and said exactly what she was thinking. "But Marc, how is it that my plans have so much influence over your promotion? Isn't it this swimwear contract that really matters?"

"Just a minute," he said, slowly, and then she heard him call to his secretary: "Kelly, would you close the door, please?" He returned to the phone.

"Iliana, I'm going to say this once." He spoke in a restrained voice, which she knew he had to do since he was at work, but she could tell he was seething. "I don't give a *fuck* about your ticket, I don't give a *fuck* about your plans, I don't give a *fuck* about anything, except that you get your *fucking ass* on that red-eye tonight!"

She felt her face turn red, as the hand that was holding the phone started to shake. Her breathing got loud and shallow. She could tell people in the lobby were looking at her, but she couldn't hide the emotion she felt. She had been married to Marc for sixteen years, had dated him for a year before that, and had never before heard him talk that way. Not to her, not to anyone. Occasionally he would throw out a "hell" or an "ass," but he never aimed it directly at her; it was only when he was stuck in traffic or describing something that annoyed him at work. It was one of the things she had always loved about their marriage—that neither one of them ever lost control to that extent.

"Don't you talk to me like that—"

"Then I'll talk to you like this," he said. "Go fuck yourself, is that better? Go fuck yourself, Iliana!" He hung up the phone.

She froze, trembling. A moment later she felt a touch on the small of her back, and jumped.

"Hey, I'm sorry, I didn't mean to scare you," Jeff said. "I was just wondering, is everything all right?" She looked at him, still shaking. "No, I guess everything's not all right. What is it?"

"Just some . . ." She looked down and rubbed her forehead with one hand. "Just some resistance."

"Your editor's giving you a hard time? Look, don't let that get to you. You're the talent, you call the shots. We have a fantastic day ahead. Let's not let anyone spoil it. Okay?"

She let out a heavy breath. What was done was done. She would have to deal with it later. "Okay," she said.

They walked to the glass doors, and he pulled one open. He stepped away for her to pass through, and then followed her out.

Chapter 16

Sitting in the blue Pathfinder that Jeff had rented, Iliana remembered a time several years earlier when she and Marc had taken the kids to a mountaintop resort in the Catskills. The day before they were to leave, a massive snowstorm abruptly changed course and headed directly toward the area where they were vacationing. The roads were closing, and guests were told that if they didn't leave right away, they could be stuck at the hotel for days. Realizing that by leaving they'd be heading into the storm's path, she and Marc decided to stay and wait the storm out. In the lobby, they watched as other families tensely loaded their cars, and staff members piled into vans to go down the mountain. The whole scene looked like a flight from Armageddon. Later that night, in a largely empty dining room with a skeleton staff, Marc and Iliana ordered champagne, and the four of them had hot fudge sundaes for dessert. A sentence from somewhere, the Bible maybe, kept running through Iliana's head: Eat, drink, and be merry, for tomorrow we die.

Iliana realized she felt the same way now as she had on that Catskills trip. She regretted getting into such a big and horrible fight with Marc. But the damage was done. Her ticket was changed, and even if she changed it back, she was still going to have to account for her behavior when she got home. So she turned to the window and quietly breathed out through her mouth, trying to calm down. She could fret all day, but what would that get her? Nothing. It made more sense to put the fight out of her mind, embrace the adventure ahead, and deal with consequences later.

"So, where should we start?" Jeff asked as he maneuvered the car out of the hotel driveway.

Iliana shrugged. "Whatever you say."

"Well, I'd like to show you everything from the old days, but not much is around anymore," he said. "But I can take you to the areas that were important to me. And maybe, if we talk a bit, maybe I can make you feel what it was like."

She nodded. It would be great to think about his life for a while.

"And as you may know, when you're talking about teenage boys and Southern California, all roads head to the beach," he added. "So, Ms. Fisher, let's start there."

They approached the 405, and Jeff merged into the traffic easily, as only someone who had spent a lot of time on Los Angeles freeways could do. The windows of the car were open, and the wind rushed through, wild and invigorating. Iliana repeatedly pushed her hair away from her eyes and behind her ears, only to have it slap against her face again. Gradually, she felt herself letting go of the conversation with Marc, surrendering to the warm wind as it pushed thoughts of him out of her mind.

"Want the A.C.?" Jeff shouted to be heard over the whipping air.

"No, I love the open windows," she shouted back.

"Okay, suit yourself," Jeff shouted, sounding amused, as though she never failed to entertain him. "But make sure you can hear me, because I have something important to tell you. I got in touch with Terry. I talked to him on the phone."

"The Dreamers' Terry?" she asked.

He nodded. "I found him online. He lives south of San Francisco. I told him about you, and he wants to meet you."

"Oh," said Iliana. "I'd like to meet him, too." It was true, she wanted to meet Terry, to see what he looked like and hear about his life. But not now. Not too soon. She wanted to be alone with Jeff. He made her feel good about herself, and she didn't want to share him just yet. The thought made her uncomfortable, as she knew it wasn't appropriate to feel that way. But she pushed it out of her mind, just as she had pushed worries about Marc out of her mind as well. She was tired of judging herself. She would judge herself later.

They turned off the highway and onto a flat two-lane road. Their decreased speed made the wind in the car less frantic.

"Oh God, I love California," Iliana said.

"Yeah? Do you get here often?"

"A few times," she said. "Mostly to San Francisco. But my favorite time was when I came here to LA with my college roommate right after we graduated. It was so exciting, being on our own, going wherever we wanted. Heading out to the clubs at night to go dancing. Never knowing what might happen or who we might meet. Whether we might run into a movie star. Whether that was the night we might fall in love." She looked down. She knew she shouldn't be talking about personal things like this, just like she knew it that day at lunch. And yet, it felt so natural. His plan to show her what his past was like made her nostalgic for her own.

He looked at her. "And there's not as much freedom now?"

She smiled. "Marriage changes things, doesn't it?"

He nodded. "Well, it was different for me. My life was never that free when I was young, because of the show. But I know what you mean. Marriage can be a real downer after a while. Both sides start off happy, but then somebody gets miserable, and instead of trying to get happy again, that person just tries to bring the other one down, too."

Iliana looked ahead through the windshield, thinking about what Jeff had said. Had she been trying to make Marc miserable because she was? Or had he been trying to do that to her? Were they past the point where they could ever both be happy together? She looked at Jeff's profile as he drove. No doubt he was thinking about his own marriage. She remembered her meeting with him in Mount Kisco, how his mood had changed when Catherine appeared. And here he was, looking so happy to see her at the hotel, so pleased to show her the California he remembered.

Thinking about how glad he seemed, she started to worry that maybe his expectations of her were too high. It was hard to know what exactly was on his mind. He was taking her to old Dreamers venues as a way of giving her information for a book. She had told him plainly that she couldn't guarantee she could get a book published, but did he accept that? Or had he convinced himself that she was too good to be turned down?

"Jeff, you know this book thing is not so easy, don't you?" she said. "I mean, I'm really going to try, but the publishing business is rocky right now, and—"

"Hey, here we go!" Jeff said, swerving way over to the right. "Almost missed the turnoff!"

The air became moist and began smelling like the ocean. Jeff made a few quick turns off the main road and finally pulled into a small parking lot, where a tan, muscular man sitting on a lawn chair beneath a clip-on umbrella took his twenty-dollar bill. He parked the car and they walked uphill along a narrow street, at the top of which was a long, concrete promenade. Ahead were some concrete steps that led toward the ocean, flanked by sand that looked like light-brown sugar. Iliana could see a line of surfers skimming the rolling waves, while sunbathers—families, pairs of women, groups of teenagers—lounged on vibrantly colored beach towels and under striped umbrellas.

Jeff turned and started to walk along the promenade, and Iliana followed him, the beach to their left and fanciful surf shops, poster galleries, and bars on their right. It was a busy place. Women and men in high-tech gear and expensive sneakers ran past, some with dogs by their sides, while bicyclists weaved among mothers with strollers and attractive couples in bathing suits holding hands. Some young men in dress shirts and slacks walked slowly and aimlessly, as though they dreaded going back to the office, while others with ponytails displayed beaded jewelry for sale on square bridge tables. Iliana noticed a homeless woman in an overcoat, sitting on a folding chair, her cart with all her belongings next to her.

Jeff was looking down, his hands in his jeans pocket.

"What is it?" she asked.

"You know, there used to be hundreds of people right here behind police barricades, just trying to get a glimpse of us," he said. "Crying and screaming, calling our names. All they wanted was to be noticed. All I had to do was wink or wave in their direction, and they acted like I gave them the moon. God, what a time that was."

He shook his head and began walking again, and she followed alongside. They strolled in silence, listening to the ocean, watching the people. He looked so sad that she felt sorry for him. It was as though the show had been canceled yesterday and not years and years ago.

Eventually they came to a restaurant, with an awning-covered stone patio that held several wrought iron tables and chairs. "Hey, are you hungry?" Jeff asked. "How about some lunch?"

They ordered two glasses of wine and a couple of upscale sandwiches, and Iliana rested her chin on one hand. The area brought a host of fond memories to Jeff's mind, and he entertained her with them, one after another. He recalled the afternoon that he and Terry had to swim into the ocean for a scene. "They took us out beyond the waves in a motorboat," he said. "But what we didn't know was that Terry couldn't swim! He never told us. Anyway, he's flailing around, and it takes us twenty minutes to realize that he's not kidding around, he's drowning! The guy starred in, like, a million commercials that took place on the beach—suntan lotion, potato chips, Coca-Cola—but he hates the water! I had to jump in and rescue him!" He laughed out loud, as she wrinkled her nose and shook her head.

"Then we were shooting a night scene on the beach, and during a break, Terry takes one of the script girls into the dunes," he said. "Well, the rest of us run up behind them and steal his clothes. So we're about to start shooting again and the director calls for Terry and we're all hysterical. Finally Terry shows up wearing nothing, just covering himself with a rock!"

As he leaned back and laughed out loud again, two women approached the table. They were a little older than Iliana, and both very slim, with spaghetti-strap tops and flat, strappy sandals. But while their outfits were youthful, their complexions gave away their age. Both had the plastic look of too much work having been done.

"Excuse me, but weren't you on TV?" the first woman asked, as the other woman clasped her hands together under her chin.

"Yes, I was," Jeff said, standing up. "Hi, ladies. I'm Jeff Downs." He shook hands with them, holding each woman's hand a moment longer than Iliana thought was appropriate.

"Oh my God, I knew you were. Didn't I tell you?" the first woman asked her friend, who gave a few quick stamps of her feet and clenched her fists as she giggled. "I loved *Guitar Dreams* when I was a teenager," the first woman continued. "I know it's a cliché, but I was definitely your biggest fan."

"Can we trouble you for your autograph?" her friend asked.

"No trouble at all," Jeff said grandly, as though he hoped other diners would look up and recognize him, too. Iliana felt a little embarrassed for him, because he looked like an overacting guest star on an old sitcom, and all that was missing was a canned laugh track. The women handed him a few paper napkins bearing the logo of the restaurant, and he wrote, but not before glancing pointedly at Iliana's bag and murmuring, "Don't you want to take this down?" She figured he was making a joke but quickly realized he wasn't, so she reached into her bag for a notebook and pen. Still, it was hard to believe he was serious. Two women give him napkins to sign, and he wants her to take *notes*?

"So you really loved the show, huh?" Jeff asked, turning back to the two women.

"Oh my God, yes," the first woman said. "Your show, your music. It felt like forever, waiting a whole week for the next episode."

"And which episode was your favorite?"

"I loved them all, but mostly the ones about you and the girl who wanted the lead in the high school show . . ."

Iliana listened to the exchange, waiting for Jeff to introduce her. One of her favorite fantasies had always been of being with Jeff, meeting his friends, hearing him proudly tell them who she was. But he never did. Instead he just handed her their cell phones, so she could take pictures of the three of them. Finally the women thanked him for being so nice. He took their hands again, first one woman's and then the other's, looking directly in their eyes as he did so. It was the same way he had taken Iliana's hand when he said good-bye that first day in his showroom.

He sat down with a sigh, appreciatively watching the two women from the back as they grasped each other and giggled and shook their heads. Then he pointed to her notebook. "Did you get it all down?" he asked.

Looking at him, his eyebrows raised and his eyes wide, she was reminded of Matthew on the day of his very first orchestra concert, when he saw that she was just taking her phone. "Don't you want to bring the good camera?" he asked. She nodded and hurried to the hall closet where the electronic equipment was, to prove to him that of course he deserved the good camera. Of course he was that important.

Jeff, she saw, was asking for that same reassurance. And yet Jeff was a grown man. He shouldn't be acting like a ten-year-old boy.

"Don't worry," she said. "I got it."

He looked at the two women leaving the restaurant, then turned back to her. "So you were really a fan?" he asked. She nodded. He leaned his elbows on the table. "Tell me what that was like," he said.

"What it was like to be in love with you?" she asked, an edge in her voice. It was an insanely narcissistic question.

"No, I don't mean it that way," he said. "I just want to know. We were always being swarmed by millions of girls, and I was always wondering why they were there. What they were thinking. Because if I had understood . . . then maybe I could have prepared myself for when they all left."

It was actually an interesting question. She perched her chin on her hand and thought for a moment. "You helped me get through middle school," she answered.

"I did? How?"

Iliana continued, rediscovering things about herself as she relayed them to him. "When I got to sixth grade, my best friend began hanging with a rich and popular crowd of girls, and I was . . . dumped. I was nothing but a follower. I followed her and her new friends because I had nowhere else to go. None of them noticed me. None of them cared if I was there or if I wasn't.

"But you cared. In some crazy way through the television screen, I thought that. I felt like there was so much inside of me that nobody ever saw. But I thought that you would see it. I thought if you met me, you would want to be with me. You would think I was special." She stopped, realizing that she was talking not just about the long-ago past, but about the recent past, too.

"And then what happened?" Jeff asked.

"Things changed," she said. "I got to high school, joined the school newspaper, made some new friends. Got a boyfriend. I guess I didn't need you anymore." The words surprised her. But it was true—she had needed him, and then she hadn't. Without even realizing it, she had changed her life in a way that freed her from him. And now, decades later, she had needed him again. Why? Why couldn't she do this winter what she had done in high school without even thinking—change her life and be happier? Why was it harder as an adult?

Because things were different back then, she told herself. Once she left middle school and escaped from the tyranny of the rich girls, it was like she'd been given a book with blank pages to fill. Every decision sprang from a wealth of choices—what classes to take, what clubs to join, what to do with the money she made from babysitting, where to hang out on Friday nights once she and her friends had their driver's licenses. And then there were all the college and post-college choices—what subject to major in, what boy to date, what career to choose, whether to marry, where to buy a house, when to start a family. Life could be a very creative project when you were young.

And now she was a grown woman who had had a career, who had fallen in love and gotten married, who was raising two children. Did she really have no choices left to make? Couldn't life still be a creative project? If so, then why had she chosen for so long to spend each and every day of her life shopping for groceries, chauffeuring kids, and putting the stuff she really wanted to do on hold? Yes, it was hard to run a household, take care of two kids, and still find the time to do something else. Yes, there were only twenty-four hours in a day. But giving up wasn't the answer. She loved her children, she loved her life, she even still loved Marc, although she had a lot of hurt. But abandoning herself shouldn't be the price she had to pay for that love. She realized now that this trip to California was a game changer. She could never go back to living the same old way again.

Jeff was deep in his own thoughts as well, turning his credit card over in his hands. "You didn't need me anymore," he finally said, sounding resentful. "None of you did. You all just left me. Do you know how that felt? If I could have walked away when *I* was ready, oh man, Iliana, my life would have been so much better. But suddenly all of you were gone, and I was a has-been. The girls who came next, they were all into the guys who came next. New Kids on the Block. Menudo. Kirk Cameron. Ricky Schroder. You all just dumped me."

"We . . . didn't mean it," Iliana said tentatively, recognizing the absurdity of apologizing for the millions of girls in America who had decided to change the channel. "We had to get on with our lives."

"Yeah," said Jeff. "You teenyboppers, what a cruel lot."

He signed the bill and they left the restaurant, walking back to the parking lot in silence. In the car, Iliana watched Jeff drive. Although she had certainly suffered in middle school, she suddenly believed that when all was said and done, he had probably had a rougher time of it. After all, she had had *him*—or felt she had him—when she listened to his albums or watched *Guitar Dreams*, or examined her collection of magazines with his photo in them. They had used him, she and the millions of other teenage girls like her. They had used him when they needed him. Maybe she was using him again now.

They were quiet on the way back to the hotel. Jeff looked straight ahead as he drove, somber and seemingly deep in thought. She had revealed something to him that he may have suspected but had probably never heard articulated. That he was dispensable. He had most likely been hoping that she would give another reason that she and her peers had abandoned him in high school. He probably wanted her to say that it became too hard to keep loving him, that it was too discouraging to love him yet know there was no chance of ever meeting him. But that's not what she had said. She had told the truth. That they had outgrown him. But he had stayed locked in the past. He was locked there still.

She glanced over at him. He looked positively shell-shocked, and she felt sorry for him. She hadn't meant to hurt him.

"You know, when I watched you singing on *Guitar Dreams*, you used to do this cute little thing with your chin," she said, wanting to lift his spirits.

He was still pouting. "Yeah?"

"Yeah, you used to sort of dip your chin and then thrust it slightly forward in time with the music. It was really sweet. All the girls loved it."

"I don't do that," he said, brushing her off with his hand, but smiling.

"You do," she said. "I'll prove it. Go ahead, sing!" He sang a few bars of "The Best of Times," and she watched as his chin dipped in time with the song, like a canoe oar skimming through water. "See?" she said. "You're doing it!"

"No, I'm not!"

"Yes, you are!"

"You're crazy."

"No, you did it, you just did!"

Soon they were at the hotel. A valet took their car, and they went through the glass doors and to the elevator. The lobby had an atrium with an enormous fountain lit from within by colored lightbulbs. It had been turned on while they were out, and the rush of water made a terrific racket. She could barely hear Jeff suggest that they meet back in the lobby at seven.

"And that's when you'll get your surprise," he added.

The doors opened on his floor. As they began to close again, she watched him swagger down the hall. Her mention of his head-dipping mannerism had clearly shaken him out of his melancholy, and he was on top of the world again. It scared her to think how much he loved being the center of attention, and how much he seemed to relish thinking he was once again the center of *her* attention. What kind of a surprise did he have for her—and what was he expecting to happen that night?

Chapter 17

In her room, Iliana washed her face and put on a T-shirt and sweat-pants, then checked the time. It was six thirty in New York, and she knew Marc would be on the train. She decided to call home. Since he was so furious with her, she thought it best to talk to just the kids.

"Hello?"

"Hi, Matthew honey, it's Mom. How are you?"

She listened as he told her about his day at school, the math test that he thought he aced and all the points he scored in the basketball scrimmage against Somers. Then she talked to Dara, who complained of too much homework and went on to say that it was her friend Karen's birthday tomorrow, and she and some of the other girls were going to decorate Karen's locker with candy and signs. Iliana loved hearing how different Dara's middle school experience was from her own. Even though she and Marc had their problems, the kids were fine: happy and self-sufficient, as they should be. They had great kids, and they were good parents. She loved her children so much.

"Say hi to Daddy for me," she added. "I'll be home late tomorrow night, so I'll see you first thing Friday!"

She hung up and crawled between the sheets of the king-size bed. It had been good to talk to Matt and Dara, but now she felt strange, hollow, like an empty tin can. She missed them. At the same time, guilty feelings about leaving them worked their way through her system, like a fire burning through the edges of a sheet of newspaper in the fireplace. Picking up the remote from the night table, she clicked through the TV stations to see if there was something on to distract her. Life never stopped being complicated. She found an old Cary Grant movie and watched a bit, dozing on and off.

At six, she got out of bed and took a shower. The stall had a flimsy plastic wall, and the towels were thinner and smaller than she would have liked. In the dressing area, she opened the closet, where she had hung her good clothes. It was hard to get dressed, though, because it felt as though she were getting ready for a date. It didn't matter that she had often stayed in hotels and dressed for business dinners with attractive men, even after she was engaged to Marc. Back then she was having dinner with men who seemed old to her, men she wanted to be with because they could tell her about new products or management changes. But Jeff was different. They had opened up a lot to each other today. She had seen so many sides of him. She had seen him preen like a peacock when the women at the restaurant asked for his autograph, and she had seen him crumble when he talked about how it felt to be forgotten. He was real to her now—charming, but also vulnerable and flawed. She didn't know what he was expecting from dinner tonight. She was scared that by allowing them both to open up so much, she had given him the impression that she wanted to let their relationship get more personal.

She pulled out the outfit she had brought for dinner, a sleeveless white tank top and a swingy black skirt with tan espadrilles. She had thought it was sophisticated and stylish when she packed it, but now it seemed suggestive, almost provocative. It wasn't businesslike, and it didn't feel like the kind of outfit Jeff should see her in. But there was no

choice; it was all she had. At the last minute she decided to take along
the black blazer she had traveled in from New York. She knew she didn't
really need it, but at the least, she could use it to cover up in case she
felt too exposed. She left her room, hearing the lock on her door click
behind her.

Jeff was leaning on the marble concierge counter when she stepped
off the elevator. He looked up and grinned when he saw her. The deep
green of his button-down shirt made his face look golden tan, reminding her of that first love of his, the neighbor Wendy, and her long,
tanned legs. His eyes showed flecks of green that she hadn't noticed
before.

He kissed her cheek, and she felt his warm lips on her face. "You
look beautiful," he said. His fingers on her skin felt electric. Why hadn't
she put the blazer on before she got downstairs? The fountain in the
lobby shot streams of color toward the skylights above. The scene was
just so overwhelmingly romantic. She felt the urge to touch his face, to
feel his jaw, to close her eyes and melt into a long kiss on the mouth.
Maybe she had been deluding herself earlier tonight when she worried
that Jeff would want to be intimate. Maybe she had been deluding
herself back in New York, when she tried to convince herself she was
coming out here for a story. Maybe this was really what she had been
hoping for all along. But no, it didn't feel right, not at all. She was married with a family, and so was he. It was wrong. It had to stop.

She felt him pick up her hand and stroke her fingers with his
thumb. She pulled it away and clumsily opened her shoulder bag.

"Anyway, I have questions," she blurted out. "More questions. For
you."

He looked at her as though he were amused. "We're still working?"
he asked agreeably. "Okay, shoot."

She took a couple of steps back as she pulled out her notepad and
pen. Then she put on her blazer, stalling until she could come up with
something. "Okay, let's see . . . merchandise! That's what I need to

know about. More about, I mean. Because we talked about it at lunch, I know. But how, or what . . . or what kind of money did you make, from all that?"

"Like I told you at the house, none, believe it or not," he answered, turning more serious. They began to walk farther into the lobby, Iliana trying to steady her hand to write. "You know, it all has to do with how smart you are when you negotiate these things. And everything was less sophisticated then. Merchandise tie-ins were nowhere near the kind of business . . ."

It took her a moment to realize that Jeff had stopped talking. When she looked up, she saw him staring past her. "What is it?" she said.

"Oh man," he answered. "It's Terry."

"What?"

"I invited him to have dinner with us."

"He's here? Terry's here?"

"Will you look at him," Jeff said, shaking his head. "Son of a gun."

She turned to see Terry walking toward them, with the fountain bursting in the background. Iliana recognized him immediately but was struck by how different he looked. The years hadn't been nearly so kind to him as they had to Jeff. It was as though parts of him—his full lips, his blue eyes—had been superimposed on an old, misshapen body. He had gained a lot of weight, all above the waist, so he had an enormous torso on top of short legs. His face had expanded while his features stayed the same size, so his cheeks and forehead were huge, and his eyes, nose, and mouth looked tiny and squished together. His hair had darkened to a mustardy brown and lost all its curl. It looked thin and greasy, combed back from his forehead. He wore a dark-blue button-down shirt tucked into too-tight pants and had a thick, tacky gold ring on his left pinky.

Iliana watched as Jeff walked past her and grasped Terry warmly by the shoulders. Terry lifted his hands to hold Jeff's shoulders, blinking away tears. His mouth twisted to the side as he sniffed a few times. Then they pulled each other closer, coming in for a real hug, patting each other on the back. Iliana lowered her arms, letting the notebook and pen hang from her hands. She was stunned by Terry's changed appearance, and also by the emotion the two men were showing. Even other guests were looking over. Some walked closer, forming a ring around the two men.

"Hey, Jeff," she heard Terry whisper between little gasps. "Hey, Basketball."

Jeff was the first to break away. He motioned toward Iliana. "Terry, man," he said. "This is her, the writer I told you about. Iliana Fisher. She's really here, like I said she would be."

Iliana put out her hand. "Hi, Terry," she said.

"Iliana Fisher," Terry said. "You know what you are? You're a dream come true."

Twenty minutes later they were sitting at a round table in a warm, dark Italian restaurant, drinking red wine while Terry talked about his life. He had spent the first ten years after the show severely addicted to cocaine, and the next ten trying to get clean. He was twice divorced, and he had a fifteen-year-old daughter who lived with his first wife in Atlanta and hated his guts. He'd been diagnosed last year with a chronic form of leukemia, and although he was in remission, he required transfusions every three months that left his arms spotted with angry purple bruises.

Gripping the edge of the table as though it were a lifeboat, Terry talked for a long time. His speech was punctuated by present-tense half sentences—quick three- or four-word phrases that were missing subjects or verbs but sounded like they ended in exclamation points.

"The *Bye Bye Birdie* gig? Fired in two weeks. Stranded in St. Paul! Not even a plane ticket home. Good drugs, though, plenty good. A week later—back in LA."

He told them he had tried to use his old connections to make a living in the music business, primarily by discovering and promoting young, talented bands he saw in small clubs, but none took off. Nobody in the music industry had much respect for his opinion. He worked for a while as a DJ at a small club, and when he was really desperate for money, he worked as a telemarketer, too. He also tried to start up an Internet business, buying and auctioning off old cassettes and records. That did well for a short time, but eventually failed. "Kept the website, though. Good thing. 'Cause old Basketball here tracks me down!"

"So what have you been doing lately, buddy?" Jeff asked.

"Teaching," Terry answered. "Yes, sir. Old Terry a teacher! Alternative high school . . . you know. Vocational. Kids do all right. They come out engineers, technicians. For radio stations, recording studios."

"That's so interesting," Iliana said, glad that he had finally succeeded at something. She felt a little responsible for him, since she was clearly a key reason why he had come down to LA, and she found herself rooting for him, the way she'd silently root for Matthew at his baseball games. *Shoot! Pass!* It was strange, feeling this way. She'd always imagined herself as the girlfriend of a Dreamer, not the mother. But hearing Terry talk made her see him in a new light. He had been the daredevil member of the group. She'd never realized what a naive little boy he probably was then—and seemed to be now. Just like Jeff.

"It's okay," Terry said. "Pays some bills, you know what it's like. But then"—his tiny eyebrows lifted onto that huge forehead, his tiny blue eyes lit up, and his speech became more normal—"then I got your call, Basketball. And I can't think of anything else. I see it all happening. A whole new start."

"Exactly," Jeff said, leaning forward.

"Yeah, baby!" Terry exclaimed, banging his leg into the table so the glasses and plates made a sudden, loud clank. Iliana instinctively reached out her hands to catch any glass that might tip over. Neither Terry nor Jeff even acknowledged the noise. "You know, man—a comeback," he continued. "Iliana's book comes out, and boom! We're a hit! Pull Peter off the farm, find Bruce wherever the hell he landed, launch a reunion album, a tour. We're back on top, man. Back on top!"

"That's just what I'm thinking," Jeff said. Iliana could imagine the same relationship between the two men years ago: *We'll take all the newspapers from all the machines!* "*That's just what I'm thinking!*" But this time it wasn't just all in fun. Terry was really counting on her to publish a book about them. And now it seemed even more unlikely to happen than ever. Terry's life was a mess, and he looked terrible, too. How did he expect to actually make a comeback, let alone have a book written about it? How did Jeff not see that this was all so unrealistic?

"Yeah," Terry said, pounding on the table with one fist to emphasize his words: "Because. It. All. Starts. With. The. Book! The book, man! I mean, look, Iliana works for the *Times*. The fuckin' *New York Times*!" He turned to Iliana. "A bestseller, right? Could you get us on Jimmy Fallon?"

Iliana felt her breath speeding up. Her cheeks were hot, and not from the wine. She felt as frantic as a trapped animal, which she sort of was, her chair pressed against the wall in this crowded restaurant, the two men blocking her path to the door. Now she was supposed to book them on late-night TV? "Hang on, Terry," she said, trying to let out a casual-sounding laugh. "As I'm sure Jeff told you, it's just a book *idea* at this point—"

"I even wrote a reunion song for us!" Terry said, tossing an unlit votive candle in the air.

"A *song?*" she said, trying to sound like this was a happy surprise. And what did he expect her to do about that—get someone to sing it on *The Voice?* Terry was on another planet. This was getting out of hand.

Jeff laughed, a big, sudden "Ha!" then turned to Iliana. "If there's a way to get attention, leave it to Terry to find it." He shook his head and chuckled, but Iliana thought he actually sounded a little annoyed.

"It's not just attention, man! Jeff! It's a real song!" Iliana noticed that he used Jeff's real name, for the first time that evening. "I worked on it 'round the clock. Collaborated, you know? With one of my students. So it's more *now*."

Terry grasped Jeff's arm on the table. "And get this. This kid once worked for a music producer here in LA. And when he tells the guy about the song, the book, the guy says, 'Stop by!' We got an appointment, all three of us! Tomorrow morning! Nine o'clock!"

"No!" Iliana said. "I mean I can't . . . I have a plane . . ."

"Not until the afternoon," Jeff said. "Don't worry, there's time."

Terry raised his wineglass and exclaimed so loudly that two couples from a nearby table exchanged amused glances, as though they thought he was drunk. "Here's to Iliana, for making dreams come true!"

Jeff lifted his glass, too, and they waited, expectantly, for her to raise hers. She reached past her plate and somehow missed the stem of her glass, nearly knocking it over with the back of her hand before she caught it. Then she lifted it and clinked it with theirs, not knowing what else she could possibly do at the moment.

"Here's to Iliana," Terry repeated.

She nodded and tried to muster a smile, but could only produce a small lengthening of her lips. "Thanks, you guys," she said. "I'm glad you're happy."

Chapter 18

And then they were in a taxi on the way back to the hotel. Jeff had decided not to drive so he wouldn't have to worry about directions or parking, and Iliana had thought it was a good idea when they left for the restaurant. But now things were different. Relaxed and somewhat drunk, Terry took up far too much room in the backseat of the cab, spreading his legs and gesturing grandly with his arms as he emphasized how excited he was. Iliana leaned against the backseat door, but Jeff—who had politely offered to sit in the middle—was nevertheless pressed against her.

Iliana nervously flexed her feet.

"You okay?" Jeff asked.

"I just get carsick in cabs," she said. She had to get out of the meeting tomorrow. There was no way she was going to continue with this charade in front of yet another person. Who would Terry want her to see next? She was a good writer, and she would give this book a shot, but she wasn't some magician who could make old dreams new again. She was mad at herself for carrying this whole situation way too far. She thought about calling Jeff's room in the morning to say she didn't feel well. Or she could tell him something had come up at home and she had to get right back to New York. But she'd still have to deal with him at some point; she was in too deep to disappear now. The bottom line, she knew, was that it was time to tell him the truth. She needed to tell him that she wasn't a *Times* reporter and she was very sorry for leading him on all these weeks. And she had to step back for a moment and figure out the best way to do it, so maybe he would understand and forgive.

She was still trying to decide how to proceed when they arrived at the hotel. "Anyone for a nightcap?" Terry asked.

"I can't, you guys," she said. "I'm exhausted."

"Just come to my room," Terry said. "A minute! Just hear my song."

Jeff looked at Iliana hopefully. "How 'bout it?"

She shook her head. "No. You go ahead."

"Come on, isn't this the kind of material you need?" Jeff teased. "Don't you want to be there when Terry plays the song for me? Where's that reporter's instinct?"

"Please, Iliana," Terry said. "I came all this way. Just for a minute."

They weren't going to take no for an answer. She smiled and threw up her hands in submission. "Just got my second wind," she said. "Let's do it."

They got on the elevator. Iliana watched the numbers light up, looking longingly as they passed her floor. She knew that with every moment that she spent withholding the truth, she was digging a bigger and bigger hole for herself. She wished she had the courage to fess up right then and there. She was sure that if they accepted her for who she was, she could go on to craft a great story about them: *Terry Brice gripped Jeff Downs's arm, where it was resting on the table at the dark Italian restaurant, searching for a connection that once was there. It had been years since the two men had seen each other. They had parted ways without even saying good-bye, too desperate to save their own skins to worry about one another's. But their youthful optimism never faded, and here they were, about to become Dreamers once again . . .*

Terry slipped his key card into the lock and opened the door. He walked in, and Jeff moved aside and gestured for her to enter. She hesitated. She felt like she was in one of those dreams in which she was wandering inside a building, trying to find the exit but only getting farther and farther away from it. All the years she had traveled for *Business Times*, she had never gone into a man's hotel room. She would always meet up with people or say goodnight in the lobby. Finally she stepped inside, breathing through her mouth so she wouldn't smell anything. This was way too personal a space. She didn't know how she'd be able to look at Jeff if she realized that they both were recognizing the scent of Lectric Shave or Right Guard.

Terry hurried across the room and tenderly picked up his guitar. It was resting on an armchair by the beige-draped window. He bent his knees and squinted under the shade of a thin standing lamp until he finally found the switch. On the small table next to him was some sheet music with handwritten notes, and he sat down on the chair and began to strum. Jeff sat down near him, on the foot of the bed, and because there was nowhere else to go, Iliana sat next to him. Then Terry began to sing:

> *Ohhhhhh, it feels like long ago,*
> *But in some ways more like yesterday.*
> *Yesterday . . . yesterday,*
> *Yesterday when it all began.*
> *Where did it all go?*
> *And can we get it back?*
> *Get it back . . . get it back,*
> *Oh, yeah, get it back.*
> *Back to where it all began.*

Terry looked at them as he sang, and Iliana nodded and smiled encouragingly. It was a nice sentiment, the idea of going back to where it all began. That was surely a theme people could relate to. And his use of repetition, that was good, too. The way he sang "get it back" three, even four times, one right after the other? It was good that the repetition happened all at once, right in the beginning of the song. That would get the theme of the song out really quick.

Yeah, right, she thought. Who was she kidding? She was no music expert, but even she knew Terry's song was like a bad poem someone wrote in high school. Amateurish. Embarrassing. And Terry's voice didn't help much. The resonant, slightly gravelly quality that had sounded romantic and a little dangerous so many years back now came across as hoarse and old. His range had decreased as well, so his voice was weak, even squeaky, when he tried to hit the higher notes, and fell off-key when he held any note for more than a beat.

Iliana looked at Jeff, assuming they would exchange unimpressed glances. But to her surprise, he seemed to like it. He was nodding his head with the rhythm and said a quiet "Yeah!" after the first verse. He actually liked the song.

As Terry started the next verse—filled with so many repeats of "get it back" that Iliana was sure she'd be hearing it in her sleep for nights to come—he motioned to Jeff to join him. Jeff looked at him questioningly, pointing at himself, as though the room was crowded with fans and he couldn't believe he'd been singled out. Terry nodded and even called out a quick "Come on!" as though he were ad-libbing in the middle of a concert. Jeff popped up and leaned over Terry's chair, and Terry helpfully pointed to the right spot on the sheet music. When the next line started, Jeff began to sing along, rocking his hips in time to the beat. He looked at Iliana and gave her a thumbs-up.

Iliana reached in her bag for a pad and pen, thinking Jeff would expect her to take some notes. But she could only bring herself to write a few words: "new song," "singing," "guitar." She didn't want to write what she was really feeling, because she didn't want to insult them in case they wanted to see it. But the truth was, the whole scene reminded her of a *Saturday Night Live* spoof, or a bar mitzvah where the grown-ups have had too much to drink. Jeff's singing voice was thin and consistently off-key, with none of the richness of his speaking voice. It reminded Iliana of watery coffee. The few notes of "The Best of Times" she had heard Jeff hum back in his office had given her no clue as to how little singing talent or rhythm he had. Had he lost it, or had he never really had it to begin with? Had the marketing machine that created him been able to fool a whole generation of girls into thinking that this cute guy with the great smile really had talent?

Terry was swaying now as he played, his eyes closed, and Jeff was biting his bottom lip in concentration as he tapped a kind of drum accompaniment on the small table. When Terry got to the end of the song, he strummed more chords as he called, "Let's try it again now, a touch faster. Let's not lose it, man."

"Got it, faster," Jeff answered, still swinging his hips.

Iliana continued to watch, holding back the groan she felt building in her throat. She saw clearly now that Jeff had been picked for stardom not because he was especially talented, but because he was lucky. He had a certain smile that appealed to a generation of girls at a particular moment in time. It was something she never would have been able to see back when she was eleven or twelve. She was just supposed to enjoy her first experience falling in love. No wonder Catherine wasn't thrilled that Iliana wanted to write about his *Guitar Dreams* days. Catherine had known for years that Jeff Downs was infinitely better off as a mature, self-sufficient businessman than as an aging heartthrob chasing a teenager's dream. And Jeff had pretty much accepted that, too. That is, until she came into his life.

But why did you change your mind? Iliana wanted to shout at him. Why had he come to respond so completely to her interest in his celebrity? She hadn't expected the maturity and judgment he'd shown when they first met to be so fragile. She hadn't realized how close to the edge he was, how easily he could be drawn to the glamour, the youth he had put behind him. How it would take just a few meetings with a reporter to undo all he had worked on since *Guitar Dreams* went off the air. But then again, maybe what had happened to him wasn't so hard to understand. After all, she, too, had let herself be seduced these last several weeks by the power of her own youthful dreams. She had remembered what it was like to be whisked away from the real world by the TV image of a guy with a cute smile, and to believe she was special—the most special of all!—because that fantasy guy in her head said that she was. She had withdrawn from reality and embraced a fantasy world these many weeks, instead of finding a way to fix what was wrong in her life. But she was an adult, and her fantasies had hurt others. She should have known better.

And no, it wasn't entirely her fault that there were now two middle-aged men in this hotel room, singing off-key to a practically tuneless song. They were adults, too, and they were responsible for their own choices. What *was* her fault was that she let herself get caught up in Jeff's plans for a comeback that day at the coffee shop, not because she actually thought it was a good idea, but because she had co-opted his fantasy. She had immediately linked the Dreamers idea with the book idea she had thought about for years but had never gotten around to writing. It had been easy to grasp onto Jeff's idea, much easier than developing her own. But that wasn't the kind of writer she wanted to be. She wanted to embrace stories because she had uncovered them herself, and they had value; not because some cute guy dropped one into her lap and flattered her with an invitation to LA.

Jeff turned to her and raised his eyebrows: *You okay?* She nodded and waved her hand. Nevertheless, he tapped Terry on the shoulder. "You know, Iliana's still basically on New York time. And you look tired, too, Terry."

He was right, Terry looked pale and winded. "It's been a long day," he agreed. "How about we meet downstairs for breakfast? Like, seven?"

Iliana grabbed her blazer and bag, and Terry walked them to the door. As he opened it, he kissed Iliana's hand. "So great," he said, his voice trembling with emotion. "Thanks, Iliana."

Across the room, Iliana could see the night sky through the window, black and vast, behind the light of the hotel lamp next to Terry's guitar.

Chapter 19

She stepped into the elevator and pressed the button for her floor, with Jeff right behind her. They both turned to face the doors. She could feel Jeff's eyes looking sideways at her. Did he know she was upset? Was he waiting for her to talk? She didn't know what to say, she didn't even know how to go about thinking up something she *should* say. She just felt sad and drained.

The doors opened, and Jeff followed her down the hall. She had been hoping he'd stay inside and wave as he went on to his room. She needed to take stock of everything that had happened and figure out what to do next. She was too tired to deal with any of it tonight, but she didn't want to just proceed with the plans and go with Jeff and Terry to the record producer's office tomorrow. What was the alternative? Next to her, Jeff began singing a few bars of Terry's song, dipping his chin in an exaggerated, teasing motion. She smiled a little and nodded.

They stopped at her room, both of them facing her door. She stood still, hoping he would just leave.

"What's up—don't you have your key?" he finally said.

She nodded and reached into her bag. She knew he was right to expect to come into her room. She had been leading him to this moment from the day she agreed to come to California, or even earlier—from that morning she first came to his office and didn't correct him about the *New York Times*. She wished she could go back and relive everything, undo all her smiles and flirty glances, correct all the irresponsible conversations that had led them to this moment. But that was still fantasy thinking. Now was the time to face him and own what she had done.

Inside, the bathroom caught her eye. The fluorescent light over the sink was on, and a stick of deodorant and white cotton bra were visible on the countertop. If this had been a TV movie, or even just a fantasy in her head, the deodorant would be a bottle of perfume, and the white bra would be black lace. But reality kept intruding. Even now, she couldn't stop thinking about how foolish Jeff had looked, swaying his hips like some Elvis wannabe and singing off-key to Terry's awful song.

She pulled the bathroom door closed and backed up against it. The king-size bed in the center of the room seemed lit up, the way the correct vowels flickered hot pink on the computer screen when Dara studied her Spanish words. The rest of the room was now dim, lit only by a table lamp, which gave the ice bucket and glasses next to it a golden glow. Spots of light were also reflected in the blank screen of the TV, which sat in a wall unit nearby. The drapes were closed. Iliana braced herself, expecting Jeff to walk over and put his arms around her, getting ready to tell him to stop.

But instead, he pushed the room door so that it closed with a harsh, metallic click, and plowed right past her. "Whew! We can finally talk," he said as he flopped down on the bed with his back against the headboard and his legs outstretched, his shoes still on. "I was scared to say anything in the hallway. Who knows who was listening?"

"Talk?" Iliana asked. Was *that* what he wanted to do?

"Yeah, hey, thanks for looking so tired. It was a great way to get us out of there."

"But I *am* tired."

"Oh, I know, and I really appreciate what you're doing," he said, getting up and giving her a friendly kiss on the forehead before walking into the center of the room. "We'll just come up with a plan, real quick, and then you can get some sleep."

She paused, trying to figure out what the hell he was talking about. "Jeff, I don't know—"

"Yeah, I should have warned you, but I didn't expect him to be like that. Fuckin' Terry, man, he'll never change. He was always that way. I got a close-up, he wanted two. I got three scenes, he needed five. I call him to LA, he writes a song and gets a record producer. What an asshole!"

It was as though she and Jeff had spent entirely different evenings. "I don't understand," she said. "What do you think he wants to do? Make a . . . what? A bigger comeback than you?"

"I *know* he does!" Jeff said, pointing a finger at her. "But I'm not going to let him do it. I'm not gonna let him steal this chance from me. I got the idea, I got the writer, I got the book . . . I'm the one who's gonna make it, not that son of a bitch!"

"Wait a minute," she said. "You *got* the writer?"

"No, no, no, I just meant I invited you here," he said, opening his palms toward her. "Don't start getting all insulted now, this isn't between you and me, it's between me and that . . . dick two floors down."

She leaned back against the wall, stunned by his outburst. "But I thought you liked each other. I thought you said he was a good guy—"

"Yeah, well, good guys don't send you on a wild-goose chase to find newspaper machines while they sneak back to the studio for a two o'clock call. They wrote me out of two scenes that week because Terry told them we were in my car and I was in charge. Even way back then he was scared of how big I could become." He was pacing around the room now, pumping his fists and talking mostly to himself. "I just need an idea, not to cut him out completely, just to keep him where he belongs—"

"Jeff," she said, walking toward him. It scared her to see him like this. He was tearing himself apart over some old jealousies and seemed to be building this rivalry up to absurd proportions right before her eyes. She hadn't realized how angry he could get, particularly toward this old, sick friend who barely looked like his former self. "Aren't you overreacting? I mean, he's not exactly . . . you know, he's not exactly a Hollywood type anymore, is he?"

"Shit, Iliana, a good publicist will staple his stomach and throw a wig on his head and in two months he'll be pushing Adam Levine off the cover of *People*!" He took her hand and jiggled her arm. "Come on, help me. We've got to think. We've got to come up with a— Hey, your book! That's it, you'll just write it. Write the first chapter tonight!"

He pulled her to the desk and pushed her into the chair, switched on the desk lamp, and began opening and slamming shut the drawers. "Shit, there's gotta be paper here," he continued. "And a pen. There's always paper and pens in these damn desks!"

"Jeff, this isn't going to work—"

"You're right, there's gotta be a faster— What am I thinking? Did you bring a laptop with you? Where the hell is that thing?"

"Jeff—"

"Look, you'll call your editor at the *Times* in the morning and tell him he has to run the first few pages this week. Like an excerpt— newspapers do that all the time. It'll build excitement for the book." He pushed away an armchair and lifted the drapes, ignoring her as he continued to look for a computer case. "We'll email the chapter first thing—" He grabbed her shoulders as she stood back up. "Please, Iliana, you have to help me. For everything we've been through, please."

She looked at him, at how desperately his eyes searched hers. She felt bad for him—despite his ego, despite his vanity. He was so, so lost. But even if she had been a top *Times* reporter who could secure a book deal with a phone call, she could never do what he was asking her to.

No writer could whip out a chapter like that. Or at least, no writer who actually cared about writing.

"Jeff, it's impossible," she said. "It doesn't work this way."

He let go of her, and she watched his shoulders sink. Then he sighed and walked back to the bed. He sat down heavily, leaning over so that his elbows were on his knees, and he dropped his head into his hands. "You have no idea how lucky you are," he said. "You're a writer, you have talent, you do something that other people can't do, and they admire you for it. You *have* that."

He paused. "Damn it, I spent a minute becoming Jeff Downs and the rest of my life hoping that people would remember that I'm still him." He shook his head. "And that he still matters."

She watched him, with his head hanging down. *He* was the one who had no idea. No idea that she knew just how he felt. She remembered emailing Stuart a few weeks back, expecting him to be wowed by her idea, waiting for confirmation that the old Iliana, the successful Iliana, still mattered. The truth was, she was just like Jeff. Even though he had grown up being worshipped and she had grown up worshipping him, they were two of a kind. Even though they had met just weeks ago, she knew him very well. She remembered poring over science books from the library as she sat at the writing desk her father had picked out, trying to get to the bottom of the M&M's controversy. She truly believed she could shake up the world with that article. She wanted to shake up the world still—that's what all this mess had been about.

She walked to the bed and sat next to him. "You are still him," she said. "And he does still matter."

He looked at her. Then before she knew what was happening, he took her face in his hands and kissed her.

It started off as barely a touch at first, but then he pressed his mouth closer. At first she didn't stop him. One thought kept running through her head: *Jeff Downs is kissing me. JEFF DOWNS IS KISSING ME!* It felt like the start of those long, luxurious kisses she had enjoyed back when she was in high school, when kissing was an end in itself and not just a prelude to lovemaking. She imagined the last moments of the auditorium episode of *Guitar Dreams*, the part where the girl finds out she's gotten the lead, and she runs down the hallway to embrace Jeff again.

But Jeff was hardly the romantic kisser Iliana had dreamed he'd be. In fact, he was a disappointing kisser, intrusive and sloppy. His mouth was open too wide, and his big tongue pushed too deep into her mouth. His lips felt thick and droopy, instead of nicely firm and pliable. Just another cosmic reminder that childhood dreams were no reflection of reality. And she'd been foolish to put her stock in them.

He grasped her shoulders as he pressed his mouth harder against hers. It surprised her how quickly he changed moods—one moment he was devastated, and the next, he was totally absorbed in their kiss. Maybe all men could be like that. Or maybe he hadn't been that upset at all—maybe he had acted upset to seduce her. She didn't know. But either way, this was ending right now. She had no desire to sleep with him. She needed to get back home and begin finding a way to matter more, whatever that way turned out to be. And she needed to let him get back to reality, too.

She pulled her face away. "Jeff, I have to tell you something," she said, struggling to be articulate as he craned his neck to keep kissing her. "I'm not what you think I am."

He reached behind her head to pull her back. "I know, you're not some superwoman writer, you can't write the book tonight. I get it."

"No, it's more than that," she said, more firmly.

"It's okay, I know—"

"Jeff, listen to me. I don't have an assignment about you for the *Times*."

He stopped trying to kiss her. "What? Are you mad at me?"

"No, of course not," she said. "I just don't have an assignment."

He pulled back a little more, his face registering no emotion but confusion. "What?"

"I came across an old rerun of *Guitar Dreams* on TV, and I wanted to write about you," she said. "So I called your office and said I was *trying* to write an article, for *Business Times*, my old magazine, not the *New York Times*. And Rose misunderstood."

"What are you talking about?"

"I had to meet you," she continued. "I thought I could get back into publishing if I wrote a great article about you. And I was feeling like a has-been, and I thought meeting you could help me get back on track, since you were a has-been, but then you weren't—you reinvented yourself into a business owner." She gave him a moment to say something, but when he just kept looking at her, she went on. "And what I didn't realize was that you maybe weren't happier selling blankets after all. And instead of me learning something from you, you got carried away along with me. And everything just spiraled from there."

It was hitting him, she could tell. His eyes narrowed and his jaw grew longer. He looked like he wanted to punch her. He was more frightening now than he had been when he was ranting about Terry, and she was starting to get very scared. When you came right down to it, she didn't know the real Jeff very well at all. She had no idea what he was capable of. She remembered how Marc spoke about the lawyers he opposed in merger deals, how he always gave them time to talk because silent adversaries will do much more damage to a deal than talkative ones.

"What—what are you thinking?" she asked.

"What am I thinking?" Jeff said, staring at her. "What am I thinking? I'm thinking, what the hell is this? That's what I'm thinking." His voice grew louder as he stood and ran his hands through his hair. "I'm thinking you're a lunatic. I'm thinking you're a fuckin' stalker, okay? That's what I'm thinking!"

His temper was terrifying, because unlike when he was complaining about Terry, now he was angry with *her*. If he could yell at her like that, what else could he do? Push her, hit her? She didn't want to get hurt, and she certainly didn't want to go home with a black eye or broken arm that needed explaining. She thought about trying to leave the room but changed her mind. He was standing between her and the door, and she didn't want to get any closer.

"No, I'm not a stalker," she said, standing up so she'd be nearer to the door if she got the chance to leave. "I'm a writer. A good one. I had a good run with *Business Times*, you saw all those articles I wrote. And I've been sending out queries—article proposals—to different magazines, and I know I can write a great article about you. But I'm not sure . . ." She paused; how was she going to say it?

"I don't think what you've got here . . . is a book. And even if you did, I couldn't guarantee I could get it published. I know you thought I had that kind of clout. But the truth is . . . I don't."

He took two steps backward. "I knew it," he said, holding his head with his hands. "I FUCKING knew it! How could you be a writer for the *Times* when you didn't even have one fucking byline? But I believed all your lies! I fucking trusted you!" His voice sounded like an explosion in the quiet room. She resisted the urge to shush him because she thought it would make him even madder. "You were going to write a book about me," he said, charging at her, shaking his finger in her face. "You were going to make me famous again. You were going to make women want to hear me sing again!"

She held her palms up defensively. "I never said that. I *never* said that I could do all that. I only wanted to help."

"I knew you were a phony!" he exclaimed, running his hands again through his hair. "I knew it! You never even took out your notebook until I reminded you! You're no writer, you're no reporter, you're . . . you're . . ." He stopped, grasping for words, pulling at his hair. Then he lunged at the little table near the window and fiercely swept the lamp off it, along with the ice bucket and glasses. They flew into the air and crashed into the wall unit, shattering into pieces. She squeezed her eyes at the sound of the impact. She had never, ever seen such a violent act in real life. The angrier Marc was, the more he withdrew, just like those silent lawyers he dreaded. Even when she had changed her flight and made him madder than ever before, all he had done was throw out a lot of curse words and hang up on her. She didn't think Marc could ever do what Jeff had just done, and the thought made her wish she were back home, long before she ever saw the Downs Textiles website. Breathing in short, frightened gasps, she ran to the door, but Jeff got there first, and he held it shut.

"All these weeks, all we talked about? Everything a goddamned lie?"

"Not everything, just the *Times* part, and I'm sorry," she said, starting to cry with fear. "I'm so, so sorry, please let me go."

"Let you go? What are you, kidding me?" He grabbed her by the elbow. "I took you into my home! I told you about my dad, my wife, my daughters! I fuckin' made Terry come down here to meet you! That poor, sick bastard who—"

"Poor, sick bastard?" she blurted out before she could stop herself. "After all you said—"

Suddenly there were three sharp knocks on the other side of the door. "Open up!" a man's voice said. "Security!"

Iliana looked at Jeff, who was looking back at her, his face softening. She knew that they *both* knew that they were going to have to work together, at least one last time. He stepped back and opened the door. A small man dressed in a short-sleeve shirt and tie entered the room, followed by two large men with crew cuts, each wearing a shirt with a "Security" patch on the shoulder. The large men approached Jeff, who backed up to the wall.

The smaller man put his hands on his hips and surveyed the broken glass in the center of the room, then looked at Iliana. "Are you all right?" he said.

"I'm fine," she said.

"We got some reports of shouting and glass breaking."

Iliana looked at Jeff, trying to tell him with her eyes that she was going to protect him. "I was carrying . . . I wasn't looking where I was going, and I bumped into the table and knocked all that over. I'll pay for it."

"*You* knocked it over?" the man said, as though he didn't believe it. "You both staying in this room?"

"No, this is my room," Iliana said.

"Where's your room?" he said to Jeff.

"Twelfth floor."

He turned back to Iliana. "This man bothering you?"

"No, no, he's not, sir. It was all an accident. I'm sorry, it won't happen again." She looked at Jeff. His lips were pressed together. She could tell that he knew he needed her right now, and he hated it.

"Do you want me to call the police?"

"No, really, thank you," she said, trying to sound calm. "No need at all, really."

"Okay, let me see some ID," the man said. "Both of you."

Jeff reached in his back pocket for his wallet, while Iliana picked up her bag from the bed. *Please, please*, she said to herself. *Please let this be over. Please let me go home.*

The man examined their licenses. "Ms. Passing?"

"Yes," she said.

"Mr. Downs?"

"Yes," Jeff said. She thought she saw Jeff's eyebrows rise, as if even now he was hoping to be recognized.

"When are you checking out?" the man said.

"Tomorrow," Iliana said.

"Friday," Jeff added quietly.

The man walked toward the door. "I think it's time you went back to your own room, don't you?" he said to Jeff. "And any more trouble, I'll make sure you're arrested. Got that?"

"Yeah. Yes, sir," Jeff said and walked out, his head down.

Iliana went to the door as the other men also left. There was an older couple in bathrobes standing in the hallway, as well as two blond women who looked like flight attendants. A family with twins about Matthew's age was peeking out the opposite door. The kids looked shocked.

So I'm finally the center of attention, Iliana thought to herself wryly as she closed the door. *I finally matter. There's a corridor full of horrified onlookers to prove it.*

Chapter 20

Iliana hardly slept that night, waking up every hour or so. One twenty, two forty-five, three thirty. Sometimes she'd wake and lie in bed for a few peaceful moments. But then she'd remember where she was and what had happened right there in her room, and the realization would hit her in the stomach, as though she were on an elevator that unexpectedly and forcefully plummeted down.

She felt as if she were seeing the events of the last few weeks for the first time, and she didn't like how she appeared. She had been unhappy for a long time, there was no doubt about that, but she had chosen a selfish, childish way to deal with it. She had lied and used a bunch of people she hadn't even known. Life might not have been exciting, revolving as it did around such tedious questions as what to serve for dinner and how to squeeze in Dara's orthodontist appointment and still get Matthew to basketball practice on time. And Stuart's rejection of her original email was pretty harsh. Maybe it was reasonable that she had been vague with Rose on the phone the first day she called. But she should have come clean pretty soon after that. At least then she could have gone ahead and written her article. But now, she felt too guilty to even think about it.

And what was worse was that she had done so much damage to her marriage. Yes, she had a right to be angry with Marc. He was wrong to order her around, to tell her where to be and when to get there and what to say, to belittle anything she tried to do that didn't support him and his career. But she made life rough for him, too. He was right—she never would have wanted to leave New York for Cleveland, and if they had ultimately decided to go, she would have brought it up repeatedly as a sign of how much she would give up for him and how little he would give up for her. They had both been so proud of each other when they were younger, so happy for one another's achievements—for her cover stories, for his assignment to key projects. He had put her professional photo on his credenza for that very reason. When had it all turned to resentment? He asks her to help him out by meeting the wives of some of his bosses, and she interprets this as an insult to her identity; she asks for a couple of days in LA to pursue a dream of her own, and he acts like a child convinced he's getting the short end of the wishbone.

Maybe disappointment was inevitable as time passed and opportunities naturally shrank, she thought. Life could never be as thrilling as it was when they were both first starting out. But if disappointment was the normal course of things, wouldn't she prefer to face it with someone she loved at her side? The answer was yes, and she knew that meant that she had to give her marriage a shot. She and Marc had to commit themselves to talking things out, over and over if that's what it took, to try to find common ground and reclaim the love that brought them together in the first place. Instead, over these last few months, she had pulled away from him and held a grudge, she had lied and snuck around, and she had walked away from a promise she had made to him. He had behaved badly, too, there was no doubt about that. But she had also secretly forged a relationship with another guy and flown across the country to be with him, knowing that there was attraction on both sides. That was the most horrendous thing of all.

At four a.m. she woke up, sweating. She wanted to go home. She wanted to make sure that home was still there for her. That Marc would be willing to work with her to make things better. She truly had no idea what he might do when she walked into the house. She imagined him flinging her suitcase out the door and telling her in a quiet, tense voice to get out. Marc didn't get mad often, but she'd seen just yesterday how intensely angry he could get. He had told her to go fuck herself. She was still surprised he had actually said it.

She reached for the remote and switched on the TV, hoping to make the time go faster. The light shot out from the screen in bright rays, and she had to squint for several seconds before her eyes adjusted. The "E" channel was on, and she caught the end of a segment about Ansel Elgort, the young star from the movie *The Fault in Our Stars*. Iliana grimaced as she watched. Another teen idol. Just what she needed.

Turning the TV off, she got up and took a long shower, scrubbing herself twice with soap and washing her hair twice, too. The drain at the bottom of the shower looked green with rust, and as she brushed her teeth, she noticed that some of the grout between the sink and wall was black with either grime or mold. Her stomach was bubbly and her arms felt heavy and weak. She put on the jeans and T-shirt she had planned to take the red-eye in. She packed up her shoes and toiletries and put her notebooks on top.

At five thirty, she gathered her bags and left the room. She figured she could get a cup of coffee in the lobby and then head right to the airport. Jeff had gotten her booked on a one o'clock flight, but maybe she could get on an earlier one. She desperately wanted to get out of the hotel before Jeff and Terry came down for breakfast. She was scared that they'd humiliate her, that they'd call her a stalker so that all the people in the lobby would turn and stare. Maybe a security guard in the lobby would overhear them and would grab her elbow and escort her roughly out of the building, warning her to never come back or she'd be arrested.

At least if she left early, she'd have a chance to escape quietly. If she was lucky, Jeff would have decided to sleep a little later.

She scanned the lobby as she stepped off the elevator. There was no sign of Jeff or Terry. The lobby was mostly empty, in fact; nearly all the people were hotel employees, going about the kinds of after-hours jobs that most guests never saw them do, emptying trash cans and polishing the floor. Two men with squeegees nodded politely toward her as they expertly swiped the large sliding doors.

At the front desk, a young woman in a crisp gray suit bade her good morning and asked if she had had a pleasant stay as she retrieved her bill from the computer. She then asked Iliana to wait a moment and went to confer with a man in the doorway of an office behind her. Iliana felt a rush of panic. What if Jeff had made a police complaint after he left her room last night? What if the clerk had been instructed to notify her boss when Iliana tried to check out, so they could call a patrol car? Could it be that she actually had done something that she could be arrested for? She felt her cheeks redden and her legs get weak. She considered running past the squeegee guys and out into a cab. But no, the clerk returned and told her to have a good day.

Forcing herself to take deep breaths and try to relax, Iliana walked to the front of the hotel, conscious of every step. She wheeled her overnight bag to the bellman and asked him to call her a cab. As he went outside into the light of early morning, she bought a cup of coffee from a smiling, young clerk at a kiosk. A few people rushed by her in pairs or groups, talking in animated tones about business deals. She could hear isolated words and phrases—shipping dates, backlogs, deadlines, receivables.

Iliana realized that she had become used to traveling with her family, encouraging the kids to watch their step, hold on to the railing, stick together, look at the fountains, see the tall buildings. She had forgotten how lonely it could be, even in the middle of big cities, to be traveling alone. Looking down at her coffee, she decided she really wasn't in the mood for it. She was walking to a trashcan near the elevator bank to throw out the cup when a set of elevator doors opened. She looked up, startled. Inside were Jeff and Terry.

Iliana gasped when she saw them, and they looked stunned, too, so that the elevator doors started to close before they got out. Jeff reached out a hand, and the doors reopened. The two stepped out and stood opposite her. There was no one else nearby. She didn't know how angry Jeff was or what he was capable of doing. She was scared he might smack her into the marble wall nearby, or blast her verbally, calling her a crazy bitch or something uglier.

But the worst he did was shake his finger at her. "Now you stay away from me," he said, speaking more loudly than he needed to. "Do you hear me? I will call the police. I will file a report against you, do you understand?" The speech sounded rehearsed. Maybe he had come up with this script last night. Fine, she thought. Let him frame her as a lunatic, if then he'd leave her alone. It was no skin off her nose to let him relive his glory days as a stalked performer for one more morning.

"No problem," she said, starting to walk away.

"I can make life very difficult for you. I know you have a husband and children," he said, following her, raising his voice still more. Evidently his performance wasn't done. Iliana turned back. Jeff looked smug, enjoying the attention he was drawing from the hotel staffers. He wanted to publicly embarrass her, and it was working. A few businessmen who had come out of a nearby elevator were looking over, as were some women walking through the front doors. The squeegee guys had stopped working and were stealing sideways glances over, too. Terry was rocking back and forth on his feet uncomfortably. His eyes were long, droopy ovals.

"Listen," Iliana said in a low, angry voice. "We *both* were somewhere we shouldn't have been last night—"

"I should expect it by now, and God knows I should be flattered," Jeff said as he walked past her, ostensibly talking to Terry but clearly playing to the people in the lobby. "I guess it comes with the territory, but sometimes you just wish these fans would get a life."

He put on his sunglasses and shook back his hair, a move that would have seemed more useful back when his locks were long and shaggy. The lobby was filling up more, and several people were looking at Jeff and whispering, as though they couldn't quite put their finger on who he was.

Watching him with a mixture of anger at how he had embarrassed her and relief that he hadn't done anything worse, Iliana felt a light tap on her shoulder. She turned and saw Terry right next to her, his forehead sweating, the buttons of his checked shirt straining over his belly.

"Terry, I—" she said, starting to apologize.

"I'll make sure he leaves you alone," he said quietly, then walked off to join Jeff. Iliana felt her eyes fill. It was hard to believe that this poor sick guy, whose life had essentially collapsed after the Dreamers, was feeling sorry for *her*.

She arrived at the airport to find that all the earlier flights were booked, so she wandered around the gift shops and snack bars until her one o'clock flight was finally called.

Back in New York, it was cold and drizzly, and the traffic on the Grand Central Parkway was stop-and-go all the way to the Whitestone Bridge. She tried to lean her head back and close her eyes, but the vinyl upholstery felt sticky and uncomfortable, and the taxi's fitful starts and stops jerked her shoulders and head first one way, then the other. The shocks on the car were practically nonexistent, and her low-grade headache turned into a burst of sharp pain each time the car slammed into a pothole, which seemed to happen every two or three minutes.

She was anxious to get home, but scared, too. Scared of what would happen with Marc. Scared that they'd never get past this week. She didn't want to lose him, she didn't want to break up her family. She wanted to find a way that she and he could move on together.

By the time she arrived home, it was almost midnight. The lights in the front of the house were all out. After she paid the taxi driver, she made her way to the front door, wryly thinking as she entered how relieved she was that the locks had not been changed and her key still worked. She hauled her bag past the door and took a few steps into the living room. She was about to collapse into a chair when she noticed that something was different. There was a strange smell in the room, sort of woody, like furniture—no, it was a little lemony, too, like furniture polish. She turned on one of the table lamps, looked around, and gasped. There in the corner was a small cherry writing desk with pewter drawer handles and a roll-down top.

It was just like the desk her parents had given her for her twelfth birthday.

Chapter 21

"What's the matter?" Marc said dully from behind her. "Don't you like it?"

Iliana turned around. By the dim light of the lamp, she could see him walking down the stairs. He was wearing his jeans and a white dress shirt, the top buttons unbuttoned and his sleeves rolled up. *Her* Marc. Maybe things would be okay after all.

"You bought me a desk?" she asked.

"Yeah, I bought you a desk," he answered, rubbing one eye. "I heard you wanted it."

"Who told you that?"

"Jodi," he said, reaching the landing. His hair looked mussed, as though he'd been sleeping. He was barefoot. "She dropped by on Tuesday evening to make sure I had gotten home in time to give the kids dinner. She said you fell in love with it when you saw it at the antiques store near the coffee shop."

"It was seven thousand dollars," she said. "You bought it for me?"

He lifted his cheek in a kind of smirk. "Of course, I called and paid for it *before* you told me you decided to stay in LA an extra day."

She saw the smirk as an overture, and she smiled back a little. "And you sure used some choice words to tell me how you felt about *that*," she said.

He backed up and sat down on the sofa. "I was so mad at you," he said. "I don't think I've ever been that mad in my life. But there was something you said on the phone that I kept hearing over again in my head. I told you that if you didn't go to the Connors thing it would hurt my chances of getting promoted, and you asked why your attendance there mattered more than what I did with the swimwear contract. And of course it doesn't."

He shook his head. "I really screwed up on that Seattle thing. I should have done more with that contract when I first got it. I kept thinking that if you made this great impression at the cocktail party and the Connors thing, it would mitigate the mess I made. Or just make everyone forget about it. But it's not your responsibility to get me a promotion. And I'm sorry."

She walked over and sat down next to him. "I shouldn't have broken my word at the last minute like that. I'm sorry, too."

He leaned over, his elbows on his spread-out knees, his fingers interlaced. "I don't think I'm getting a promotion, Iliana. Not this year. I think Dan's going to get it. But not me."

She stroked his back. "So you'll get a promotion next year," she said. "Or you'll get a better offer somewhere else. Come on, it's not the end of the world. You're a smart, talented lawyer. You've got a long career ahead."

He rubbed his forehead. "When did everything get so hard? How did it all change? I was one of the top recruits out of law school. When I got to Connors Holdings, they were constantly throwing money at me. Everyone wanted me on their project team. I was a rock star."

He sighed. "I guess we're all rock stars when we're young. At least in our own minds."

She smiled, tilting her head. "You'll be a rock star again, I know it. I have no worries about you.

"But speaking of jobs, Marc, I need to tell you that I'm going back to work," she said. "Not just dabbling with a couple of queries between carpools. For real. It was great being entirely here for you and the kids, but they're getting older, and the time for that is ending. You're all going to have to take care of yourselves a little more. I don't know whether it's going to be as a freelancer or on staff, but I'm finding a way back into publishing."

"I know, I get that," he told her. "And I'm not surprised. I mean, I was surprised when you went to California even though I said all those things to stop you. But I was impressed, too. That was a bold move, going all the way there to find a unique story."

She looked down. "That's not exactly what I did."

"It got me thinking about how it was when you were working. You were good. I was wrong to say you weren't."

He walked over to the desk and began rubbing a spot with his finger, evidently trying to reassure himself that he had noticed a smudge and not an imperfection. "So I take it things went well out there," he said. "Got a lot to write about?"

"Not really," she told him. "I didn't come back with anything. It was a dead end."

He turned around. "Not anything? But you said something was going on. That's why you stayed the extra day."

She looked down, knowing how easy it would be to backpedal, to say she had come back with some good ideas, to nod and deflect his attention when he innocently asked her in the coming days whether she'd been able to get any magazines to bite. But she wasn't going to dig herself back into that hole. Marc had been honest with her from the moment she walked into the house, talking about his fears and disappointment, how they had made him act the way he had. And they were drawing closer now as a result. She owed him the same honesty. She didn't want to cause distance between them anymore.

"Actually, what happened in California is a little more complicated than that," she said.

He walked toward her, his hands on his hips. "What does that mean?"

She took a deep breath. "Okay, it all starts back when you were in Chicago. I emailed Stuart at *Business Times* to ask for a freelance assignment, but he wouldn't even talk to me unless I had a good story. A celebrity story. I was so frustrated. What kind of celebrity story could I come up with?"

"Yeah, so?"

"I had seen a rerun of that old show *Guitar Dreams*, and I found out that one of the guys, Jeff Downs, had this company in New York selling blankets. And I thought it would be a great story, because he used to be a star and millions of girls were in love with him. So I called his office and he agreed to talk to me because he thought I was with the *New York Times*."

"You said you were from the *Times*?"

"No, but it was what he believed. So he kept inviting me back. It was the only way I could get him to talk to me."

"But why did you— Iliana, what's wrong with you? This sounds nuts."

"It's not 'nuts,'" she said, standing up. "It's what somebody does when they're feeling desperate."

"So what did you do?"

"I interviewed him a few times. And then I went to California. To learn more about his life. Because I thought I could write a book about him."

"*That's* why you went to California? Why didn't you tell me?"

"Because I thought you would belittle me. Sort of like what you're doing right now. I didn't think you'd understand, and I didn't want you to ruin it." She looked down. "Even I didn't entirely understand what I was doing. But now I do. And once I figured out it was all based on some delusional old dreams I had—that's when I couldn't wait to get home."

Marc shook his head in disbelief. "I don't even know what to say. This is crazy. So what's going on now? Does he still think you're with the *Times*?"

"No, I told him the truth."

"And then what happened? Man, he must have been pissed."

"Marc, what is wrong with you?" Iliana said. "Why do you care if he was pissed? I'm telling you that this is how bad things were between us. I'm telling you how confused I was!"

"So you spend all this time with this guy, letting him think you're someone you're not, and then you travel all the way across the country, and . . . Wait. Was he with you?" Marc looked at her, hard.

"Yes."

"And is there a wife? Was she there, too?"

"No, she wasn't there."

He paused. "Iliana, did you . . . have an affair with him?"

"No," she said firmly.

"That's hard to believe."

"But it's true."

"Then why were you with him?"

"Because I thought it would make me a writer again. At least that's what I told myself."

"Well, did you stay in the same hotel?" She nodded. "You went all the way to California and stayed in the same hotel and nothing happened?"

"Nothing happened," Iliana said. Marc looked at her. "Nothing," she repeated. She waited a moment. "Okay, we kissed, but that's it. I kicked him out after that—"

"You kissed?" Marc said. "You *kissed* him?"

"It was a mistake, and I ended it right away," she said. "And I'm sorry I let it happen at all. But I'm not sorry about going to California. I learned a lot about myself while I was there, and it's going to make our marriage stronger—"

"But you *kissed*?"

"Yes, we kissed, but haven't you heard anything else I said?"

"Oh, I've heard plenty," he said, walking to the steps. "Plenty enough to know that I'm leaving. Go live in your little writer fantasy, Iliana, because I've had it. I'm gone."

She sat down on the sofa and listened to him upstairs, packing. He wasn't frantic and furious, the way he had been on the phone. Just calmly hell-bent on leaving her, which was even more devastating. A short time later, she heard him come back down and walk out the front door.

She went upstairs and checked on her sleeping children. Then she went into her bedroom.

And it was after she saw his chest of drawers, with the empty space where his wallet and watch should have been, that she lay down on the bed and sobbed.

Chapter 22

"Daddy brought home Dunkin' Donuts for breakfast yesterday," Dara said as she picked a piece of blueberry skin out of her teeth.

Iliana handed her a napkin. "I guess he's the better parent."

"Even chocolate frosted, the ones that are 'toxic,'" Matthew added, putting down his cereal bowl and placing the word in air quotes.

"That's right. That's what they are," Iliana said.

"Would you *ever* buy us Dunkin' Donuts for breakfast?" Dara asked.

"Never."

"Not even for, like, a birthday?"

"Nope."

"Not even a *birthday*?"

"If you're done, will you please clear your place?"

Dara carried her cereal bowl and juice glass to the dishwasher. "What's wrong with you? You're so mean today."

"I'm tired, I got home late last night. Let's go."

"So what was with all the shouting?" Matt asked as they climbed in the car. "I was half asleep. I didn't know if it was real or I was dreaming."

"Sorry if we were loud. It was nothing." Iliana backed out of the driveway.

"Did you guys have a fight?" Dara asked, sounding hungry for drama. "Is that why Daddy was gone this morning?"

"He's usually gone before you get up," Iliana told her.

"What time will he be home tonight?"

"I don't know." She shrugged. "I don't really know what his plans are."

"When the parents got in a fight in *Good Luck Charlie,* the mom sent the kids to a movie and set up the dining room to look like the place where they had their first date," Dara said. "Mom, why don't you send us to a movie tonight and make the dining room like your first date?"

"You moron," Matthew told her. "It doesn't work that way in real life. That's just an old TV show. Are you really that stupid?"

It was a question that Iliana had asked herself all morning, and answered to herself as well. Yes, she had been that stupid to get carried away by a TV show. But she wasn't anymore.

For the rest of the day, she tried to decide what to say to the kids when they got home. She would have to tell them that Marc might not come home that night, and she thought it was better to do it sooner rather than later. But in the end, she didn't need to explain it at all. She was setting the table with only three plates for dinner, and the kids were in the family room watching TV, when she heard his key in the front door.

"I didn't want to come back," he told her, as they stood in the doorway. "But I didn't want to *not* come back more. I missed you guys. I want to be here."

He looked horrible—tired and pale, his overcoat unbuttoned, his tie askew. She stood next to him, not daring to even touch him yet for fear that she'd drive him back out. She was so glad he was home. She didn't want to live her life without him.

"Marc," she said. "I love you. I always have."

Later that night, after the kids were in bed and she had finished cleaning up in the kitchen, she found him in the living room, staring into the dark. She walked over and curled up on the couch next to him, wordlessly. She didn't know what to say, and she suspected he didn't know either. They had spent so much time blaming each other—him, for pushing her to end her career and make his the priority; her, for holding him back and ruining his chances for greater success—that it was almost as if they needed to learn a new way to communicate. Iliana didn't know how long the two of them sat there on the couch. But at one point, she placed her hand on his leg. At one point, he put his arm around her shoulder.

The thing was, when she really thought about it, she wasn't even sure he had done all that she accused him of. Maybe he was right, maybe *Business Times* wasn't as big a deal as she always thought, and maybe Stuart would have gotten promoted over her even if she had stayed, just as Marc said. Maybe the reason she hadn't done much as a writer wasn't only because she was too busy doing errands and taking care of her family, but also because she got discouraged too quickly. And maybe Marc was seeing things differently, too. Maybe he realized that part of the reason he'd always wanted her home was that he found her success threatening, and maybe his concerns about financial security were partly about exerting control. And maybe Jeff Downs didn't really save her sanity in middle school. Maybe the rich girls weren't so, so bad, and she would have been fine if *Guitar Dreams* had never existed. The past was a funny thing; in some ways, it was as unknowable as the future.

The next day Iliana went back to Chelsea's Home Details and arranged to return the writing desk. It was far too expensive for them. They needed to be careful with money, since Marc wouldn't be getting a promotion this year, and there was no way of knowing how much time it would take for her to start working and earning some money. But more important, she didn't need it. She didn't need some desk—some sentimental, knockoff piece of furniture, as Jodi had said—to provide some cosmic connection to the dreams of her childhood. Romantic notions like that belonged on TV.

Marc called that afternoon to suggest that she reach out to Jena Connors and say that she didn't have time to participate in her program. But she told him she'd rather apologize for missing the first meeting and plan to go to all the rest. As long as she was making time to actively look for work, what difference did a couple of afternoon sessions in New Jersey make? Once she stopped seeing the workshop as a threat to her identity, she realized she *wanted* to help Marc. And Jodi was right. It would probably be fun to play around with flowers.

After sending off the note, she went into her browser and took a look at some boutique hotels in Manhattan, finally settling on a small one two blocks from Marc's office. She made a reservation for the following week, and then called Marc and invited him to meet her there for a lunchtime rendezvous. She imagined walking into the hotel and spotting him, sitting in the corner of a darkened bar, waiting for her. With his top button unbuttoned and his face aglow from the light of a single candle, he would look irresistibly handsome. After all, he was the man who had built a life with her, made a beautiful family with her, and then come back home to pick up the pieces with her, all because he loved her. He was her husband. And that was better than any dream.

A few months later, Dara tiptoed into their bedroom late at night and tapped Iliana's shoulder.

"Mom, my belly hurts," she whispered.

"Do you need to go to the bathroom?" Iliana whispered back.

"No, I just tried."

"Any of your friends sick?"

"Jayden was absent today."

Iliana pulled back the covers. "I heard there was a stomach bug going around. Okay, let's go downstairs and see what we can do."

She took Dara to the kitchen, where she poured her a glass of ginger ale, and then settled her on the family room couch, covering her with the wool throw. She reached for the remote and turned on the TV. Keeping the volume down, she flipped through the channels.

"Ah, *Sponge Bob*," Iliana said. "Dara, this should take your mind off your troubles."

"Thanks, Mom," Dara said and lowered her head onto Iliana's lap.

A few minutes later, she was fast asleep. Not wanting to disturb her by bringing her upstairs, Iliana picked up the remote again and flipped quickly through some more channels to find something interesting to watch. There was a travel show, an old episode of *Friends*, a few sports shows, a talk show, some music videos, another talk show, and—

Suddenly she sat up, as straight as she could with Dara curled against her, and went back a few stations to the face she had recognized. *Oh my God!* she thought when she found the right channel. It was Terry, and he was being interviewed on *ET*. She never would have guessed it was possible. He really did it. He really got himself back in the spotlight.

". . . and the greatest song we ever recorded was 'The Best of Times,'" he was saying. "We really reached our peak with that one. It had a nice melody and a good beat. But the real reason it took off was that it really captured that time in everyone's life when things couldn't be better—you're young, you got your girlfriend, you got the beach, and the road keeps rising up to meet you . . ."

Iliana leaned forward, listening to him thoughtfully discuss the Dreamers' most successful pop song. He sounded smart, much more analytical than she would have ever guessed he could be. And he looked good, too. Not that he had changed so much from when she met him in LA. He was still overweight, with thin, combed-back hair. But he was more relaxed, less desperate than he had appeared the night they went out to dinner. His calm demeanor brought out his eyes, which were as clear and blue as they had been back when *Guitar Dreams* was on the air. She was glad that Terry was pulling himself together. He really had been sweet to her.

"Terry tells us he'll be appearing for two weeks at Bally's in Las Vegas with other former recording stars," the reporter was saying. "Check out TerryBrice.com for dates and details."

"But Terry is not the only Dreamer cashing in on former glory," another reporter said, as an old close-up of Jeff appeared on the screen. "Sources tell *ET* that Jeff Downs, known as the gentle-mannered member of the group, has reached out to the other two bandmates and is close to signing with an indie film company to produce a documentary of the group's reunion tour, which is scheduled for sometime next year. It's a complete Dreamers affair, as a source with knowledge about the deal tells us that the tour will be managed by Downs's wife, Catherine, who had a small, recurring role in *Guitar Dreams*. Terry added that he and Jeff got together a few months ago in LA."

The image switched back to Terry. "This all came about because of this writer friend of Jeff's," he said. "He met her in New York, and she convinced him that people still cared about us. So I met up with the two of them in LA, and things just skyrocketed from there. I hope our paths cross again. I'd love to tell her thanks."

A new reporter came on-screen and as she began to talk about celebrity pregnancies, Iliana felt herself break out in a big smile. How about that? Terry was fielding interviews, the Dreamers music would be back on the market, the group was scheduling a tour, and Jeff and Catherine—the wise, fame-averse Catherine—were planning a documentary. In spite of everything that had happened, and even in spite of how scary Jeff had been that last night in the hotel, she couldn't help but feel glad that he was getting the comeback he wanted and that Catherine was okay with it. Life was never short of turns and twists, and people never stopped landing in the most unlikely of places. It was the reason she liked being a writer.

With that in mind, she wriggled off the sofa, placing a throw pillow under Dara's head and covering her up again with the blanket. Then she tiptoed over to the dining room and turned on her computer. With the streetlights shining through the windows, she went to the hall closet and fished her digital recorder from her shoulder bag. She put it on the dining room table and opened a blank document on her laptop.

For a moment she considered writing up Jeff Downs's story. She could write it from her own perspective—which, after all, was certainly unique. She had been the only one around when Jeff had hatched his comeback plan and when Terry had shown up to join him. And now that he and Terry were back on the entertainment industry's radar, maybe it would be more marketable than when she had tried to pitch it to magazines before. All of her impressions from California were still in her head, and all he had said to her in Mount Kisco about his *Guitar Dreams* days was saved there on the recorder.

But then she closed the computer. No, she thought—that ship had sailed. Jeff's story didn't merit a book or even an article, at least not by her. It was a story of looking backward, of glomming on to past fantasies, and she had no interest in doing that ever again. If there was anything productive that had come out of her time with Jeff Downs, it was the realization that she could be passionate and determined. Now it was time to find a writing project that was entirely *hers*, and that warranted her passion and determination. Maybe, she thought, she would move ahead with the book she had always intended to write, about four distinct people striving to make it in New York. Maybe it didn't have to be four, and maybe it didn't have to be about New York. But it should be about people taking a chance and making an impact. She had always loved to uncover what made people tick.

She decided to think more about how she wanted to proceed tomorrow. For tonight, she had an under-the-weather daughter to take care of. She turned on the recorder and, with a quick touch of a button, deleted Jeff's interview. Then she went to take Dara upstairs.

Leading her daughter to the stairway, Iliana thought about the teenage world that Dara was about to enter. It was so different from when she was growing up. Back then, she had to wait for the monthly issue of *Teen* to find out what Jeff Downs was up to, and the news was always G-rated. These days, a person couldn't go more than a few hours without hearing about drug busts, DUI arrests, rehab stints, and ugly breakups and hookups involving any number of hot young stars. Was Dara more jaded than Iliana had been? Too jaded to fall in love with a guy simply because he looked good on TV?

She thought that the answer was yes, but when she reached Dara's room, she realized that it actually was no, not at all. Iliana hadn't focused on it for a long time, but on the bulletin board right above the bed was a photo of Dara with Brandon Ryde of Amplify, taken after the concert she had treated Dara to last month. He had put his cap on Dara's head just as Iliana snapped the photo, and Dara had transferred the photo to her Instagram account, where she had gotten more than eighty "likes" from her friends and classmates. Then she had posted the photo on his Facebook fan page, and he had "liked" it there. She came downstairs the next morning exclaiming how awesome he was to have "liked" her photo, inferring from his technological handiwork all the wonderful personality characteristics that Iliana had inferred from Jeff Downs's unique smile. And so it began.

Iliana helped Dara into bed, covered her with her comforter, and kissed her cheek. Dara would be thirteen in a few weeks, and Matt would be fifteen a month after that. Driver's licenses, prom, college . . . Matt was at the starting gate of adulthood, and Dara was right on his heels. How long would it be until a flesh-and-blood boy replaced the charismatic singer on the bulletin board?

She watched Dara sleep for a bit, then quietly left the room. It was fine if Dara dreamed about pop stars—for now. But someday soon, her dreams needed to center around who she wanted to become and what wonderful things she wanted to accomplish. And Iliana was determined to teach her that *those* kinds of dreams were the ones that mattered. It was a lesson that she owed her beautiful daughter.

Acknowledgments

I am so thankful to my mentors and good friends, Patricia Dunn and Jimin Han, of Sarah Lawrence College's Writing Institute, for their extraordinary teaching and unending support. Thanks, too, to Cynthia Manson, the best agent a writer could have, and to her immensely gifted editorial assistant, Nancee Adams-Taylor. I couldn't be more thrilled to have Danielle Marshall of Lake Union Publishing as my acquisitions editor and Tiffany Yates Martin as my developmental editor. Their insights helped me discover and explore elements of the book that I never even realized were there—and working with them has been pure pleasure! My gratitude extends to the entire Lake Union team for all their help and expertise. Finally, I send a huge thank-you to my wonderful husband, Bennett, and our three amazing children—David, Rachel, and Alyssa. You four are my dream come true!

About the Author

Photo © 2015 Andrea Harnick Tuchman

Barbara Solomon Josselsohn is a magazine writer specializing in articles and essays about home and family. Her work has appeared in the *New York Times*, *Consumers Digest*, *Parents*, *American Baby*, and *Westchester Magazine*, as well as on numerous websites. She and her husband live in Westchester County, New York, and have three children and a lovable shih-poo. *The Last Dreamer* is her first novel.

Connect with Barbara at www.barbarasolomonjosselsohn.com.